PRAISE FOR

The Thread of Destiny Series

"Beyond the diverse, richly-imagined world, the heart of this story is its characters, particularly Evelaine, who struggles to balance her yearning for revenge, her desire to protect her friends and family, and her responsibilities as a wielder of plant magic. The result is a thrilling adventure story that also pulls at my heartstrings."

— Bridgette Portman, author of *The Twin Stars*

"The series continues with a heart wrenching, action packed story that draws you in and keeps you on the edge of your seat with every emotional pitfall Evelaine and her friends encounter."

—Aiden Murray, author of *Knight of Elysia*

"Claire's lush prose transports readers to a diverse world where 'blessed ones' attempt to find their place."

—Austin Valenzuela, author of *Tournament of Hearts*

"The Threads of Destiny series is a masterfully crafted, inclusive fantasy tale."

—Sarah Madden, author of *Lucid*

"Devastatingly powerful!"

—R.J. Castille, author of *Goddess*

Use QR Code to View Full-Color HD Map:

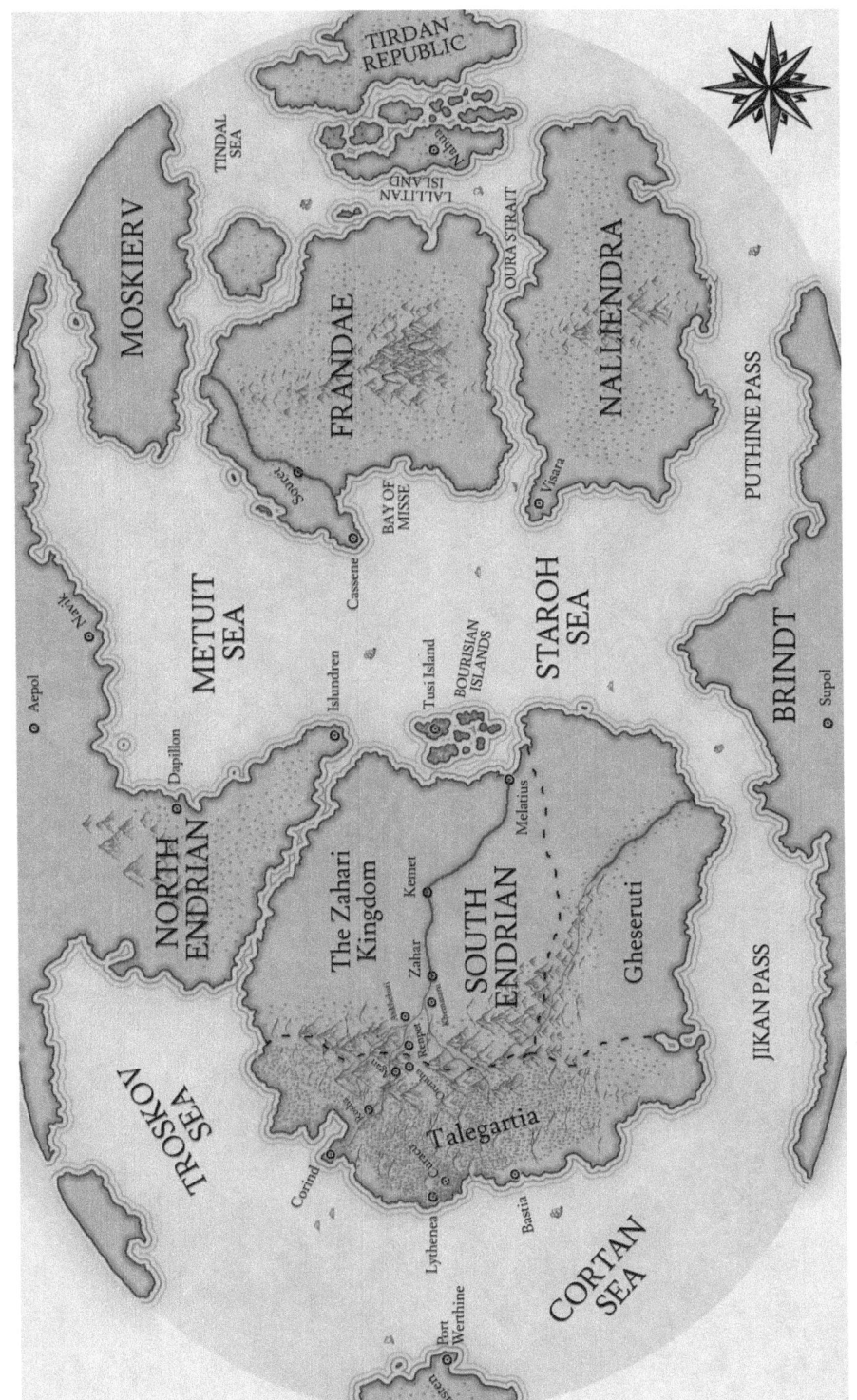

.

To
Reap
What
Is
Sown

CLAIRE E. JONES

THREADS OF DESTINY BOOK 4
CLAIRJOYANCE PUBLISHING LLC

Published by Clairjoyance Publishing LLC

www.claireejones.com

Copyright © 2025 by Claire E. Jones

Cover Art by Carlos Ortega-Haas

Map by Claire E. Jones

ISBN:

979-8-9989893-0-8

Library of Congress Catalog Number:

2025914873

Hardcover, Paperback, eBook editions / October 2025

To Cris Hassold,
thank you and I'm sorry.

DAY ONE

Evelaine slipped into the masses once the dingy merchant ship she had bought passage on arrived in Port Werthine, her lip curled in disgust at the expected stench of rotting fish and unwashed sailors assaulting her senses. She had spent the entire journey across the Cortan Sea avoiding everyone on board, choosing instead to cultivate her plots for retribution in dank corners that suited the black pitch filling her chest. She was just a few steps away from tearing down those who had taken everything from her and she refused to lose sight of her goal.

Relying on instinct, she wove her way through the dilapidated buildings and crumbling walls that cluttered the docks like cursed barnacles, disappearing farther into a city that she truly doubted had seen better days. The teeming port was like every other metropolis in the great Tirdan Republic: battered and bruised attempts at survival that were squashed at every opportunity by those who sought power, influence, and riches at the expense of everyone and everything.

Both the people and structures she darted past bore their doomed fates upon hunched shoulders, the creases of their facades lined with dirt and soot that spoke of years of suffering under the weight of the tyranny of the privileged few, who rose like oil above the murky waters. She pulled her hood low, keeping to the shadows like a second skin. It had been far too easy to revert to her muscle memories, her past life as Mistress Satine's top assassin cloaking her movements and focusing her attention on the singular purpose that drove her forward:

Nydas Sutherland must die.

She had been here once before, on a mission to take down the criminal headman that had been interrupting drug shipments meant for the Satine Rouge in Risten. It was a task that the Mistress had entrusted to Evelaine as a way to protect her business interests, but now Evelaine was undertaking the mission a second time around for an entirely different reason. When she had found Nydas five years prior, he had been much more prepared than anticipated for her assassination attempt. Turning the tables on her, he had wiped all of her memories away with a powerful sedative, then had shipped her off across the sea like a crate of produce. She had narrowly escaped in Talegartia and, guided by divine powers beyond her understanding, had somehow stumbled her way to the long-lost plant village her ancestors had originally been from.

To Reap What Is Sown

As someone who came from the bloodline of those blessed by the Plant Goddess Tabriara, she had been readily embraced by the villagers as an answer to their prayers. While they had viewed her as a savior to lead them in their time of need, she had found a safe haven for her confused amnesia. Spending a handful of blissfully ignorant years with them, she had dulled her edges and found false comfort in the innocent love that had blossomed between her and the oathed guard that had been assigned to her upon her arrival.

Nees had been a steadfast partner, grounding her and providing the foundation upon which she could recover and heal from both the visible and invisible scars that haunted her. Although she had had no memories of what her life had been like up until that point, she had been plagued by vague nightmares and fleeting feelings of terror, uncertainty, and grief. She had somehow known that she had lost more than she could imagine, but the exact details had been inaccessible until Rakhmet, one of the fire blessed, and his guard had shown up and urged them to delve into the sacred plant temple—an ill-fated journey that had brutally ripped her out of the fanciful lie she had been living.

Yes, her goddess had restored her memories and set her back on her rightful path, but watching her beloved Nees die right in front of her had almost been too much to bear. However, she was no stranger to transforming her pain into something more worthwhile, into a weapon that harnessed the poison inside of her. Because that was who she was at her core, her blessing twining through every fiber of her being with a need to consume and conquer.

3

Nothing would stand in her way.

Thanks to the naive fire blessed, she now had both the freedom and resources to finally make her mark on the world. It had been a pipe dream of hers for as long as she could remember, to rise above the pitiful existence of relying on others for survival in a hostile country that had refused to see her as anything more than a bastard orphan of a courtesan turned heartless killer. Little did they know that they had been creating the means of their own destruction.

With her purpose clear, Evelaine found what she was looking for wedged between a rusted iron bridge and a sluggish canal, an inconspicuous inn that could provide a roof over her head while she searched for Nydas. Its peeling sign was unremarkable, only barely visible through the grime covering the building's weathered timber, and the windows were small and shrouded, their glass panes smudged with streaks of muddy water.

The air was thick and sour as she pushed through the entrance, desperation leaking like steam from the scattering of patrons hunched around scarred wooden tables. The dimly lit lamps showed a bar stretching along the back wall, behind which stood a bartender with a face as lined as the city's streets. He polished a chipped glass with a rag, his puffy eyes sharp despite his distracted frown. They instantly found her as she crossed the threshold and approached, all of her senses on high alert.

"Room for one," she murmured.

"Aye, three silver." He grunted. "Five if ye want a meal."

She narrowed her eyes, daring him as a tense moment passed. His hand slowed just a fraction as the rag circled the rim of the glass and the crease on the left side of his mouth deepened.

"Fine, four." He scowled, and she knew without a doubt that he was internally cursing her.

She almost smiled at the thought, more than happy to play the villain. It made the coming bloodshed easier to bear. Satisfied, she nodded and dipped her hand into her pack to grab and drop the coins onto the worn wood.

He grumbled as he turned and drew a key from the board behind him, tossing it in her direction. "Upstairs, third door on the left."

The key vanished into her hand, and she was gone before he could utter another syllable, her steps silent as she ascended the stained stairwell at the end of the bar. She secured her room the minute she entered, checking every dust-filled crevice and wedging the lone chair underneath the doorknob to reinforce its shoddy lock. She only removed it when a short knock came about an hour later, the thump outside telling her a meal tray had been deposited. Waiting until the sounds of steps retreated, she retrieved the sad excuse for dinner and replaced the chair once again.

It wasn't like she couldn't afford better accommodations. She carried enough coin on her to rival even the deplorable leaders of this ugly city, but she had better plans for it than her own momentary comfort. Plus, keeping a low profile while on the hunt was in her best interests. She didn't want Nydas or any of his cronies getting even the faintest whiff of her presence. She had thought she had the element of surprise in her favor the first time around. Now, she was determined to make that true.

She ate methodically then sat on the edge of the insubstantial bed, sharpening the edge of a dagger that she tried not to think about too much. Its glittering green gem at the end of the pommel whispered unwelcome memories to her as she waited for the muffled midnight bells to toll in the dark night. And yet, images of the past sprouted despite herself, tiny shoots of green pushing their way through the cracks that she tried so valiantly to keep mortared.

It had been an excruciating process, attempting to integrate her long-gone past with whom she had become in that strange village in a strange land. When the goddess had so suddenly restored her awareness, her mind had fought against it instinctively. Thrashing in denial against the glaring truth of all she had lost. It had been simply too much information to process in such a short amount of time, but the recalled faces of those she had been so callously ripped away from had been like a thousand blades to the heart. Her soul had been shredded in an instant, leaving behind only pure black rage.

Her destructive anger in Tabriara's throne room had been defensive, a knee-jerk reaction to the anguish that had been buffeting her as multiple realizations had hit. Not only had she been forced to abandon those most dear to her, but she had further betrayed them by going on to live a blissfully ignorant lie, enjoying her peaceful security within the warm embrace of the plant village. Unforgivably, she had forsaken them twofold by letting herself fall in love with Nees, only to have the guard brutally taken from her as well. There had been no winners in the end, no scrap of accomplishment to rest her laurels on. Both she and Nees had lost far too much.

The overwhelming shame and grief had thickened around her like hardened sap, continuing to remind her of her treachery with every step she had taken since. The sheer effort that it took to simply keep moving forward was immense, her teeth gritted and shoulders hunched in determination, but the fury fueled her. The potential for revenge, the possibility that she could maybe, somehow right at least some of the wrongs she had committed was what kept her focused. That was why she had to keep going. That was why she had to do whatever it would take.

Only the occasional sound of a chair scraping across wood filtered through the floorboards as she stood and tucked the dagger into her hip holster, drawing her cloak tightly around herself and opening the dirty window that looked out over a littered alleyway underneath. Using her blessing, she called forth a single seed from her hand, set it on the windowsill, and urged it to grow into a thick vine that crept its way down the stone wall to the ground below.

She remembered how confusing it had been when she had first begun to find random seeds and smears of pollen in her bedsheets as a young girl. Initially, she had assumed that they had come from the scattering of overgrown, potted plants that her mother had left behind when she had died a couple years prior, but after they had appeared several nights in a row, she had examined them more closely and discovered that the variety of species were well beyond what the pots contained.

Her mother had always had an affinity for plants, her precious flowers and herbs sprouting in abundance despite the lack of light and nutrients available in their cramped room at the Satine Rouge. Evelaine had thought it was just an unusual skill that had been passed down in the family, evidenced by the modest prominence to which her grandfather, Otis, had risen to with his apothecary in Risten with the small, attached greenhouse where he spent most of his hours. While he was not renowned by any means, he had a loyal base of customers that regularly sought out his plant-based remedies and tonics year after year.

Mystified, Evelaine had gathered the seeds and brought them to him, seeking answers that had ended up changing her life as she had known it. He had been saddened but not surprised, his expression tender as he had carefully explained her birthright. A secret that her mother would have revealed when Evelaine had come of age. A blessing passed down through the generations that made her fundamentally different from everyone else around her. Another reason why she would never be truly accepted into the disdainful society that had raised her.

Shaking her head with a huff, she pushed the distracting thoughts away as she slung her leg out the window and quietly climbed down into the alley. Once she reached the ground, she directed the vine to grow further, tangling around the window's latch to secure it closed while she was out.

The cracked streets were relatively empty as she made her way across town to the shipping district, where she had last found Nydas's hideout in a seemingly derelict

8

warehouse, a large, indistinct building sandwiched between a slaughterhouse and a chemical factory that easily veiled the criminal leanings of the headman's activities. When she managed to locate it, she carefully circled the block a few times and took in the subtle differences the last five years had wrought.

Not much had changed, to be honest. It was still as depressing as before, just now with more grime and soot wedged into their tired fractures. While the slaughterhouse was shuttered for the night, the chemical factory still had a couple of chimneys belching thick clouds of gods knew what, but there was only one window that seemed to be lit up. She made sure to steer clear of the single slice of illuminated street below as she tucked into the slim walkway leading to the back dock of the slaughterhouse, where carts lined up during the day to haul away the many pounds of dead flesh.

Glancing around once more to confirm that no one was around, she leapt up onto the first-floor roof overhang with all the stealth of a cat, then gradually scaled the wall until she could tuck into the gabled cranny that she remembered from before. It gave her a direct but hidden viewpoint from which she could see into the dark windows on the upper floors of Nydas's warehouse, and there she waited, attentively watching for any signs of life coming from within.

She had done the same song and dance years ago, but she had been almost fatally fooled so she kept her eyes peeled for any movement. Yet, in the still darkness, she couldn't help her mind returning to the question that had been bothering her ever since her memories had been restored:

how had Nydas been so prepared for her? Up until him, her targets had always been too arrogant or stupid to invest much beyond the usual defenses that deterred run-of-the-mill brutes and thieves. But Nydas had not only had hidden traps, but he had also deployed that glass wall to block her pollen cloud.

It had been far too specific of a contraption to be brushed off as a coincidence. What use would a glass wall do him against someone without her special abilities? It was a physical barrier, sure, but his guards had also had those cloth masks for their noses and mouths readily at hand, saving them from inhaling her toxic spores. Nydas had somehow known that she, specifically, would be coming for him and he had had precise knowledge about her that extremely few people did. She had been careful to only use her blessing against those that would never live to tell the tale, so how had Nydas found out?

The lack of answers was disquieting, and her instincts were screaming, thorned frustration tangling in her gut. She struggled to swallow it down, forcing herself to focus. Where she had seen a figure or two patrolling the hallways before, she now didn't sense a soul, as if the building itself were an empty echo of what it once was. Her hands clenched in fury, her chance at retribution seeming to slip through her fingers like fistfuls of dried grain.

As the distant clock towers struck two, her resolve to wait it out lost the battle against the poison filling her lungs, and she hastened toward the hatch that she knew was on the top roof. She still kept low out of habit, fully realizing that she could be walking into another clever trap laid by an enemy that had a regrettable history of outsmarting her. But all was quiet as she carefully pried open the stiff hinges, the only sound the soft grinding of rusted metal.

She waited again, holding her breath as she peeked inside to the shadowed hallway beneath her. Here and there, she spied signs of tiny trails in the dust collecting on the floor, most likely rodents searching for their next meal, but nothing else caught her attention, so she slipped inside and dropped down on silent feet. Immediately drawing her dagger, she held in a crouch as her eyes adjusted.

Only grim silence greeted her as she straightened and studied the doors lining the walls, most of them open and lonely. Not even the dust was disturbed on the thresholds, telling her that none of them had been moved in a long time. Her anger doubled and she scowled, heading in the direction of where Nydas's office had been. The main hallway was one of those that followed the outermost wall with a few intersecting interior passages leading off to other areas, and she left footsteps behind her as she crept toward the back of the building, but she couldn't bring herself to care.

She slowed as she neared open doorways just in case, though, flattening her back to the wall and peeking around the edges of the jams. Some rooms were completely barren, some possessing a chair or table that had been pushed to the side or tipped over and lay forlornly on its side. A scene of desolate abandonment that had her hand clenching around the pommel of her dagger, twitching vines unconsciously weaving around her fingers and wrist. She wanted to scream, the emptiness too similar to the vacuum inside her chest.

Eventually, the door of Nydas's office came into view and she stopped, staring at the closed panel. She stood there for long minutes, unwanted memories budding inside of her as she forced herself to breathe through the fury. She couldn't shake the feeling that she was too late, and a resentful howl built in her throat. The silence around her was deafening and her muscles were aching for a release as she fought to get a hold of her emotions, but she forced herself to move forward. Her free hand landed on the doorknob, and she drew in a tight breath as she pushed the door open, taking in the scene in front of her.

All of the furniture was gone except for his imposing desk at the back of the room, waiting for her in the dark, but signs of a tussle were everywhere. There were holes in the walls where errant crossbow bolts meant for her had landed, a few floorboards where javelins had pierced through were splintered, and even the trap in the floor was exposed. The rug that had been hiding it had vanished, but the red stains that surrounded it were still there. Haunting remnants of blood that had pooled around her, laid low by their prepared assault.

She eyed the traps and carefully sent out a few probing vines, testing them, but nothing moved so she stepped inside, avoiding the holes as she approached the desk. Her footsteps were loud and sharp, the urge to stomp forward and tear the place apart a seething need inside of her. A single paring knife had been thrust into the top of the desk, pinning a small note to its surface, and she circled to the other side in order to read the elegantly scrawled message:

"Checkmate."

Her jaw clenched even further and the rush of blood in her head was far too loud as she stared at the piece of paper. She couldn't move, her thoughts whirling in a thousand directions.

How dare he, she wanted to scream.

How dare he deny her her rightful revenge.

How dare he rip her life away in mere seconds and get away with it.

How dare he leave this forgotten shell of a building, just like he had left her a lost shadow of her former self.

He had had no right to do so, and she wanted him to pay in blood just like she had, yet he had refused her once again.

He had destroyed everything she had held dear and had gotten away with it. Just like that.

Before she knew what she was doing, her hand ripped the knife from its place and it flew across the room as an inhuman sound tore from her throat. It landed with a thunk, sticking into the doorframe and quivering for a second as her fury echoed through the deserted building. Her chest heaving, she became aware of distant doors opening and closing. It seemed as though someone might have been alerted to her presence in the factory next door and it was time to make herself scarce, yet her feet were rooted to the floor. Literally.

She suddenly realized that long tendrils of thorned vines had grown from her, snaking across the room. They had tangled into a thick bramble and covered everything in sight. Shaking her head, she forced them to dissolve as they dried and crumbled into dust. She couldn't let herself get distracted—she had to stay focused. She would be damned if this was the end of her plans.

Barely reining it in, she made haste as she quickly rifled through the drawers of the desk and looked for anything that had been left behind. She cursed, finding nothing as she spun to search the rest of the space, but it had been picked clean. Only the empty wooden shelves of a formerly well-appointed office mocked her in silence.

The muffled sounds of people talking in the back alley reached her and she choked down her frustration as she hesitated, hunting for something, anything that would give her a clue as to where Nydas had moved his operations. Her eyes darted around, but she had to face the facts of reality. There were no signs of the fucker beyond that one word laughing at her anger. All she could do was shove the piece of paper into her pocket with a sneer.

She cursed again, lurching forward as more voices joined those in the alley. She didn't bother with stealth as she retraced her steps and ran back to the hallway hatch, jumping up to hoist herself over the edge and onto the roof in one swift motion. Closing it once more with a soft groan of metal on metal, she kept low and scurried away from the voices to the front of the building.

With a peek over the edge, she waited for one lone pedestrian to disappear around the corner on the street below before urging another vine to snake down the facade. She double-checked that the coast was clear then rode it down, letting it crumble away the second her feet met cobbled stone. Drawing her hood tight and tucking her hands inside her cloak, she forced her pace to be casual as she slipped back into the shadows.

To Reap What Is Sown

The district's bleak warehouses and drab storefronts became a blur as she walked, her throat choking with indignation. Did she think it was going to be easy? That she would simply be able to waltz into Nydas's office and slaughter him in cold blood where she had failed before? Self-disgust bloomed, threading with the barbed thistle of spite that tightened around her lungs like a vice.

Did she think that a little freedom, money, and conviction were going to fix everything? It hadn't been enough before, when she had been one of the most feared creatures of the night as the Mistress's assassin. She had thought she had everything she needed back then. She had thought that she had all the answers. She had had a job, a safe roof over her head, and a family to go home to. But it had all been taken away in an instant.

Now, she had even more power, more training, more leeway, yet she still couldn't reach what she wanted. She needed a target, someone to blame. Someone to rip to shreds just like she had been. She could easily lay fault on everyone and everything that had led her to this anticlimactic fury. She could clearly see the long line of betrayal after betrayal that had paved the road to her anguish, but she knew there was only one place she could go to for answers.

The next logical step unfolded in the front of her mind as she wove her way back toward the decrepit inn, but she didn't want to accept it. She didn't want to revisit her past. She didn't want to look into the faces of those she had failed and commit to a longer-term plan, digging even deeper into the decomposing remains of her lost life.

But it would require her to return to where it all started.

DAY THREE

I t had taken her a whole three hours of debate, pacing the short distance between the sad bed and filthy window, but the fact of the matter was, she needed answers and she knew exactly who she would have to face in order to get them. So after two days of loathing in silence, tucked away at the bottom of another ship, this time sailing inland up the Ferus River, Evelaine forced herself to get on with the plan. The piercing headache that besieged her once they reached the outskirts of the city she used to call home, however, should have been her first warning that things were only going to get worse.

The nausea hit first, her stomach rolling as she fought to keep down her breakfast of lumpy gruel, but it was the sharp pounding in her skull that had her staggering down the gangplank as they disembarked, the familiar yet unwelcome sight of the towering capital of industry rising in front of her. White haze crowded the edges of her vision as she struggled to push through the crowd around the docks, looking for somewhere to catch her breath, and she teetered for several blocks, getting as far away as possible from the overwhelming sensations that brought up memories she didn't want to recall. The smell of oil and the acrid stench of smoke mixed with the clash of metal on wood, shouts of weary sailors, and grumbles of laborers made her wince and hold her ears until she couldn't stand it anymore. Her legs finally gave out as she lurched into a shadowed doorway, her knees hitting the cold ground with a jarring impact as she groaned in pain.

No one cared to notice as she collapsed into the mildewed corner, gasping for air as a buzzing numbness overtook her and left her dazed. She blinked slowly and forced her fingers to unclench, her skin feeling oddly stiff and detached, but managed to suck in a deep breath and ordered herself to focus.

Counting down from ten, she started with the basics. She felt the chilled stone beneath her, grimaced at the worn stones that supported the opening above her, and squinted beyond to the oppressively overcast sky that peeked through between tattered roofs. She listened to the conversations that reached her: a petty argument about the price of wool, a hushed warning of theft in the night, an aggressive reminder to store the crates in the right place this time.

She breathed in again, noticing the subtle scents of rust and mold underneath the wafting aromas of roasting meats and spiced tobacco. Finally, she was able to bring herself back to her body and probed at the disassociation that made her limbs as heavy as trunks. It was somehow recognizable, and she gasped when it hit her. Immediately, she reached for her powers and tried to call forth a single seed, yet the request went unanswered as the cavernous space inside of her simply echoed it back.

Her blessing was gone.

Just like how it had been in the plant village before the fire blessed had arrived to explain the corruption that had plagued her sacred temple and blocked her connection to her goddess. She choked, trying to catch her breath as her sluggish mind stumbled to conclusions. Rakhmet had said that the corruption was blocking many of the sacred temples across the world, that any blessed who were in the proximity of such a temple would fall prey to its influence. Which meant that it was very likely that there was one nearby, somewhere in or around Risten.

But she had never heard of such a thing. Granted, she had known very little about her blessing beyond what her grandfather had told her as a young girl. Most of her knowledge had actually come from studying under the village elders in Curacu over the past five years, and all of their information had been strictly based in Talegartian history.

Here? In Risten?

The only other blessed she had known in her previous life was Corsair, and he had never mentioned anything about a temple either. She wondered if his powers were dampened as well, if he was still around, but that thought was quickly chased away by another realization as anger bloomed inside of her: her powers were gone.

The very critical edge that she had in her fight against Nydas was inaccessible. She was effectively neutralized. Now, she had nothing but her wits and blade, and the reality of her situation shoved her to her feet as fury filled her. Her mouth dropped open as rage scraped its way up her throat and her chest heaved in an attempt to keep the howl from bursting forth.

She had lost again. Her carefully reseeded plan has been thrown out the fucking window before she had even had a chance to enact it. Clawing at the sides of her face, she spun in place as she searched for an answer that wasn't there. This couldn't be it. She wouldn't be stopped. Not now. Not ever.

Her eyes were wild as a passing woman in a faded dress with muddy hems glanced at her and quickly looked away. Evelaine ground her teeth together and frantically reached for a thread of logic, planting her hands against the wall and fighting to keep herself under control. What the fuck was she going to do now?

Her mind jumped from one possibility to another, seriously considering how bad of an outcome it would be if she marched into whatever hole Nydas was currently hiding in and tried to rip off his face with her bare hands. It would never work. She had been unable to best him even when she had had her blessing the first time around. It would be a suicide mission if she attempted it without it.

Maybe he wasn't in Risten, though. Maybe he was somewhere else, somewhere she could have access to her powers. But that was a fool's dream, and she couldn't base a reasonable plan on something as flimsy as hope. She stepped back, threading her fingers through her short hair and pulling.

Good gods, everything was crumbling around her and she had no leg to stand on.

She thought of the mass of coins tucked away in her pack and realized she could hire someone, a hitman or a group of mercenaries to back her up, but the solution tasted sour on her tongue. She wanted to be the one that did it. She craved the surge of pride and accomplishment and triumph that it would be to take Nydas down herself. Plus, the more people she involved, the harder it would be to get away with it with no one finding out.

That was why she had always worked alone as an assassin: there had been no one around to snitch or leave a trail that the authorities could find. It had always been better to just handle it herself. Other people complicated things.

She groaned, her frustration a thick bramble that crowded her chest. Dropping her hands, she clenched and unclenched them at her sides. The next immediate steps in her plan hadn't changed, she told herself. She still needed to find out where the fuck Nydas was in the first place. Figuring out how exactly she was going to bathe in his blood would be a problem for future Evelaine.

Turning back toward the street, she absently watched as more people passed in the pale light of late winter, hustling away from their own demons wrapped around their shoulders and whispering ill tidings in their ears. She could sense coming rain in the air and knew she needed to reach her intended destination before long, the resolution coiling low in her belly. She had to keep going. Shaking her head and drawing her hood low on her forehead, she pressed her lips into a grim line and stepped out of the doorway to find the thoroughfare that she knew would lead her in the right direction.

The capital of the Tirdan Republic rose overhead like a monstrous, metallic beast, its towering smokestacks and iron scaffolding piercing the skyline with arrogance. It was the proud heart of the country's industrial power, a hub of innovation and wealth where the elite perched above the masses like predatory birds, both literally and figuratively. Where in other cities, the affluent separated themselves from everyone else with walled-off neighborhoods and enclaves, in Risten, they had built themselves an untouchable city in the sky.

Their grandiose mansions, glittering with polished brass filigree and expansive glass windows, had been carefully constructed on top of the rest of the populace. Looming above Evelaine as she walked was an intricate network of bridges and support columns that connected their opulent dwellings, shadowing the tangled web of narrow alleys and crowded streets that made up the lower districts underneath. Below, the architecture was a patchwork of haphazard constructions, left to their own devices. Above, the powerful feasted in luxury on high.

While the sprawling metropolis was centered around the Urdian Spire, an immense clockwork mechanism that ticked day and night with relentless precision, that was not where she was headed. Instead, she turned southward toward the Market District, an area of the city that housed the immense glass structure where the haves shopped and dined on the upper floors and the have-nots bartered for their food and wares at ground level. Last time she'd checked, her grandfather's apothecary had been tucked into a side street nearby, and she soon found the familiar corner, taking care to avoid a certain alley a few blocks away that she was desperately trying not to think about.

She slowed as she neared the entrance, the same old, worn wooden sign hanging discreetly above a leaded glass door that she had sometimes glimpsed in her dreams while in Curacu. A vision that she had somehow known was integral to her history without knowing why or how. Her heart pounded as she came to a stop a few doors away, the feeling of déjà vu making her head spin.

Breathing deeply, she filled her lungs with the scents of fried pastries, tanned leather, and pungent spices wafting over from the market, just barely covering the ever so slight presence of herbal tinctures and earthy loam that she recognized from her childhood. Before her courage could fail her, she strode forward and pushed the door open, the tinkle of the shop bell making her wince despite herself.

She stuttered to a halt, arrested by the sight of crowded shelves filled to the brim with eccentric collections of jars, bottles, pouches, and boxes stuffed next to plants of all sizes and kinds—a veritable smorgasbord of concoctions, remedies, and aids for anything a person might be in need of. It almost brought tears to her eyes, the sound of distant fumbling in the back something she had never thought she could forget.

Swallowing her emotions, she cleared her throat and tapped her fist against her thigh awkwardly. Her feet were telling her to run right back out the door, but she knew what she needed to do and ordered them to approach the long counter that stretched along the rear wall. The office door creaked open, and she held her breath as the expected puff of white hair and lined eyes behind thick-lensed glasses appeared. A bleary green gaze met hers, instantly widening as shock splashed across her grandfather's face.

"Lainey?" His voice wavered, cracking on the last syllable.

"Gr—" She cleared her throat again, letting her hood fall back as she tipped her chin up. "Grandfather."

"Oh, blessed goddess," he murmured, bumping into the edge of the counter in a hurry to get to her. She stiffened as his calloused, wrinkled hands clutched at her cheeks and his searching gaze shone with unshed tears. "Oh, Lainey, I knew it. I knew you weren't gone."

She forced her shoulders to relax, attempting a reassuring smile that likely looked more like a grimace as she wrapped her fingers around his bony wrists. "It's alright, Grandfather. I-I'm alright."

"I knew the goddess would keep you safe, dear girl," he rasped, stepping back and holding her at arm's length to inspect her. "How are you? Have you been far? Where were you hiding? The Mistress said—"

"It's a long story," she cut him off, already overwhelmed by his questions. She glanced around the shop. "Is it safe here? Has anyone come looking for me?"

"Well, of course. You have been missed greatly. Mason was the first to—"

She held up her hand and backed out of his tight hold, her heart clenching. "Let's go to the back and I'll tell you everything. Can you close up early for the evening?"

24

"Oh, yes, yes, of course." He shook his head, then hustled over to the front door and slid the heavy locks in place. Drawing the faded curtains over the windows, he turned and gestured for her to lead the way to the back, where his personal rooms were. "Please, I'll get some tea started for you. Have you eaten?"

Something softened inside of her as she let herself droop and started in that direction, her grandfather's offer one that she had heard a thousand times before and yet had been terrified that she would never hear again. He was the one person she could always trust, and the bone-weary exhaustion that she fought so hard to ignore made her steps heavy, the comforting smell of his cozy sitting room greeting her like a long-lost friend. It was truly a sight for sore eyes.

She watched, almost in awe, as he rushed to set a fresh kettle of water above the large stone fireplace that took up the majority of the rear wall next to the glass door that led to the greenhouse and started digging around in his pile of tea canisters crowded in the corner of the kitchen area. As her aching gaze drank in the familiar scene, her limbs acted without her conscious direction, the movement rote as they tossed her cloak to the side and dropped her into the faded, oversized armchair that she had spent a good portion of her childhood in.

It felt surreal to be back, her focus catching on all the insignificant details she had never paid much attention to before. The ceiling was cluttered with bundles of herbs hung out to dry, and there was the usual assortment of scattered teacups, notebooks, and fermenting tonics patiently awaiting his attention on every surface. On the walls hung botanical illustrations and handwritten recipes alongside the knobs that held his aprons and coats, still the same worn canvas ones he had owned for years and years because why spend his hard-earned coin on something that didn't need to be replaced yet?

Her eyes pricked and she blinked rapidly, shoving the tears away as she leaned forward and picked up one of his half-finished papers to distract herself. It was a recipe-in-progress for a salve intended for a skin disease she had never heard of, and as expected, there were scratched out ingredients and additional notes crowding the margins in his familiar scrawl. More clanging raised her head as her grandfather drew out a loaf of bread from a cabinet and began adding new bits of vegetables, herbs, and stock to the hanging cauldron he used for his personal cooking, freshening up the perpetual stew that she was sure would keep him fed until his dying day. Satisfied, he nodded to himself then brought a tray of cups over to her, setting it down on top of the papers that covered the low table in front of Evelaine.

"Now, dear girl, tell me." He settled into the settee next to her. "What have the years brought you?"

"Oh, Grandfather." Her voice was too thick for her liking. "Too much . . ."

He watched her struggle to find the words with kind eyes that saw more than she wanted, patting her hand. "Just start from the beginning, alright? We can take it from there."

She gave him a sad smile and squeezed his hand on top of hers before sitting back in her chair with a long exhale.

"Well, you know that I traveled to Port Werthine on a mission."

He nodded, waiting for her to continue.

"It was to take care of someone who had become a problem for the Mistress." Her grandfather had known that she had been under the employ of the woman who ran the Satine Rouge, and he had been somewhat aware that her job duties had been of the kind that would have gotten her into big trouble with the authorities if they had known, but she had kept the exact details from him, letting him believe whatever he had chosen to.

"It . . . did not go well." She glanced at him to watch his reaction. "They managed to . . . capture me in the process."

His forehead creased slightly but he nodded again, staying silent.

"They shipped me off to Talegartia, actually."

"Talegartia?!" His brows shot upward. "My gods."

"Yes, well, I managed to escape after we landed there and somehow . . ." She shook her head, still confused as to how it had all unfolded. "Somehow, I made my way to the plant village."

"Wait—" His jaw dropped open as realization struck him, the only person alive in Risten who would be able to make the connection. "Curacu?? The village where your blessing comes from??"

"That's the one. They have not been doing well since the council came into power over there, since the revolution, and they interpreted my arrival as the answer they'd been waiting for. Apparently, they hadn't had a blessed in the

27

village for quite some time, so they were quick to welcome me."

"I mean, my mother said—I didn't truly believe—" The steam whistle for the hot water went off behind him, and he got up distractedly, shuffling over to pour it into their cups. "But why didn't you return home? Did they keep you there?"

"No, I . . . I lost my memories." His wide eyes shot to hers as he put the kettle to the side. "The sedative that was used on me when I was captured left me with a severe case of amnesia."

He pursed his lips with a frown as he sat back down and picked up his tea to blow on it. "A sedative that powerful is rare indeed. I only know of a few myself, and even then, the ingredients are very hard to come by."

"I was going to ask you about it. How do you think they got a hold of something like that?" That had been one of the items on her list, a possible lead for tracking down Nydas.

"They were in Port Werthine, you say? I've never heard of any apothecary in that city who would be remotely capable of creating a sedative of that caliber. Here, in Risten, I'm the only one that I know of and I would never sell it, no matter how much I was offered." He shook his head adamantly. "They must have imported it somehow."

Evelaine's teeth clenched at the implications. It meant that Nydas's operations were potentially international, not just relegated to the Tirdan Republic. That or he had connections spread far and wide. Apparently, he wasn't just some domestic headman, which made him a lot more dangerous to tangle with.

"So you were in the village for the last five years?" Her grandfather interrupted her thoughts. "How did you regain your memories?"

"Yes, the villagers set me up as their de facto leader, since I was the only blessed that they knew of, and I spent all that time training with and learning from them. I learned so much, Grandfather." That had been an exciting time, she had to admit. Honing her skills and exploring the full extent of what she was capable of. She had been able to harness what was naturally inside of her and turn it into an art. "But a little over three years in, my blessing started to fade."

"Fade? What do you mean?" Her grandfather had taught her everything he knew about plants when her powers had first started to present themselves, just like he had with her mother, but his teachings had only been able to go so far. The blessing only showed up in the women of the bloodline, and his own mother had been the first he had known, so he had never felt what it was like to truly tap into the powers that flowered through her veins.

"I lost access to it." She frowned, thinking of the echoing vacuum inside of her. "At first, it was as if it was weakened, like I couldn't draw from it as easily as I had been able to. But then these storms came and they washed away my powers completely. I was unable to do anything until one of the fire blessed showed up a few weeks ago."

"A fire blessed? My, my, I haven't come across one of those before. What were they like?" Her grandfather's eyes brightened, his innate curiosity instantly stoked.

"He was . . ." She thought back to her impression of Rakhmet. "He was powerful and skilled, an formidable

29

fighter. He came with his guard, and he's apparently the heir to the Pyrantus throne in Zahar."

"The Pyrantus throne?" His gaze grew distant as he searched his memories. "The Zahari used to be ruled by the fire blessed, did they not? I thought they had all gone into hiding after the revolution."

"Well, they're back in power." Evelaine could still see the exact moment Rakhmet had accepted the Fire Crown from Tabriara and wondered how his reception had gone upon his return to his capital. "This fire blessed, Rakhmet, and his guard were on a mission to seek out the sacred plant temple because the fire temple, and others around the world, have somehow been corrupted in the last handful of years. It was first discovered at the water temple. The moon and sun blessed apparently joined forces with the water blessed to clear it."

"Goodness, I've never heard of so many blessed coming together like that. It's this . . . corruption, you say, that's bringing them out of hiding?"

"Yeah, that was what had been blocking my powers at the plant temple. His guard and the water blessed had been successful in clearing the fire temple and restoring his powers, so they had traveled to Talegartia to find my temple and clear it too. And, well, it worked . . . sort of." Her stomach soured at the memories, the bitterness still a festering wound on her blackened heart.

"What do you mean, sort of?" He watched her, having many years of experience interpreting her expressions.

"It was . . ." She looked away. "It was a really bad fight. Some . . . Some of our party didn't make it out. But the temple was cleared, I got my blessing back, and we ended up . . . We were met by the Plant Goddess."

His eyes rounded. "Blessed Tabriara? You spoke with her?"

"She's the one who restored my memories."

"Dear gods." Her grandfather trailed off, stunned.

"I was . . ." She swallowed the knot in her throat. "I was so angry when I remembered everything I had lost, everything I had left behind. I never meant to leave. I—"

"I know, I know. It's alright," he immediately comforted her.

"No! It's not alright. I had responsibilities here. I had . . . I had . . ." She couldn't even bring herself to say it.

"They've been doing okay, Lainey. They're staying safe and healthy. They still come to vi—"

She held up her hand again, but it was shaking. "Please, I don't . . . I don't want to know."

Her grandfather eyed her, his expression growing somber. "You have to return to them now that you're back. That girl needs her mother."

She stood in a rush and paced to the other side of the room, feeling like she was going to throw up. She couldn't face them. There was no way. How could she possibly explain to them that she had failed, leaving them to survive on their own with no warning while she'd traipsed thousands of miles away in a happy, little delusion. No word from her in over five years. Her betrayal was inexcusable.

"I-I can't. I—" She clutched at her stomach, the part of her that still bore traces of the daughter she had left behind. Her body had remembered her even when Evelaine's mind hadn't, and she had tortured herself in Curacu, racking her brain for any clue as to why she'd felt like she was missing a limb all those years. The stretchmarks had told her a story that she hadn't known the punchline to. The loose skin had taunted her, telling her that there was a piece of her that she had somehow lost along the way.

Her daughter, her darling Estella.

"You must, Lainey." Her grandfather had risen, coming up behind her to lay a steadying hand on her shoulder. "Mason has been asking about you, even after all this time. They still come to visit every weekend, and Ella has grown so much. You'd be so proud. She needs you, though. Her powers are starting to show and there's only so much I can tell her. She needs her mother. You can't let her face it by herself."

Evelaine's head whipped around. "Her p-powers? She has the blessing?"

"Of course she does. You knew it was going to happen one day. It was inevitable." His forehead creased with sadness. "Your mother couldn't be around for you, but you can guide Ella. Be her support. She needs to know she's not alone."

Evelaine's throat clogged with emotion, her fingers digging into the fabric of her shirt. A part of her had been terrified that Estella would inherit the blessing, yet she had known it was only a matter of time. Of course, her daughter would be about twelve now and that was exactly the age when Evelaine had begun to find errant seeds in her own bed. Her stomach clenched as she imagined the confused expression on her daughter's sweet face as she was mystified by the strange tingling sensations in her fingers. The odd pull toward the herbs and flowers crowding her great-grandfather's apothecary.

"She loves to spend time in the greenhouse with me, just like you did. She has grown into a bright, inquisitive thing, always asking the most interesting questions. You can give her the answers she seeks," he said gently, a soft smile on his face.

Evelaine drew in deep breaths, trying to calm the riot of her heartbeat as she realized that it would only further her betrayal if she left her daughter to figure out things on her own. She had hoped that she would be able to handle her business before bothering them and opening that old wound, yet it seemed like she couldn't avoid it. She had wanted her fight with Nydas to be over and done with before she attempted to earn a modicum of redemption from them, as she knew she would only bring trouble to their doorstep until then. But as painful as it would be to look into the faces of those she had abandoned, it was her duty. It was her responsibility as a mother. As a blessed.

Her anger rose as she thought of the other blessed out there, the moon, sun, fire, and water who had stood back and watched as she had been the one to lose so much in that battle at the plant temple. She was fully aware that Rakhmet had chosen to help his own guard over coming to Nees's aid back there. It was crystal clear where his loyalties were. And the others? Where had they been? Back at home safe and sound, only sending Rakhmet and Hara to support Evelaine in clearing her temple.

They had no idea what she had sacrificed, and still they had asked her to give even more. They wanted her to focus on the temples, help them find Corsair, and forget about all the other things that needed her attention. That was why she had refused to accompany them back to Zahar, why she had gotten on a ship back to the Tirdan Republic as quickly as possible. She had shit she needed to do.

"I'll speak with them. I promise." She sighed, removing her grandfather's hand from her shoulder. "But I need to take care of some things first. I have to finish this business with the person who captured me. That's why I'm here. I need to gather information on him."

Otis studied her expression and let out a long exhale, knowing that he wasn't going to succeed in convincing her otherwise. "Alright, how can I help?"

She gave him a grateful look and started pacing again. "I need to speak with the Mistress, see if she has heard anything about him or knows where he might be now. I also need somewhere to stay in the meantime, if that's alright with you?"

"Of course, you know you're always welcome here." He motioned to the side door that led to his bedchamber. "I'll bring out the cot for you. Who exactly are you looking for, if I might ask?"

"His name is Nydas Sutherland. He's of the criminal type. He's likely keeping a low profile wherever he is."

"I haven't heard of anyone by that name, but I'll be sure to keep an ear out for you." The smell of stew was becoming stronger as he glanced over his shoulder and shuffled over to the cauldron to ladle out portions. He took away the tea she hadn't touched and set the bowls on the table with the bread, bringing out a pot of butter and some utensils as they sat to eat. Her hunger was elusive, but she forced herself to consume the calories she knew she would need. Weakening herself further would do her no good.

"Do you think he's in Risten now?" her grandfather asked as they chewed.

"I honestly don't know," she admitted. "He has obviously vacated his hideout in Port Werthine, but I'm hoping the Mistress has been keeping tabs on him. Considering the job she sent me for wasn't finished, she may still be having issues with him, unless she hired someone else to take care of him."

She desperately hoped not. If Nydas had met his fate at the hands of someone else, leaving her without her retribution, she would be furious.

"But I do have a problem that I need to solve before I can do anything about it." She hesitated, glancing over at him. "It seems as though I have lost access to my powers once more, upon my arrival to Risten."

"Your blessing is gone? But I thought you said it was restored?" Her grandfather's brows furrowed.

"Yes, well, it seems as though there may be a corrupted temple nearby blocking it. I had it when I was in Port Werthine, but the minute I got close to Risten, it faded again." She huffed, frustrated. The trouble with the temples was a thorn in her side, disrupting her carefully laid plans.

"A temple? In Risten? I've never heard of such a thing."

"I know, me neither. Things seem to only get more complicated each step of the way. I just want this to be over and done with." She rubbed her forehead, annoyed with the increasingly long list of things she needed to figure out.

"You know who you'll need to speak with then." He eyed her over his bowl, sopping up the last of his meal with a chunk of bread.

She met his gaze and swallowed. "You can't be serious. He's still around?"

"Of course he is. Where else do you think he'd go? It's the only home he has." Her grandfather huffed. "He does come and see me sometimes, you know. Whenever the ladies need their refills."

She sat back in her chair, setting her empty bowl aside. Corsair, the metal blessed she had grown up alongside at the Satine Rouge, had been one of those few outside of her family who had known who she truly was. His mother, Serphine, was also a courtesan there, at least she had been last Evelaine had checked, and Corsair had also started showing signs of his own abilities around the time he had reached puberty, about a year before Evelaine had.

They had been like siblings to each other, being the only kids scampering around the Rouge at the time, and had awkwardly disclosed their unexpected developments in bits and pieces once they had realized that what was happening to them went beyond the usual hormonal changes. Corsair had accompanied her to her grandfather's, and Evelaine had spoken with Seraphine quite a few times, trying to get a better idea of what their oddly shared histories meant for them.

As they had grown over the years, Corsair had proven himself useful as a bouncer-in-training for the establishment, while Evelaine had turned to the more discrete protection services that the Mistress required, but their bond had never faded. They had spent many an afternoon holed up in one of their rooms, Corsair chain-smoking cigarettes and Evelaine sharpening her daggers while they had bitched about the people around them and dreamed of better days.

Her heart ached for him, too, although she didn't know if she could ever admit it to him, his smug, teasing smirk a frustrating yet beloved cousin to her ever-present scowl. But he had been abandoned by her as well, and she desperately hoped that the years hadn't poisoned him against her.

"Do you think he'll know anything about a temple?" she asked, bringing herself back to the issue at hand.

"He hasn't breathed a word of it to me, but you never know." Her grandfather looked pensive as he gathered their bowls and began washing them in the sink.

"I'll go to the Rouge tomorrow and speak with them. Hopefully I can find something out." She slumped back into the chair and rubbed her forehead again. She needed to focus on her plan or else the heavy dread that all of her pain had been for nothing would overtake her like weeds devouring a grave.

"Please stay safe while you are here," her grandfather urged, glancing over his shoulder. "Without your blessing . . ."

"I know." She sighed again. "I'll be careful. I promise."

He only nodded, his eyes sad as he turned back to the dishes. She could promise that she would be careful, but she couldn't promise that she would be reserved in her quest for vengeance. She was going to do whatever it took to see Nydas and his operation pay for what they had cost her. She would make sure of it.

DAY FOUR

Rising with the sun, Evelaine spent the morning poring over her grandfather's ledgers and daily journals, looking for any clues into ingredients that could have been used for a sedative powerful enough to erase memories. She had questioned Otis the night before about possible combinations and recipes, trying to figure out where the mixture could have come from.

But, by the time midday arrived, she hadn't found anything of use and was in a sour mood as she made her way through the city to the northern Gildan District, where she knew she would find the Rouge proudly perched above the masses that sought out lower-fare entertainment every night. She blended in easily, her dark cloak a passing shadow as she wove her way past theaters that boasted salacious shows for only a copper or two and dance halls with poor ventilation, their walls stained with years' and years' worth of tobacco smoke.

She debated as she walked but ultimately chose to use the staff entrance to the Rouge, scurrying up the creaky metal staircase that led to the rear of the massive, shining beacon. At night, it lit up like a sunrise, spotlights trained on its polished red exterior and elegantly draped windows, but it was no less impressive during the day. The Mistress obviously took pride in her business, not sparing any cost when it came to enticing patrons to enter the towering great hall at the front, decorated with sensuous fabrics and plush furnishings.

In the rear, however, there were discrete doors tucked into molded archways, and Evelaine let her hood fall back as she approached the guards stationed there. She recognized one of them, a fellow named Wexit, who had been hired a few years before she'd left, and his brows shot into his forehead as his watchful gaze landed on her. The other guard reached for the sword at his hip, but Wexit held out an arm, stopping him.

"I'm glad to see the years have treated you well," she greeted him casually, her lips curved in the slight smirk that had been her go-to mask during her time at the Rouge. It had always been better to act the part of the self-assured right hand to the Mistress whenever she'd been on the premises, never letting her facade fall until she'd been in private. She noticed a new scar on Wexit's jaw and a few more lines creased around his eyes, but otherwise he was the same bulk of a man she remembered.

"Evelaine—" His jaw dropped open. "It's been a while."

"I'm here to speak with our dear Mistress. Is she in?" she asked, jerking her chin up to the top corner, where her offices were.

"Yeah, but—" He blinked, trying to gather his thoughts. "Is she expecting you?"

"Not exactly, but I'm sure she'll want to hear my report." She left it vague, not entirely sure what kind of reception she'd be receiving, but he didn't need to know that.

"Sure, of course . . ." He turned to the other guard. "Wait here."

She crossed her arms and leaned back on her heels, looking bored as Wexit disappeared into the door behind him and the other guard eyed her with an expression caught between mistrust and curiosity.

"And your name is . . . ?" she asked him after a moment.

His brows furrowed as he considered whether he should answer, but he came to some sort of decision as he rumbled: "Rocan."

She hummed noncommittally in response and looked him up and down. His guard uniform was the same as they'd always been, dark burgundy pants tucked into sturdy leather boots with a thick leather chestplate atop a black, cotton, long-sleeved tunic. The only difference she noticed was the sword and dagger holstered at his hips. They were much nicer pieces than she remembered, and she briefly wondered if Corsair had had anything to do with the upgrades.

Swallowing the knot that arose at the thought, she focused back on the guard's face and met his intense stare. It turned into a battle of wills as she narrowed her eyes and dared him to say something, her slight stature dwarfed

41

by his weight, but something in her face made him flinch slightly as he quickly glanced away, unnerved.

The smirk returned as the door opened once more to reveal Wexit, who motioned to her. "She'll see you now."

Evelaine didn't bother responding as she crossed the familiar threshold, the hushed whisper of Rocan behind her asking who she was cut off abruptly as she was closed into the silent hallway that led to all sorts of doors at the back of the building. At midday, she knew that not many were up and about yet, and she had planned her visit accordingly. Beyond the cleaning crews, day cooks, and required guards, most of the inhabitants of the pleasure house were still asleep or just waking, used to operating on nocturnal hours due to the nature of their business.

Glancing to the left, she eyed the barely lit passage that would lead her to the staff quarters but shook her head. There would be time for that later, she told herself. For now, she turned right and headed to the stairwell that would take her upward, her boots echoing in the empty wooden hallway that was worn from decades of courtesans, maids, attendants, servers, dealers, and guards rushing from one task to another at the Mistress's bidding.

She kept her mind carefully blank as she ascended, memories crowding around her and pleading for her attention with each step she took. She passed one floor, then another and another, refusing to look down the carpeted corridors that peeked through gilded openings, before she reached the end of the stairwell and paused. Her skin itched as she took in the opulence, a richly appointed hallway that promised decadent indulgence and clandestine pleasures with curtained archways leading off to secret spaces where the privileged few could satiate their appetites. It turned her stomach just like it always had, that unignorable feeling of unfairness tangling in her gut with distaste.

She had never understood why there were some who could enjoy comfort, safety, and easy acceptance at the service of those who were constantly plagued with worry about whether their next meal would be enough or if they would need to yield even more of themselves in order to ensure their survival. For years, she had watched her mother leave their room with brightness in her eyes that was dulled and tired by the time she returned in the early hours, her skin carefully scrubbed clean. She had seen the eager faces of newly hired maids and attendants harden as the weeks of their employment went by, oftentimes increasing their scant earnings with a requested favor here and there that left them haunted and twitchy. She had heard the whispers of what happened when an "accident" caused a staff member to disappear suddenly, sometimes returning with internal scars that never healed, sometimes never to be seen again.

Elemona and Seraphine had been exceptions that caused some of the staff to look at them with envy and bitterness, some with disappointment and pity. As a result, Evelaine had grown up with a stinging need to stay out of the way, whereas Corsair had adopted a more direct approach to the stares. Yet, their chances outside the Rouge hadn't been much better, with the vast majority of the populace finding that they had to sell their labors somehow in order to make do. At least within these walls, they were surrounded by people who understood that however their coin was earned was their own personal business. Plus, the Mistress paid better than most.

Evelaine breathed through the mess of emotions until she could reach an intentional distance again, then continued toward the intricately carved double doors at the end of the hall and knocked with a sharp rap. She heard a distant invitation to enter come from the other side and gripped one of the gilded handles, firmly placing her smirk in place as she walked in.

She was greeted by an expanse of white: a creamy carpet filled the room, framed by pearlescent walls lined with gold moldings and accented with pristine couches and chairs piled with silky pillows. At the opposite end of the space was a wide window that looked out over the Gildan District, the surrounding halls and high-end residences glinting in the soft winter light, and settled right in front of it was the Mistress, sitting regally at her eggshell, lacquered desk. Her hands rested casually on the top of it, her delicate fingers idly holding a feather-tipped quill, also in pure white, and her piercing blue stare was trained directly on Evelaine as she crossed the carpet.

Evelaine almost couldn't breathe as she took in the sight of the Mistress's carefully piled blonde hair and rich cerulean dress that clung to her curves with exactness. Although she must be well past middle age, she had always been a stunningly beautiful woman and had used her looks as equally as her wit to support her business interests over the years. She had used every resource she had at her disposal to assure her success and it showed.

"I must admit, I was quite surprised when Wexit told me that you wished to speak with me, my dear. How long has it been now?" the Mistress purred, her gaze drinking in every detail as Evelaine came to a stop in front of her desk.

"Five years, I believe, Mistress," Evelaine answered, forcing her tone to remain even.

"Five years, indeed." The Mistress hummed as she leaned back in her elegantly carved chair. She tilted her head to the side and played with the quill in her hands, the pads of her fingers sliding across its smooth surface. "And what do you have to report after so long an absence?"

Evelaine felt the need to clear her throat but resisted it, knowing full well that she couldn't let any of her anxiety show. "The Nydas mission didn't go well. He was much more prepared for me than anticipated and succeeded in capturing me. He shipped me off to Talegartia, and I was unfortunately unable to return until now."

The Mistress hummed, setting the quill aside and straightening it so that it was perfectly parallel to the pile of correspondence in front of her. "And you wish to enter under my employ once again, I see."

"Well . . ." Evelaine shifted her weight on her feet, and the Mistress's attention dropped to her muddy boots. She cursed internally. "Not exactly."

The Mistress's bright gaze shot to hers. "Is that so?"

"I have managed to do well for myself in the interim, and while I will always be grateful for your past support, I am only in need of information for now." She held her tongue as she waited, the Mistress studying her expression closely.

"What kind of information?" The question was deceptively casual.

"I wish to know if you are aware of where I might find Nydas. I have a score to settle with him." Evelaine watched as the gears turned in the Mistress's eyes, her mind ever calculating.

"If I'm understanding you correctly, you failed in your mission, ended up across the sea, somehow earned enough that you are no longer in need of us, yet could not return until now, and are now asking for confidential information that is no longer your business as it pertains to the employment you are no longer interested in." Her gaze sharpened, and Evelaine held in her grimace.

She considered her answer carefully. "What do you request of me?"

The Mistress smiled, pleased by the response. "It was quite an inconvenience to lose you, my dear. Your specialized services have been difficult to replace, you see. I've had to rely on the less . . . subtle attempts by my hired men to accomplish what you did for me so skillfully. It's been . . . unideal."

Evelaine stayed silent, wholly unwilling to offer her services to the Mistress again. That was a trap she was determined to remain free of. Her blessing had been a secret at first, something that she had only shared with those closest to her, but it had quickly become obvious that she had more advantages than others when she had begun training under the Mistress's former assassin as a teenager. Before she could fully control them, her powers had erupted from her instinctually as a protective mechanism when threatened, which had happened quite often as her trainer had beaten her into fighting shape.

It hadn't been long before the information had found its way to the Mistress, and the revelation that such a valuable asset had been hiding right under her nose soon made Evelaine their employer's favorite pet, causing the older woman to dote upon the aspiring assassin with a beguiling warmth that had hidden the harsh truth. The young, motherless girl had simply been another shining weapon in the Mistress's armory, and there was no way she would lock herself in that gilded cage once more.

The smile faded as the Mistress realized that Evelaine wasn't going to offer herself up as a solution. It was extremely rare, if not inconceivable, that one of the Mistress's prized tools eluded her grasp, and her expression grew hard. It was time for a business negotiation. "I was able to solve the issue of Nydas indirectly, but your loss has been costly overall. Considering the lifetime value of your services, minus the cost of your weapons and supplies, I would estimate that I would require 1600 gold as compensation. Plus another forty for the information on Nydas."

Evelaine clenched her teeth together and breathed through her nose, struggling to rein in the rising anger as she stared the Mistress down. She had fucking walked right into the trap that she was looking to avoid and it galled her. Of course the Mistress would try to twist her arm into coming back, but Evelaine had stupidly thought that the woman who had been a cruel mother figure to her for so many years would be the most direct route to getting the information she needed. Gods forbid she provided help to her long-lost pet out of the goodness of her cold heart.

What did she mean that she'd solved the issue of Nydas indirectly? Was he already taken care of? Would this all be for nothing? She should've never come here. She should've known better, looked for answers elsewhere, and it was going to cost her. There was no way the Mistress would let her go free now that she knew she was alive and well. Evelaine herself had often been the one to track down the valuable runaways that had tried to escape the Rouge's contracts. She knew exactly what was waiting for her if she refused to bargain.

Narrowing her eyes, she stared the woman down, hoping against hope that there was still a seed of tenderness for Evelaine after all these years, but her old employer refused to break, her shrewd gaze glinting with the challenge. It was clear that the Mistress believed that Evelaine had nowhere near that amount of coin and was certain that Evelaine would have no choice but to become her employee again, with the dangled promise that she could possibly be able to enact her plans for revenge under the Mistress's orders.

What she didn't know was that there was a fortune in Evelaine's pack that could cover the price, plus some. It would be the majority of what she had, though, and Evelaine's knee-jerk reaction was to hold onto as much as possible. She had plans for that money, and she warred with herself as she deliberated.

She swallowed, straightening her shoulders. "Nine hundred even."

Evelaine watched as shock rolled through the Mistress's expression, her eyes widening a fraction, but it was quickly hidden as one of her brows arched with superiority. "Eleven hundred."

Evelaine briefly closed her eyes, holding in her fury as she forced herself to breathe. This was a fucking waste of her coin, but she didn't see any other choice. She had walked into the trap, and she would get herself out of it. She grounded herself and locked onto the Mistress's intense blue stare. "Deal."

The Mistress let out a light laugh, another smile curving across her face. "My, my, my. This day is full of surprises, I suppose."

She raised both of her eyebrows and pointedly glanced down at the surface of her desk, indicating that she needed the coin to be presented before she would continue.

Evelaine worked her jaw as she silently said goodbye to some of her plans, then shrugged off one of the straps of her pack, letting it fall to her side as she reached inside. She drew out only one of the pouches she had divided her coins into, not wanting to let the Mistress know how much she truly had, and deposited the negotiated amount on the desk, using up nearly all of the platinum she had received from Rakhmet.

The Mistress slid the piles over to herself and counted through them twice before nodding, satisfied. She scooped them into one of her drawers and then folded her hands on top of her papers with a pleased expression. "Nydas took up residence in Risten shortly after your failed attempt in Port Werthine and has been holed up in the Brookton District under the protection of the Waltzin family since then."

Time stopped as the words registered, her heart pounding in her head. Nydas was a mere three miles from where she currently stood, and she had just given away the majority of her money to learn a piece of information that she could have easily discovered herself if she had

49

simply looked around first. Her fingers twitched toward the blade strapped to her side as wrath began to bloom out of control inside of her, her breath catching as the Mistress's attention dropped to her hand.

"Ah, ah, ah, dear girl. We made a deal. You have exactly what you came for," the Mistress chided, her lips curving farther as one of her hands disappeared underneath her desktop.

Evelaine fumed, her fingers tightening into a fist. She knew full well that the bitch had a whole building of guards who would rush to her aid the minute she pulled the alarm bell tucked into the underside of her desk. Evelaine had once been one of those that ran full speed toward those double doors the second the ringing sounded in the staff hallway, and she desperately didn't want to add more weight to her shredded soul by attacking those she'd once worked alongside, good fighters who were just doing their best to survive in an unkind world.

Swallowing, she counted to ten and forced herself to breathe. From a distance, she watched as her hands absently secured her pack to her back once more as her mind churned over the information. The Waltzin family was one of the premier merchant households in the city, with a history of claiming influential political positions that ensured their continued amassing of wealth. They owned a dozen or more stores and trading outfits that they ran with ruthless greed from their glittering compound in the northwest corner of the capital. Why they would be protecting Nydas was a question that Evelaine would have to find the answer to, without the Mistress's involvement.

But she had to ask: "What do you mean that you dealt with the issue indirectly?"

The Mistress's posture relaxed a little, her hand reappearing from below the desk as she tilted her head and considered Evelaine for a moment. She apparently came to a decision, the smile on her face telling Evelaine that she was deigning to give her the answer. "I contacted my supplier and intimated to them the importance of better ensuring the safe and secure arrival of my goods. They were more than willing to agree, of course."

Evelaine dipped her chin, confirming what had been left unsaid: the Mistress had intimidated her partners into conforming to her will through brute force and manipulation. The savvy businesswoman who ran the Satine Rouge always got what she wanted, one way or another.

"Right, well, thank you for your . . . assistance," Evelaine rasped, the ingenuine gratitude tearing her throat with its thorns. Her feet were itching to bolt, and she needed to get out of there before she did something she regretted.

"Of course, my dear girl, but before you leave, you know I must insist." A piece of parchment was extracted from the drawer to her right and slid across the desk's surface.

Evelaine dropped her attention to it, recognizing one of the Mistress's nondisclosure contracts. They'd specifically been written with the standard stipulation that the unlawful activities her staff were often involved in would be revealed to the authorities should the agreement be broken. The Mistress had spent decades carefully developing her network of connections within the legal and political structures of this great city, allies that she compensated generously in exchange for pulling certain levers at her request. If enacted, those who broke her contracts sometimes ended up arrested by the same individuals that they'd serviced under the Rouge's roof.

With unusually valuable employees, like Evelaine, a threat of immediate execution was also tucked into the fine print. There was no way the Mistress would let her go without assuring her favorite assassin's silence. Evelaine's feet carried her to the desk, her movements wooden as she bent and took the quill offered to her. Signing her name in a messy scrawl, she tossed it down and retreated quickly.

"I do hope you will visit from time to time. I would very much enjoy hearing your story of apparent success in the years that separated us so inexcusably." The Mistress's white teeth shone against the backdrop of the cityscape behind her. "And best of luck on your future endeavors."

"Thank you, Mistress." Evelaine bowed out of habit, hating herself for it, but her muscle memory was too strong in the presence of the woman that had molded her into the cunning assassin she had become. As she backed up toward the doors, her eyes darted over to the poised figure a final time as her heart thrashed around in her chest. Bitterness mixed with her fury, but there was also a pathetic strain of yearning that she didn't want to acknowledge.

She shut it out as firmly as the door closing behind her, her chest heaving as she rushed down the hall and away from the choking opulence. She was running before she knew it, blindly flying down the stairs at a rapid pace, and didn't even spare a glance to the startled attendants she passed, everything a blur of red and gold. Suddenly arriving in front of a familiar door, she stuttered to a halt and stared at it as she caught her breath.

Her boots had carried her there without conscious thought, and she found herself at a loss for words. What could she even say? There was too much to apologize for, and yet she somehow needed to try. Sure, she had her grandfather to return to. He would always accept her, even with her many failures, but a craving for reassurance from someone who truly understood her pain clutched her heart in a tight vise.

Her shaking hand reached up, knocking on the door in a pattern she had used countless times before. It was a special greeting they had devised as kids, and she held her breath as she heard the squeak of bed springs on the other side. There was a long pause, and she could see him in her mind's eye, standing there and gripping his dagger in indecision.

Another moment passed and then the door cracked open, a steely gray eye peeking around the edge and then widening with shock.

"Holy shit," came the mumbled greeting as the door was flung wide. Corsair's eyebrows grazed his hairline as he stared with his mouth wide open, the expected dagger hanging from his hand. He was shirtless, per usual, his bare feet peeking out of the bottom of loose pants and his long, dark hair mussed from sleep and brushing the tops of his muscled shoulders.

"What the fuck?" he croaked, rubbing one eye with his fist and blinking at her in confusion.

"Hey, fucker." She attempted a smile but felt it waver, the expression foreign on her face. "How's it going?"

"Evie," he rasped and grabbed for her, his thick arms squeezing as he wrapped her in a bear hug, and she awkwardly patted his shoulder. "Holy fuck, where have you been?"

He pulled back, holding her at arm's distance, and glanced her over. He took in her hurriedly chopped hair and brand-new cloak, his eyes dropping to the unfamiliar dagger at her waist and back up to the old scar on her forehead. "What the fuck, dude?"

The smile turned genuine as she relaxed. "I know, I know. It's a long story."

"You have to . . . Fuck, come in. I've got to hear this." He let her go, sweeping his arm to the side and stepping back to let her into the room.

Her smile grew as she entered and took in the usual chaos that was his private quarters. There was a single bed shoved into the corner with a desk wedged next to it and a chair backed against the bookshelf on the other side, but everything was covered in a scattering of pants and shirts and weapons. She could see the hilts of swords and the pommels of daggers peeking out here and there alongside the pouches of tobacco and rolling papers piled on the desk. A stack of empty plates and mugs completed the look, and she almost laughed at the usual smell of smoke mixed with sweat that permeated the space.

She shoved a pile of clothing to the side and sat down on the end of the bed, folding one leg underneath her and leaning back against the wall as he closed the door and turned to stare at her. He still gripped the dagger in one hand, but his other came up to thread through his hair, his expression bewildered.

"Dude," he repeated, at a loss.

She sighed. "I know."

He dropped his hand and slumped down in the chair across from her, tossing his dagger to the side and picking up a pouch of tobacco. He glanced up at her expectantly. "So? What the fuck?"

She sighed again. "The mission with Nydas was a total bust. He was way too prepared and ended up fucking capturing me and shipping me off to Talegartia."

"What?!" Corsair's eyes widened, his fingers deftly rolling the papers without looking.

"Yeah, I spent the last five years there with the plant tribe, learning how to, you know, do the thing," she explained, wiggling her fingers at him.

"The plant tribe? The fuck?" He absently licked the cigarette closed and started patting around for matches.

"I know." She rolled her eyes. "Until the fire blessed showed up with his guard and was all like, 'your temple is corrupted,' blah blah blah. 'We're trying to save the world,' blah blah blah. Long story short, I had amnesia, lost my powers, fought a bunch of these fucked-up black ooze snakes, got my powers back, and came here to track down Nydas and slit his throat."

"Wait, what? Temple? Black ooze snakes?" He took a big puff, sweet smoke filling the air, and shook his head. "What the fuck are you talking about?"

She dropped her head back against the wall. "So, apparently, there are these temples connected to our powers. Like, one for each blessing. There was this plant temple that was being guarded by the plant tribe, and these temples are being corrupted for some reason and blocking

55

off our powers. Do you have access to your blessing right now?"

His eyes widened again. "How did you know? I've been fucking useless for like four months."

"Four months?!" Evelaine sat up. "It's only been that long?"

"Yeah." His brows furrowed, smoke spilling from his lips. "It started maybe, like, seven months ago? I started to feel all weird and thought I was getting a flu or something, but the only thing that was affected was my blessing, like it was weakened somehow. Then we had these super crazy storms and poof, it was just fucking gone."

"Four months . . ." she shook her head. "Damn. Did you know there was a temple near here?"

"A temple? For what? A blessing?" He eyed her. "In Risten?"

"Yeah, my blessing also got cut off when I arrived here yesterday. I had it back in Port Werthine, but the minute I got close to the capital, I lost it again. That means there's a corrupted temple nearby."

"What is this corruption you're talking about? Like our powers are decaying?" He looked worried, his hand unconsciously going to his shoulder. He had gotten a massive tattoo on his back when he had turned twenty featuring two crossed swords and had dropped all of his savings to have the ink mixed with titanium powder so that he could use his blessing to summon the blades whenever he wanted. She supposed that with his powers blocked, the tattoo had been rendered a simple work of art.

"I'm not really sure, but it has to do with those black snakes I mentioned. The plant temple was covered in this, like, ichor that sucked everything dry. And there were these wraith things that were fucking horrifying. It was a total nightmare." Her jaw clenched, the echoes of Nees's screams filling her head.

"Dude, what? Wraiths?" He cringed back, his lip curling. "And you think that's happening here somewhere? That's why I can't do shit?"

"Yeah, your mom hasn't mentioned anything about a temple nearby?"

"No, I mean, you know, I get the power from the bastard's bloodline, so she doesn't really know much, but . . ." His eyes trailed to the back corner of the room.

"What?" she asked, following his gaze.

"The fucker left me this . . . letter of sorts. Now that I'm thinking about it, it may have mentioned . . ." He held the end of his cigarette between his teeth and leaned forward to pull the bed away from the wall. Evelaine tipped to the side from the sudden movement, catching herself before falling off as he flopped over the other end and started prying at a hidden compartment out of sight.

She heard the shifting of wood, and he brandished a handful of dusty, folded papers as he sat up, rifling through them as more smoke trailed around him.

"Here," he said suddenly and handed her one of them. It looked to be the middle of an explanation about the metal blessing, the end of a sentence cut off at the top of the paper with a drawing underneath it. It was a vague sketch of a geometric object that was equally split into squares, like they were stacked on top of each other in rows. At the center was a rough drawing of a crystal that looked oddly familiar, and she gasped as she recognized it as cousin to the one they had seen in the plant temple. The one that had revealed the doorway that led to Tabriara's domain at the end of the fight.

There was an arrow pointing to it with the scrawled phrase: "Here you will find the answers you seek when the time comes, but beware, the path is treacherous and will require the best of your abilities."

"Give me that," she demanded, reaching for the rest of the letter. She read through it, a hasty apology written by the man who had sired Corsair and left his mother to deal with the consequences on her own. It said that he had responsibilities elsewhere that he had to attend to and was deeply sorry that he couldn't be there for Corsair, but that he hoped this letter would point him in the right direction when he sought answers about his bloodline.

It detailed how to use the metal blessing, how to call it and wield the power it provided, and urged Corsair to stay in Risten where its influence was "most felt." At the end was an invitation to travel to Nahua, the capital of a large island to the west of the Tirdan Republic, and track him down in case of emergency.

She scanned the letter one more time, her eyes wide. "This is it. This is the metal temple."

"The what?" He snatched the stack back from her and read it over. "Are you sure?"

"It's your temple." She processed what it had said. "And it's somewhere in Risten. That's why he wanted you to stay here, so you'd be close to it."

The pieces were falling into place. Of course the metal temple would be in Risten, the capital of industrial power. She thought about the towering spires that decorated the landscape, the overt presence of metallic architecture that made the city famous.

Her gaze landed on Corsair, who was studying the drawing with a frown. "They're looking for you, you know."

"Who?" He startled, glancing up at her.

"The fire blessed and his guard. They said that the moon blessed had a vision about the metal temple. They believed that it was the next one they were meant to find." She frowned as well. It was another reminder of the duties they had tried to thrust upon her. But they were just a distraction from the real task at hand, weren't they?

"Oh fuck," she muttered, closing her eyes and dropping her head against the wall again.

"What?" He tossed the letter onto the bed between them and reached for his tobacco.

An unwelcome realization unfurled in her head as obvious conclusions presented themselves. "We're going to have to go there and clear it."

"The fuck you mean, 'we'?" His forehead creased as his fingers absently rolled another cigarette.

"You want your powers back, don't you?" Gods, she couldn't believe she was suggesting it.

"I mean, yeah . . ."

"Well, I need mine back too if I'm going to take on Nydas." She leaned forward and dropped her face into her hands, her frustration muffled. "And we need to clear the temple in order to do that."

Dark memories of terror and fury crowded her head like overgrown weeds and she groaned, rubbing her forehead. Gods, was she seriously considering this? How the fuck were they going to clear a temple without their blessings? They had barely accomplished it back in Curacu with two blessed plus guards. How was she and Corsair supposed to do it?

"Yeah, you mentioned that earlier, about wanting to slit his throat. What's that about?" He stuck the new cigarette between his lips and threw aside some shirts, looking for matches again.

"He drugged and kidnapped me, dude. He stole everything from me, and I'm going to fucking kill him for it," she growled, looking up at him with a scowl.

He lit the cigarette and held up his hands. "Okay, okay, I hear you, but you think we need to find this temple to do that? We're fucking badasses. We can handle a little old headman."

"Without our blessings?" She scoffed. "We need all the advantages we can get. He blindsided me the first time. I'm not going to let that happen again. He's being protected by the Waltzin family right now, for fuck's sake. Do you think we're just going to walk up to their door and be like, 'Hey, Waltzins, can we pretty please murder the criminal you're hiding? Please and thank you?'"

He whistled between his teeth. "The Waltzins? Damn. We're fucked."

"That's what I'm saying!" She threw up her hands and stood to pace. "We need a better plan. We need our blessings."

"Okay, calm down. We can do this." He scooted to the edge of the bed, waving his cigarette as he spoke. "We can find the temple, no problem. Scrub a dub or whatever, get our blessings back, and then corner Nydas somewhere away from the Waltzins and bam, take him out together. Easy peasy. He has to leave their compound at some point. He can't stay cooped up there all the time."

"No, not easy peasy. Do you know how hard it was to clear the plant temple? People fucking died. It was an absolute nightmare," she gritted at him, her fury rising to cover the desperation that she didn't want to feel.

He sighed. "Fine, then we'll get some help."

"Help? Who the fuck is going to sign up for certain death in a mysterious temple that no one's ever heard of?" She placed her hands on her hips and scowled at him again.

Now it was his turn to throw his hands up. "Well, shit, I don't know, but we can ask around, I guess. I mean . . ."

He went still, his hands dropping in his lap as his lips started curling, and he looked at her with a devious grin. "We can always ask—"

"No. Absolutely not." She shook her head. "Please tell me you're not suggesting what I think you're suggesting."

"Oh, come on. You know they'd be down," he prodded, excitement lighting up his eyes.

"Those fuckups? Nope, not going to happen. They'd only make things worse." She crossed her arms. Other people complicated things—that was her rule. She might have been willing to consider taking Corsair along with her, but the list of suitable candidates ended there.

"How would you know? You haven't been here. They've gotten their shit together, I swear. I mean, well, mostly. They are almost always productive members of society now, self-respecting citizens of the great Tirdan Republic, doing their citizenly duties. They would jump at the chance to have a little adventure in their lives. Come on, Evie," he pleaded, giving her his best charming smile.

She huffed and rolled her eyes, turning away to stare at the door. Was she seriously considering this? The whole point of coming back to the Tirdan Republic was to track down Nydas, finish the job, and then be done with it all. She would distribute her small fortune to the people who mattered, an attempt at reparation for her failures, then take her share and get the fuck out of there. Start over somewhere new where she didn't have to continue to disappoint those she had abandoned.

But things were only getting more complicated. Nydas wasn't where she had left him, her powers were functionally useless, her money was quickly dwindling, and in order to accomplish what she needed to, she now had to figure out how to clear the metal temple with no feasible plan beyond enlisting a group of fuckups that she had written off years and years ago. But who else could she trust for a job like that? It wasn't like she could go pick up a band of random mercenaries and expect them to keep their cool when faced with the nightmares she knew would be waiting for them.

"Fuck." She groaned, dropping her head back, then turned to Corsair. "You're sure they'd be up for the job? It's going to be brutal. Way worse than they've ever seen before. Like, I'm talking they may very well not make it out of there."

"Well, you made it out of the plant temple, right?" Corsair shrugged, still looking thrilled by the prospect. "How hard could it be?"

"Dude, what part of 'people died' did you not understand?" she gritted out.

Corsair's smile faded a little. "People die every day, Evie. We can at least make it count for something."

Her breath caught, the fleeting look of somberness in Corsair's expression making her think twice. His life had always been just as difficult as hers, two bastard children of courtesans with no choice but to face the world's ire and judgment, but he had never let it truly get to him. Sure, he had his vices. He smoked like a chimney, fucked for sport, and fought like a bat out of hell, but he leaned into the chase where she chose to hide in the shadows. If she was going to do this, he was exactly the person she'd want by her side.

"Fine." She sighed. "Where can we find them?"

Corsair whooped, jumping to his feet and pounding a fist into the air. "Fuck yes! This is going to be great, the whole gang back together again!"

Rubbing her forehead, Evelaine couldn't help the smile that was starting to form at his enthusiasm. Gods, she really hoped she wouldn't come to regret this.

DAY FIVE

Corsair showed up to her grandfather's apothecary late the next morning, pulling the old man into a big hug with a grin as Evelaine shrugged on her cloak. Otis grabbed Corsair's cheeks, giving them a loving squeeze, and made them take some rolls with them even though Evelaine had already eaten her fair share of eggs, toast, jam, sausage, fruit, tea biscuits, and anything else her grandfather had been able to stuff her with ever since her eyes had cracked open in the weak rays of sunrise filtering through the greenhouse's door.

More than happy to comply, Corsair was soon whistling as they headed out, his pockets bulging with breads. Evelaine side-eyed him as they walked, wondering if he was truly going to keep up the racket the whole time as they made their way through the city to the Skidden District north of the docks. It was where most of the working class lived, and even though she hadn't walked the path in over five years, Evelaine knew exactly where they were going.

They passed shadowed residences tucked alongside small shops, bakeries, butcheries, and grocers, some of them featuring the same signs Evelaine recognized, some with newer paint advertising discounts and deals to entice people inside. Folks of all ages hurried by, on their way to work or tugging kids along with dirt smudged on their cheeks, and Evelaine couldn't help but scrutinize their features, looking for a pair of bright teal eyes that she had often seen in her dreams.

Shaking her head and ignoring the pull in her gut, she hunched her shoulders against the viscous shame as they slipped into a familiar alley. Five doors down, they stopped in front of a crumbling stoop, and Corsair knocked on the peeling wood as Evelaine shifted uneasily behind him. They had to wait a few moments, and Corsair shot her a hopeful smile, but eventually there was the sound of locks turning on the other side and the door cracked open to reveal a beady brown eye, narrowing with suspicion.

"Surprise!" Corsair spread his arms wide. "Guess who's come to visit!"

The eye darted between them both, and Evelaine shifted her hood so it could get a clearer look as it widened a fraction. The door was quickly closed, and they heard the scrape of a chain being removed before it was opened again, the slim features of their old companion coming into view.

Gimlet hadn't changed one bit, his shaved head and bony shoulders showing no signs of the passing years as a sly grin curled across his face. "Well, I'll be damned."

"Look who's back from the dead, hearty and hale, and looking for her good ol' pal." Corsair grabbed Evelaine by the shoulders and pushed her forward.

She grimaced, shrugging off his hands. "Gimlet."

"Evelaine, a surprise indeed." His voice was quiet but firm, a knife between the ribs that no one ever saw coming. "What the fuck are you doing here?"

"Do we have a story for you, my good man," Corsair announced, pushing Gimlet aside and letting himself in.

Gimlet huffed dryly. "Please, come in."

Evelaine gave him an apologetic look and followed Corsair into the dark sitting room, a sole lamp illuminating the threadbare furnishings. There was evidence of a half-eaten meal on the table along with a scattering of empty bottles, but she knew that there were likely a dozen hidden blades out of sight right where he could reach them at a moment's notice.

Corsair grabbed one of the wooden chairs, turning it around and sitting on it backwards to make himself comfortable as Gimlet closed the door and propped himself against the faded wall with his arms crossed. Evelaine tipped her hood back fully, standing awkwardly to the side as she wondered where to start.

"Evie here needs our help. We're getting the gang back together." Corsair happily broke the silence as Evelaine winced at his use of her nickname. Only he had ever called her that and she wanted to keep it that way, her gaze sliding to Gimlet with a warning.

"Is that so?" Gimlet's chin lowered, his tongue running across the front of his uneven teeth as he considered her with interest.

"A deathly adventure on a mysterious mission, something I told her you'd be absolutely down for." Corsair smiled knowingly, Gimlet's attention falling to him.

Gimlet was no stranger to secret dealings, having worked as a bartender slash dealer slash bouncer for many years under the Mistress's roof. He had proven himself to be of both quick mind and feet, although his penchant for enjoying the substances he peddled had always been his downfall. His stealthy fingers had swiped many a bottle and pouch of something or another from the Rouge's stores, and after being caught too many nights two sheets to the wind on the job, he had been thrown out on his ass about a year before Evelaine had left. The Mistress had considered him more of a liability than an asset, drawing up one of her ironclad nondisclosure agreements to ensure he kept his silence in exchange for not turning him into the authorities.

"What exactly have you been up to these days?" she asked, well aware of the perpetual shadows under his eyes.

"A little of this, a little of that. I keep busy," he hedged, his eyes flicking over the sturdy shirt and pants made of a dark, heavy cotton she had acquired for herself before leaving Port Werthine. They weren't of the best quality, but they were a step above what most of the Mistress's people could afford on their scant wages. His gaze landed on the gemmed pommel sticking out of the sheath at her waist, and she could see the calculations running through his mind. He had always been a keen study of a target's ability to pay.

"Right . . ." She drew out the word, her hand landing on the end of the dagger to hide it from view as she gave Corsair a look.

"He's doing well for himself, aren't you, Gimlet?" Corsair said brightly. "Working at the tavern over on Pearson Street."

He named a respectable establishment that she was familiar with, not a hole in the wall but not one of the elite drinking halls that would be found in the Gildan District, and Evelaine studied Gimlet in return, debating whether they should trust him. She knew he had skills that would certainly be helpful. His blade work was almost as good as Corsair's, and he had always been an expert at staying unseen when he needed to. Subversion was his specialty.

"Is this a paid job?" Gimlet asked, his voice low but his gaze not breaking from hers.

"How much would you want?" She frowned, fucking tired of the amount of bargaining she was having to do in this city.

Gimlet's mouth lifted to the side again. "You haven't told me the details of this mission yet."

"Well, get this." Corsair leaned forward. "What if we told you we have special powers?"

Evelaine stiffened, sudden anxiety sprouting to life inside of her as her eyes darted to him. Was he really going to just come out and say it? Her stomach dropped. Gods, they would have to if they were going to lead Gimlet into the corrupted temple and expect him to fight otherworldly beings alongside them.

Gimlet's brows twitched together. "What do you mean?"

Corsair glanced at Evelaine, silently asking permission, and she chewed on the inside of her cheek in indecision. Was getting her blessing back this important? She shifted on her feet, uncomfortable. Maybe they could just kidnap Nydas somehow and get him out of Risten where she could take care of him away from the corruption's influence. But how were they going to do that with the full might of the Waltzins involved?

She cursed her circumstances. She was in this fucking mess all because of Nydas and she wanted him to pay, but he had already gotten away from her once before. Now he was even more protected, and there was no way she could take on one of the most influential families in the city by herself without her blessing, even with Corsair's help. As much as the thought worried her, she knew they needed allies in this fight. There was no way the two of them would be able to handle the temple on their own, and Gimlet was as good a choice as any. He certainly knew how to keep secrets and wouldn't dare snitch to the authorities for fear of exposing his own underhanded dealings.

What else could she do? Reach out to the other blessed and ask them? They hadn't even helped her when it had mattered back at the plant temple, so why would they now? When the only reason she wanted to go into the metal temple was to get her blessing back so she could take down a headman that had absolutely nothing to do with the whole corruption situation? They would never agree to it. Their motivations were the complete opposite of hers. All she wanted was to enact her bloody vengeance.

She couldn't turn back now. Her only chance at retribution was on the line.

"You have to swear to never breathe a word of what we're about to tell you to anyone, no matter what." She turned to Gimlet, drawing out five gold coins from her pack and setting them on the table one by one.

His attention dropped to the offering. "I'm listening."

"Swear it," she demanded.

His gaze slipped to Corsair, who gave him an encouraging nod, and then he focused back on her. "I swear, whatever you say will stay between us."

She flicked him the coins and he caught them easily, stowing them in his pocket in one smooth movement. Nodding, she took a deep breath. "Have you ever heard of blessed ones? Those that can wield elemental powers?"

Gimlet's expression turned pensive. "Maybe? I thought it was a myth or something. Like hyped-up tales of power from long-lost kingdoms, just something people made up to over-romanticize the past."

"Well—" She glanced at Corsair then back at Gimlet. "They're real. There are blessed ones who still live to this day, scattered across the world."

"And, what? You're telling me you two are . . . blessed?" Gimlet looked confused, trying to read the both of them to see if they were bullshitting him.

"I come from the bloodline of those who are connected to the Plant Goddess, and Corsair comes from the Metal God bloodline. Those elemental powers run in our families." Evelaine couldn't breathe, watching for his reaction.

Gimlet's brows raised, a startled laugh leaving him. "What? Two courtesan bastards? Wielding the powers of the gods? You guys are shitting me, right?"

"We're serious, Gim," Corsair said, unsmiling.

Gimlet's attention bounced between them as he waited for someone to crack a grin and tell him they were joking, but it never came, and the realization settled on his face.

"Fuck." He rubbed his hand over his shorn head. "But . . . if you guys have these wild powers, then why the fuck are you stuck in this shithole? Shouldn't you be, like, I don't know, rulers or something?"

Evelaine shrugged. "Our ancestors used to be before the revolution, I guess. My great-great-great-whatever-the-fuck-grandmother was the Queen of Talegartia, and his great-great-whatever-grandfather was the king in this area. But they were forced into hiding by the rebellion, and this is where we've ended up." It wasn't the point of all this. She had told the Plant Goddess in no uncertain terms that she had no interest in being the ruler of anything.

"Damn, that really sucks," Gimlet said, staring at them.

Corsair raised his hands as if to say, *what're you going to do?*

"So, you guys can like"—Gimlet waved his hand vaguely—"do things?"

"Well, see, that's the problem." Evelaine frowned. "At the moment, we don't have access to them. That's why we need your help."

"Me?" Gimlet's eyes widened. "How am I going to help with that? I don't know shit about any of that."

"There's a temple in Risten that's been . . . overtaken by some really bad shit, and we need your help to clear it out. It's going to be a brutal fight, and we need the backup," Evelaine explained.

"I don't know, guys. It sounds like you know way more about all this than I do. I'm just a fucking rat-ass dealer. How could I possibly be of any use?"

"Dude, you are killer with the blades. I've seen you fight. You know what you're doing," Corsair insisted. "Evie said there were these, like, wraiths and ooze snakes. Doesn't that sound like fun?"

"Ooze snakes?" Gimlet looked horrified.

"It's—" Evelaine shot Corsair a look to shut up. "It's honestly going to be really bad, so we understand if you don't want to do it. We just . . . We need all the help we can get."

"And this temple is . . . where your powers are? That's why you need to go in there? To get them back?"

"Um, kind of." Evelaine debated how much to tell him. "Our powers are, like, blocked by the things that have taken over the temple, so we need to remove them in order to be able to access our blessings."

"And you need your blessings because . . . they'll get you out of this shithole?" Gimlet dropped into the chair next to Corsair and leaned forward on the table, looking overwhelmed by trying to wrap his mind around what they were telling him.

Evelaine sighed, taking the remaining chair and joining them. "We need our powers because I have a score to settle with a headman. He's the reason why I've been gone, and I need to take him out for good."

"Who exactly are we talking about here?" Gimlet's eyes narrowed.

"Nydas Sutherland. Do you know him?" Evelaine's hope leapt despite her.

Gimlet looked at her like she was crazy. "You've got to be shitting me. You're seriously going after Nydas?"

"Yeah, he fucking ruined my life, and I'm going to make him pay one way or another," she swore.

Gimlet leaned back in his chair, a long exhale leaving him. "Shit, man. You do realize he's with the Waltzins now, right?"

Evelaine struggled to keep her fury in check, the realization that she could've learned where Nydas was just by asking Gimlet first instead of the Mistress making her push away from the table and rise to pace. She stomped to the other side of the room and cursed herself. All that money gone for nothing.

"Fucking hell," she muttered.

"What? We already knew that." Corsair looked confused by her reaction.

"I just— Fuck!" She threw her hands up, wanting to punch something. "I paid the Mistress for that information and it's just . . . that bitch obviously overcharged me."

Corsair whistled through his teeth and glanced at Gimlet, who just shrugged. They both knew full well how manipulative and deceptive the Mistress could be. They'd all been screwed over by her at one point or another.

"How much?" Corsair asked.

Evelaine closed her eyes and counted to ten before opening them again. "It doesn't matter now. Are you in or out, Gimlet?"

He eyed her, his attention once again dropping to the gemmed pommel at her waist before his brown gaze met hers with a familiar expression. She couldn't help but remember all the times that they had had each other's backs. She had often been assigned to accompany him on his supply trips under the Mistress's orders, and due to the nature of the business, they had found themselves in quite a few tussles when negotiations had turned sour.

The Mistress had always demanded that they achieve the most advantageous price for their purchases, which was almost never what the suppliers were willing to sell for. It had resulted in bloodshed more times than Evelaine cared to admit, and she knew that he carried the weight of their past actions on his shoulders as much as she did, one of the reasons why he had turned to the oblivion that the substances offered. He had been as much of a victim of his circumstances as those they had left bleeding out in dark alleyways.

"If I join you, will you get me out of here after we're done?" he asked, his features hard with the reality that was a life of trying to survive by any means necessary in the great capital they called home.

Evelaine's shoulders dropped, her anger crumbling away as she understood what he was asking. "That's your price?"

He nodded. "You got out of here, right? That's my price."

She chewed on her cheek for a moment, the weight of what they would be facing in the temple making her hesitate. Nees's pained screams echoed in her head, and she knew she had no right to guarantee that he would survive the trip. But all she could see was the plan that had been driving her forward ever since she'd been forced to return her loyal guard's body to the village. All she could feel was the poisonous hunger woven into every fiber of her being. The pitch inside her chest threatening to choke her. The need for vengeance turning her soul black.

She had to believe her plan would work. There was no other option.

She offered her hand. "I'll get you out, I promise."

A passing look of relief flickered across Gimlet's face before it was hidden by his usual cunning and he smiled, taking her hand. "Deal."

"Great!" Corsair's eyes darted between them, his enthusiasm coming off a touch too hollow as he stood and clapped his hands together to break the tension. "Tomorrow we'll be heading over to see Rikeland, if you want to come along, Gim?"

Gimlet huffed out a small laugh. "Nah, I'll leave you two to it. I've got some things I need to arrange before we leave. When do you expect we'll head to this temple of yours?"

"Let's plan on four days from now, maybe five," Evelaine hedged, starting for the door and glancing over her shoulder. They had a few more stops to make in order to gather the "gang," as Corsair had called them, plus they would need to figure out where the hell the temple was anyways. But she could only focus on what was right in front of her for now, her head too full of what-ifs to think straight.

"Sounds good." Gimlet stood, opening the door for them as they exited out into a misting rain that had taken over the city. Condensation gathered and dripped from the scaffolding above them as Evelaine raised her hood once again.

"We'll be seeing you." She dipped her chin to Gimlet. "Thank you for your help."

"I'll hold up my end." Gimlet nodded in return, leaving the rest unsaid: *if you uphold yours.*

Evelaine pressed her lips together, unease tangling in her gut as he closed the door, and Corsair slung his arm over her shoulders.

"See? Everything's coming together," he said merrily, their boots leaving a trail through the puddles as mud started to gather on the cobbled streets.

"Mm-hmm," she hummed noncommittally and shrugged off his arm. Self-doubt was trying to crowd its way into her circling thoughts and she clenched her teeth, gripping her anger tightly to fight it off.

"Want to go grab a drink somewhere while we wait out this rain?" Corsair asked, lighting a cigarette that he fished out of his pocket as they threaded their way into the thoroughfare that would take them back to the Market District.

She shook her head. "No, I'm good. I need to walk for a bit."

"Fair enough." He lifted a shoulder. "I'll meet you tomorrow at the shop?"

"Yeah, okay," she agreed, already turning away from him. She didn't wait for an answer, disappearing into a side street and fading into the shadows. They welcomed her like an old friend, helping her distance herself from the clamor in her head.

Once again, she had somehow put herself in the position of having too many people relying on her for comfort, and she desperately wished she could hide away completely.

It would be so much easier that way, she told herself, but she was in far too deep for that now. Time after time, the clawing needs of the people connected to her were too much, and she was plagued by the urge to peel her skin off and shed every piece of herself at their feet in an attempt to satisfy them.

First, there had been her mother. The bright, charming, sprite of a woman whose energies had been sapped every night by the Rouge's clients, who had sought to feast upon her blooming beauty for their own selfish gains. Evelaine had spent her entire childhood comforting her, taking care of her, and soothing her invisible wounds in the early hours, driven by an undeniable urge to protect her from the harsh world they had lived in.

Then just like that, Elemona had been gone, taken by a severe case of pneumonia when Evelaine had only been ten. After that, she had been forced to bend to the Mistress's will in order to keep a roof over her head and food in her belly, and she had clung to the older woman in her heartache. Fear had driven her to be pliable and compliant, sacrificing more and more of her instinctive sense of right and wrong with each passing year until she had no longer recognized herself. She had become a honed weapon, a tool to be used for the singular purpose of a shrewd businesswoman.

That was when she had met Mason. The kind, unassuming woodworker who had offered her a safe and comfortable life that she had never dared to dream of having. It had been a complete accident, something she had never intended to happen. A chance encounter one fall day fourteen years ago when she had entered his shop with the intention of questioning him about a target of hers. She had been on the hunt for a runaway employee of the Mistress's who had murdered one of the Rouge's clients, and the woman had been seen visiting the woodworker that Mason had been apprenticed to at the time.

He had looked at her with his clear blue eyes and tousled blond hair covered in sawdust, so trusting in his simplicity, and she had instantly forgotten why she had come there. Over the next year, she had fabricated a whole range of excuses to go visit him. Sometimes she had asked about people she was trying to find, and sometimes she had dallied about, acting like she was considering buying whatever wood project he was working on. She had even convinced the Mistress a time or two to purchase some of the shop's finer furniture, the craftsmanship of a quality that easily passed the older woman's keen discernment.

With each passing month, he had inched his way closer to her, finding excuses to brush his calloused fingers across hers and leaning into her space when showing her his work. He had been gentle, careful, and tender despite his considerable bulk, showing her that the grabbing need that possessed the Rouge's clientele was not a universal trait. She simply couldn't help falling for him.

There had only been one answer to give when he had finally asked to marry her, giving her a chance to move out of the Rouge but remain an employee under the Mistress. He had never faulted her for her vocation of necessity, not knowing the exact details but understanding that she was a skilled asset, and the Mistress had seen the benefit in lengthening Evelaine's leash, saving her the cost of housing her trusted assassin under the Rouge's roof.

She had always known that she was different from the people around her, even beyond her blessing, but it wasn't until she had been confronted with a new husband and the expectations that that entailed that she had fully realized how different she truly was. While Mason had been a considerate and sensitive lover, she had quickly learned that she did not find the same level of enjoyment in the act as he did.

A virgin until her wedding night, she had never really given it much thought. She had felt the expected love and care for her husband, but when it had come down to the physical joining of their bodies, she just hadn't experienced the rush that had overtaken Mason and sent him into blissful release. He had drawn away afterwards, worried that he had done something wrong, and she had soothed him, assuring him that it was only nerves and that everything was fine. But after quite a few more tries in the subsequent weeks, they had both had to face the fact that Evelaine just didn't find the sexual satisfaction that drove millions of people around the world to seek gratification in another's body.

It wasn't that the act was disgusting or painful for her by any means—it was simply another routine bodily function. Their skin would brush and his lips would caress her in all the right places, but there was no tingle of excitement, shuddering anticipation, or climactic crescendo for her. Even when they were united as one, there had been distance between her and the sensations of it. She had thought it was her fault and consulted courtesans and physicians alike, trying to figure out what was wrong with her, but they had all assured her that everything on her body was as it should be.

She had still loved him deeply and her heart had brimmed with genuine affection as she had gazed upon him, a soft smile on her lips as he had labored above her and found the groaning relief he needed, so they had eventually accepted that that was how it was to be. He had still adored her, and she had found comfort and joy in being his wife, and life had continued on. He would spend his days bent over his various projects in the shop, and by evening, they would curl up by the fire, chatting and smiling over dinner before she'd left for her nightly duties for the Mistress.

Every few weeks, he would give her a soft, yearning look when she'd return in the early hours and she would gladly draw him into her arms, letting his weight settle on her as he slowly entered her and gently took care of his needs. She would stroke his face and think of how lucky she was to have him, a softhearted and loyal companion who had never made her feel like she had to earn his love. Who had accepted her without pressuring her to fit a predefined mold. It had been the solace she had wished for for so many years, and she had finally found it in that sweet woodworker with a heart of gold.

A little under a year into their marriage, she had found her courses late and her breasts more tender than usual. And honestly, she had been overjoyed. The promise of a family all her own that she could keep safe and secure in their cozy quarters above the woodshop had been more than she had ever dreamed of, and she had been determined to give her husband and child a better life than she had been given.

With a baby on the way, Mason's woodmaster had happily handed over the reins of the shop to his competent apprentice and had provided Evelaine and her husband with the security they had needed for their family-to-be. But months later, as she had gazed into the face of her new daughter, her heart overgrown with soul-deep devotion, she should have known that the rewarding life she had stumbled upon had been too good to be true. She should have known that she hadn't truly deserved it. She should have known that because of her true nature, she would eventually be forced to give up the pieces of herself that mattered the most.

Evelaine had lived in that fantasy for seven whole years, keeping her duties to the Mistress far away from the beloved family that she kept free from harm at all costs and watching her daughter grow into a happy, precocious child with pride. She had always stopped by the Rouge before heading home at the end of the night, to wash off the blood and tend to any wounds, and she had even kept her blessing a secret, hoping beyond hope that she would be able to shield Estella from the ire of the world. Yet, despite all her careful plans, she had failed.

Her feet stuttered to a halt at that thought, and she suddenly realized where they had unconsciously led her as she found herself in front of the familiar corner shop just a few doors away from a window display full of carefully polished wooden chairs, toys, and shelves. Gasping, she threw herself around the other side of the corner to hide herself from view and broke into a sprint in the opposite direction. Startled passersby grumbled at her as she pushed her way through them, but she didn't care, her heart pounding with terror as she tore her way back to her grandfather's apothecary.

There was no way she would be able to face them. Not today, not ever. How could she possibly repent for her abandonment? How could she possibly explain that she had been fundamentally incapable of protecting those she loved? That she had enjoyed a comforting lie with someone else for years all while they'd struggled without her? That what was rooted deep down inside of her was a poison that tainted her beyond salvation?

She burst into the apothecary's door, startling Otis as he glanced up from the ledger he was writing in at the counter, and he started to open his mouth with a question forming, but she pushed past him and into the sitting room, not stopping until she had closed the door of the greenhouse behind her and the heavy smell of earthy loam and verdant chlorophyll filled her nostrils. Panting, she rushed to the first plant she could reach, a tall lemon tree whose boughs brushed against the very top of the glass ceiling, and shoved her hands into the soil in its enormous potted base.

She couldn't stop the angry tears that blurred her vision and trembles of fury and anguish, reaching desperately for a blessing she knew damn well wasn't there. She craved its steadying power, the deep-rooted knowledge that if nothing or no one else would be there for her, then she could always rely on its unending resilience. If she was nothing but a walking ruin, using people for her selfish revenge, it assured her she could still spread seeds that would sprout, grow, and conquer in her wake.

But it was gone, inaccessible. All she could do was accept her fate.

She was a mistake, a glaring wrongness that she could never right, and there was only one path for her to follow now. It was crystal clear to her that her true purpose was one of pain, vengeance, and retribution, a destiny bathed in blood. She could no longer afford to delude herself into believing that there was any other option for her. She couldn't bring herself to act the fool and trick anyone into thinking she was anything better than what she was at her core.

Tabriara had said it herself. *Nature feasts on the bodies that fall to the test of time.* Evelaine was the force that would be left in the end, after all else was dead and gone. It was an utter myth to believe that nature was nourishing, constructive, and generative. No, it was ravenous, greedy, and insatiable. It was predatory, all-consuming, and omnivorous.

She just prayed that she could keep those she loved safe until then.

Day Six

Evelaine was left with a bad taste in her mouth after a night of restless sleep, waking before the sun rose to pace the small floor of her grandfather's sitting room until he eventually appeared. He took one look at her puffy eyes and turned to make tea for her without asking, recognizing the worry that lined her face and shame that hung around her shoulders like a dark shroud.

She was regretting everything, from working for the Mistress and letting her control too much of her life for too long to fooling so many people into thinking she was worth their care, attention, and support. If she had just struck out on her own after her mother's death, she would've never ended up here. She would've never had so much blood on her hands. Now, she was faced with impossible decision after impossible decision.

Was she truly capable of leading a group into the metal temple, knowing what was waiting for them? Was she willing to risk them in order to gain her revenge? She had to do right by them. She could be better than she was before, smarter and quicker. She could walk into each challenge with eyes wide open this time. She might not have been able to save Nees, but she vowed to learn from that mistake.

The first step was to gain the advantage of numbers, which meant they needed to secure help beyond Gimlet and Rikeland, if he even agreed to it. Then, they needed to gather supplies and figure out where the temple even was. Firepower had been important, as had working as a group and not getting separated. It had all gone to shit when Evelaine and Nees had dropped into that hole near the center of the plant temple, forcing them to face off against the snake creatures on their own until Rakhmet and Hara could join them. That was when Nees had gotten cornered.

But it would be different in the metal temple, Evelaine swore to herself. She wouldn't leave anyone behind.

After a few hours of convincing herself and Otis insisting multiple times she eat something, Evelaine was feeling more solid in her plans, and Corsair arrived in high spirits, a pep in his step as they made their way toward a residential neighborhood that was nestled between the Market and Industrial Districts. It was a gloomy day, but the window they quickly located was glowing with warmth, revealing stacks of freshly baked breads, muffins, scones, cakes, and cookies. A short line of working-class folk waited patiently in front of the opening next to it, where a worn wooden counter was sheltered underneath a metal overhang built into the scaffolding above, all framed by two heavy shutters that closed securely at night.

They hung back for a few moments, waiting for a break in the crowd as Orlah, Rikeland's eldest daughter, handed out the orders with her usual friendly smile, and Evelaine was struck by how much she had grown. Last she had seen her, she had been an awkward adolescent, just beginning to hit her growth spurt as she'd headed into the throes of puberty, and now she was blooming into a bright young woman, some in the line darting shy glances at her when she wasn't looking. Evelaine shifted uncomfortably at the reminder, desperately trying to ignore the twisting in her gut as she focused on examining the cluttered kitchen and sitting room beyond Orlah instead.

She could see Rikeland and his wife, Patia, working diligently back there, having installed the window and counter in the side of their modest home a little over six years ago, after he had been fired from the Rouge. He had worked there as a baker for many years, also choosing to earn some money on the side as a boxer in the matches the Mistress liked to host once a month to attract a different sort of gambling crowd than those who crowded her card tables every night. Unfortunately, he had ended up severely injured in one such match with a hit to the head that had affected his short-term memory from then on out.

Afterwards, he could no longer remember key details, such as baking times or whether he had already added certain ingredients to his mixtures. Too many of his mistakes had ended in flat loaves of bread, spoiled recipes, and minor kitchen fires, and the Mistress had not found the added expenses and time lost acceptable for her bottom line. So, with one daughter already at home and another on the way, his wife had stepped up to the challenge and decided to become his organizer for a new home-run bakery. She had always had an eye for detail and now functioned as his external short-term memory, keeping track of the minute by minute while he kept his focus on the larger picture.

Behind Orlah, Rikeland stood covered in flour and kneading a large pile of dough while a very pregnant-looking Patia sat on the stool next to him, crossing out things on a piece of paper, and their younger daughter, Sorlene, cut out cookie shapes with her small hands. But there were unfamiliar details that caught Evelaine's eye as she watched: a heap of different sized boots crowded next to the fireplace, seven chairs around the dining table, and an overloaded coat tree in the back corner almost bowing from the weight of the many cloaks that were draped upon it.

She opened her mouth to ask Corsair, but the last customer turned to go and Orlah's expectant gaze landed on them, her smile widening with recognition upon seeing Corsair before sliding to Evelaine with a curious tilt to her head.

"Orlah, my dearest!" Corsair opened his arms wide as he pushed himself off the wall they had been leaning on. "Please tell me you've set aside one of those brown sugar scones for me."

She laughed, wiping her hands on her apron as she moved to unlatch the door for them. "I'll see if I can scrounge one up for you, but one of these days you're going to have to pay or else you'll eat us out of hearth and home."

"Well, good thing Evie here has agreed to foot my bill. You know she'll be good for it." He wrapped an arm around her shoulders as the door opened to Orlah's look of shock, mirrored by the stunned surprise on Rikeland and Patia's faces as they glanced up from their tasks.

"Evelaine," Rikeland started, leaving his dough where it was and moving around the worktable toward the door. "What are you doing here?"

"I thought I recognized you, but I couldn't place you. It's been so long," Orlah said softly, her hands still fluttering against her apron.

"Dear me, how have you been? Is everything alright?" Patia waddled forward, her hand pressed against her full stomach as she waved them in with the other. "Come in, please."

Orlah caught herself, stepping back from the door to let them pass as Evelaine reached for Patia, holding her elbow to steady her.

"Please sit, Patia. There's no need to get up on my account." She grabbed the closest chair and helped her settle into it, but lost her breath in the next moment as Rikeland's large arms circled her and squeezed her into a hug.

"Evelaine, good gods," he rumbled then pulled back to give her some air. "We thought you were gone."

Evelaine let out a dry laugh. "I thought I was too, but . . . it's a long story."

"Of course, you must sit and tell us everything." Patia motioned to the chair next to her. "Orlah, start some coffee and grab those scones from this morning."

Orlah had been standing back from them, uncertain, but jumped at the order, bumping into Sorlene, who had come up behind her and was clutching at her older sister's apron and peeking around her leg at the unexpected arrivals. They both squeaked, but Sorlene didn't let go, holding Orlah in place as her safety shield.

"Lenie, aren't you going to come give me a hug?" Corsair entreated with a smile, crouching down to her level.

A big grin spread across her face as she darted around the other side of Orlah and crashed into Corsair, almost knocking him to the floor. Orlah took the opportunity to put a water kettle on as Corsair scooped Sorlene up into the air and she giggled, clutching onto his neck and shoulder as gravity brought her back down. She peeked around his head as Evelaine sat and tried to give her an encouraging smile.

"You probably don't remember me, Sorlene, but I remember when you were born. You were very, very little last time I saw you." She glanced at Rikeland as he took the chair on the other side of her. "It's been a long time, hasn't it?"

"It has, it has," Rikeland answered, his brows still high in his forehead. "Where have you been?"

Evelaine sighed as Corsair sat at the other end of the table with Sorlene in his lap, distracting her with pokes and tickles while Evelaine searched for the right words.

"I've been in Talegartia but haven't been able to return until now," she began, realizing that she would have to provide these answers to everyone she talked to. She was already exhausted by the prospect. "It's been . . . A lot has happened, but I've come to ask for your help."

"My help? What do you need?" Rikeland asked, glancing to his wife briefly.

"I know you're . . . retired from the fight." She kept it vague, knowing his daughters were listening. "But we— Corsair and I—were wondering if you'd be willing to help us out one last time."

He caught her drift and leaned in, lowering his voice as Sorlene and Corsair talked about the cookies she had been making. "What kind of trouble are you in? Is it bad?"

Patia leaned in too, her hand landing on Evelaine's arm. "We'll help in any way we can."

Evelaine chewed the inside of her cheek and glanced to where Orlah was busy with the coffee, knowing she had to come out with it. She matched their tone as she asked, "Have you ever heard of the blessed ones? Who can wield elemental abilities?"

Rikeland frowned, but Patia's eyes lit up. "Yes, I believe so. They had something to do with the revolution if I remember correctly."

"Yeah, they went into hiding a long time ago, but their blessings are still showing up in bloodlines." Evelaine lowered her voice further, her anxiety rising as she took the plunge. "Both Corsair and I have abilities, but they are currently being blocked."

"*Abilities?*" Patia whispered. When Evelaine only nodded, Patia's eyes darted to Orlah as her daughter walked forward with a tray laden with a pot of coffee, cups, and a plate of scones. "Orlah, please, can you close up the shutters, then take your sister upstairs? Go over her reading with her while we grown-ups catch up."

Orlah looked confused for a moment, her gaze bouncing between her parents, but saw something they weren't saying and dipped her chin. She closed up quickly then plucked Sorlene from Corsair's grasp, heading for the stairs. "Come on, you rugrat. Let's see if you can remember your Q words."

"Quick quacks have questions!" Sorlene exclaimed happily, their voices fading as Corsair moved to join them and immediately grabbed one of the scones.

Patia shook her head at him as she poured the coffee, and Rikeland studied them closely. "So . . . 'blessed ones'? Is that what you said?"

"Yup," Corsair confirmed around a mouthful. "I can work with metal while she talks to plants."

"I don't—" Evelaine frowned at him. "Whatever. The point is our abilities are currently being blocked by something that has taken over a temple in Risten and we need help clearing it. We already asked Gimlet to come along and he said yes, but we need more people. I want to make sure we have a fighting chance."

Rikeland's surprise returned. "You want me to come along with you to this . . . temple? To help fight?"

"If you're willing to. I completely understand if you'd rather not, and please feel free to say no. It's going to be a hard fight. There're things in there that you've never seen before, the stuff of nightmares." Evelaine felt her stomach sour all over again, knowing how much she was asking.

"What kinds of things?" Rikeland asked, matching her frown.

Evelaine swallowed a gulp of coffee as it burned down her throat, hesitating, but she knew she had to give him full transparency. It was only fair. "Wraiths, black ooze creatures. I fought them alongside some people over in a temple in Talegartia. It was pretty bad, one of us didn't make it, but that's why I want to make sure we have a good group of us."

Rikeland sat back, glancing at his wife as he mulled over what she'd said. Patia lifted her brows at him and tilted her head, something passing between them. He folded his arms and gave her a look, but she lifted a shoulder in response and nudged her chin in Evelaine's direction.

He turned back to her. "Are you offering to pay for this . . . fight?"

"If that's what you want, name your price." Evelaine nodded, hoping it wouldn't be beyond what she could afford.

"We would need 250 gold," Patia answered for him.

"That much?" Evelaine asked before she could help it.

"I realize it may seem like a lot"—Patia shrugged apologetically—"but we could use the money. We've been working hard to make ends meet ever since we took in my sister."

"Your sister?" Evelaine asked, glancing at Corsair, who nodded sadly, and she suddenly realized why there were seven chairs at the table.

"She and her two sons moved in with us about a year ago, after she was injured at the factory. It was a chemical explosion and she never fully recovered. She can't work anymore but tries to help us around here as much as she can. They're out doing the shopping right now. It's a lot of mouths to feed, but we do what we can."

Evelaine pressed her lips together, reading between the lines of what Patia was telling her. Industry regulations in the Tirdan Republic were slim to none in order to maximize profit for the factory owners, and accidents happened often. It wasn't unusual for the injured workers to soon find themselves on the streets, reduced to begging for money when their disabilities prevented them from continuing in their jobs.

"With another on the way"—Patia patted her belly— "we need to figure something out until the boys are old enough to work."

"I understand," Evelaine assured them. "I can provide the gold for you."

Both of their eyes widened in shock that she hadn't tried to haggle them down, but she refused to do that to them. She knew exactly what it was like to worry about keeping your child fed, and guilt had hit her hard when she had seen Patia's round stomach. She shouldn't even be asking Rikeland to risk himself with a family depending on him, so the least she could do was ensure they were well-funded.

With the news about the sister, too, she even briefly considered just giving them the money and asking someone else to accompany them to the temple. But her options were extremely limited. She had chosen Rikeland because he was a solid fighter who stood a full head above Corsair and had limbs like tree trunks. He had been the standing champion in the boxing ring, she knew full well how difficult it was to take him down, plus he was one of the kinder souls that had graced the halls of the Rouge. She had selfishly known that he would say yes before she had even asked, a distasteful truth that made the shame thicken around her.

He had always been the first to lend a helping hand to anyone that was struggling, personally delivering warm biscuits and soup to staff who'd fallen sick or making sure the attendants' bellies had been filled at the end of their shifts, even if it had meant he'd had to stay late. It hadn't surprised Evelaine in the least to learn that he had gladly opened his home to his wife's sister and nephews. She suspected he was even the first to suggest it when the sister had lost her job. That was just who he was.

"This will be the end of it, I swear," Evelaine promised them. "Just a quick trip to the temple, then I'll never ask for anything again."

Patia nodded, looking both relieved and worried, her attention going to Rikeland. "The dough, dear."

"The dough?" he asked, confused.

"You were in the middle of kneading it." Patia nudged her chin in the direction of the worktable, and Rikeland startled, jumping out of his chair. He poked at it, testing the bounce, then tore off a piece to stretch it out and hold it to the light. Satisfied, he began shaping and cutting it into loaves as he started humming to himself.

"Thank you." Patia turned back to Evelaine. "This will really be the help we needed."

"Please, don't. I should be the one thanking you." Evelaine grimaced, the what-ifs crowding in on her. "I'm the selfish one here."

Patia gave her a sad smile and patted her hand. "If I know you, I'm sure there's a good reason behind all of this."

Bile rose as Evelaine pushed to her feet, reaching into her pack to draw out her coins. "Half now, half when we return?"

Her hand shook as she quickly deposited the coins on the table, itching to get out of there as Patia's eyes widened again at the pile. Evelaine was sure that it was roughly what Patia and Rikeland made in an entire year, combined. The full amount would be enough to put down a deposit on a larger home, and Evelaine suspected that might be why they had asked for it, knowing that the two rooms upstairs were a tight squeeze for the seven of them. She even added a bit extra to the pile, her guilt filling her lungs with overgrowth.

Rikeland turned back to them, having set the loaves aside for a final proof behind him, and jerked when he saw her. "Evelaine? My gods, what are you doing here?"

Her mouth opened and closed, unable to form the words as Corsair rose and slung his arm over her shoulders with a grin. "Rikeland, my good man, you just agreed to come along with us on a dangerous mission to a mysterious temple. It'll be fun. Patia here will fill you in."

Patia smiled and stood, sweeping the coins into her apron and holding it closed as she waddled over to her husband. "I'll write it all down for you, dear. It has been quite an interesting conversation."

Evelaine attempted a reassuring grin in return but couldn't get her face to cooperate, her feet edging toward the door. She had to believe she was making the right choice here, but the doubt was joining forces with the shame and guilt and her ears were starting to ring.

"Right, of course." Rikeland glanced at Patia with furrowed brows, then looked at Evelaine. "Happy to help."

"We'll gather you up in about three to four days' time for the festivities." Corsair waved, holding two of the scones.

"We'll see you then." Patia nodded, opening one of their flour containers and dumping the coins into it as a puff of white billowed around her.

All Evelaine could do was nod in return as she spun and opened the door, trying not to rush out into the misty air. She pressed her hand to her throat as Corsair joined her, whistling happily as they headed back to the thoroughfare. Her skin crawled at his exuberance, but he wasn't paying attention to her as her shoulders bunched and she scowled at him.

"I can't believe you," she griped.

"What?" He gave her a confused smile as he glanced at her. "We're on an adventure, Evie, just like the old days. It feels good."

"We're taking advantage of them," she urged. "**I'm** taking advantage of them, for my own selfish gain."

"Are you kidding me? Do you know how much that money will do for them?" he asked, surprised. "And Gimlet's been wanting to get out of here for ages. They all want this just as much as you do."

"And you? Why are you so happy about all of this? You just want your powers back, is that it?"

"Well, that's a perk, sure. But I'm just happy to see you all again, especially you. It's been lonely without you, dude. I haven't had anyone I could talk to about this stuff. Otis and my mom are great and all, but they don't really get it." He shrugged, a touch of darkness showing behind his gray eyes.

She sighed and looked away, the weight of all of their needs and wishes settling heavily upon her. How did she always find herself in this position? Where she felt like she was responsible for other people's happiness and was the one they counted on to provide fulfillment at the end of the day?

Rolling her shoulders to ease the tension, she knew that there was a part of her that liked it. That enjoyed being the one to supply what they needed. It helped her feel like **she** was needed. That **she** was valuable. But it was all one big lie. A huge, overcomplicated spectacle of self-indulgent pretense. They were using her to get what they wanted, and she was using them to get what she wanted. Simple as that.

Her mother had used her for emotional comfort, the Mistress had wanted financial gain, Mason had desired her as a man desired a woman, and gods only knew what Nydas had been trying to accomplish. The plant tribe? They had been in need of a leader. And thus it went on and on and on.

And yet, guilt and shame were choking her. She knew it was wrong to bring Rikeland and his family into it, but maybe what she was trying to accomplish would bring about more good than harm. Maybe taking Nydas down will benefit more than just her. She could reach even further and go after the Waltzins and other crooked leaders too, like the factory owners who had tossed Patia's sister out like old laundry.

The possibilities glittered before her enticingly, her sticky shame receding from the light of potential. Maybe she was capable of more than she gave herself credit for. She was still standing, after all. She could get Gimlet out of the Tirdan Republic, set up Rikeland and his family nicely, and do a bit of good for the greater populace.

Maybe, just maybe, her plan would work out better than she dared to hope.

———

She was trapped, thick black limbs encircling her and squeezing. Screaming, she tried to twist out of the way, but it was no use. There was nowhere to go. She strained with her full might against the force of them, her eyes wild as she yelled for help. But what she saw in the space around her confused her further.

She saw herself, frantically slicing at the ichor that surrounded her body. She had her long red hair and that faraway look, as if she had one foot in this reality and another somewhere else entirely. Wait, was this body hers? Were these long, muscled arms, struggling to break free, familiar? An extension of her? Or someone else?

She felt it, more than heard it. The crack of bone, pain radiating throughout her, and she shouted louder. Her left arm went numb and her alarm intensified, dread blooming unrestrained. She was caught, her strength wasn't enough, and she watched helplessly as the fire blessed locked eyes with his guard from across the room.

They saw no one but themselves in that moment as she—was it her? With hair that tangled around her shoulders like vines?— screamed for herself, the self that was held in a tight vise. Another resounding crack shuddered through her body, and she saw the moment her other self's eyes filled with terror, screeches of panic ringing in her ears.

Were they coming from her? Was it her throat producing these soul-wrenching sounds? The cries of agony that the gods could surely hear from their palaces beyond? Or her other self?

Nothing made sense as she felt something irreparable splinter in her hip and lower back, the world starting to spin under her increasingly blurry gaze. Her body was failing. She was failing. And both of her selves knew it.

She could tell the moment they both realized it, her jaw going slack as the air in her lungs was wrung from her. The pathetic snap of her ribs was nothing under the pressure of this abominable creature that clutched her, and all she could do was gaze upon her other self.

Her love.

Her ward.

Her blessed.

The one she was destined to disappoint after all.

The last thing she saw as darkness overtook her, her shouted name echoing into eternity.

Day Seven

She knocked on Corsair's door early the next morning, determined to forget the nightmare that whispered to her still, and was perversely pleased at his groan of protest on the other side. After she knocked again, there was the thump of something thrown at the door then a long pause. She was raising her fist a third time when a muffled curse came and a creak of bed springs signified his acknowledgement that she wasn't going to leave him be. The door flung open and he glared at her, his hair tangled and smushed to the side of his head.

"Eat one of your scones. It'll make you feel better," she quipped, shoving past him to sit on the end of his bed.

"I'm pretty sure drunk Corsair didn't leave any for me last night," he grumbled, closing the door then flopping back on his sheets face down.

Evelaine rolled her eyes as his hand groped around blindly on the desk next to him for the tin he kept his cigarettes in, and he grunted in satisfaction as he found it. He propped himself on his elbows as he opened it, and the grunt turned into a groan as he found it empty. Rolling over and sitting up, he threw some wrinkled pants to the floor as he grumpily located his tobacco pouch and papers.

"Hard night?" she asked. For once, his mood seemed to match hers.

He lifted a shoulder nonchalantly, shirtless of course, as he rolled a cigarette and stuck it between his lips, now on the search for matches as he leaned over and shoved aside piles on the floor. "You know, the usual."

"What is the usual for you these days?" When she'd been here last, he had been recently promoted to the trainer for the bouncers of the Rouge. It had been a big deal at the time, considering he had still been in his twenties back then, but like Evelaine, he had a long history of working himself to the bone in an attempt to prove his worth. Something the Mistress was willing to reward, as long as it benefitted her too.

"A little of this, a little of that." He shrugged again, now sitting in the corner of the bed with smoke starting to billow around him.

The words struck a bit hollow, literally verbatim what Gimlet had answered, and she frowned at him. "What's that supposed to mean?"

"Don't worry about it. I still do the training and all that. She's happy with my work. That's all that matters." He looked away, the tobacco sharpening his bloodshot gaze as he squinted at the sunshine just starting to peek through the small window above the desk. She continued frowning at him, and he glanced back at her. "What?"

She crossed her arms and raised her brows expectantly. It was his turn to roll his eyes, and he groaned again, slumping further in the corner like a sullen child.

"I might've started, you know . . . moonlighting. To make some extra coin," he mumbled, not making eye contact with her.

"Moonlighting? As what? As—" She stopped as it hit her. He was working in the brothel, servicing the clientele as a sex worker. Her jaw dropped open, but she quickly closed it as he peeked up to watch her reaction. She blinked several times, trying to wrap her head around it.

He had always been careful to keep his carnal activities secret, resisting the expectation that he would end up just like his mother. That stereotype had followed them both as they had grown up, other employees always gossiping about what their respective futures would hold as bastard children of courtesans. It had almost been like their career paths had been carved in stone, based on how they had talked about them.

Evelaine had squashed the rumors easily by the time she had come of age, showing no signs of any interest in that sort of physical attraction or inclination, but Corsair had begun roaming about town in search of excitement as soon as the hormones had hit him. She was sure that the Mistress must have talked to him about the possibility a time or two, especially after he had started training and developed into a muscled specimen. It had been hard to miss the keen stares that had followed him as he had walked his rounds in the gambling halls while on duty.

The Mistress was too much of a businesswoman to ignore the opportunity to add him to her roster.

And apparently, she had eventually succeeded.

"You hate it," he said glumly.

"No! No, it's not—" She held her hands up in defense. "It's just unexpected. I thought you didn't—"

He bit his lip. "It's not that bad. I get to choose who . . . you know, and it's kind of fun, the way they really want it." He gestured to himself and attempted a cocky grin. "Folks are willing to spend a whole lot of money for all this."

"Of course, that's great. If it's what you want, I mean," she tried to assure him.

He reached for his tobacco pouch to roll another cigarette. "It's whatever. It passes the time, fills my pockets. Just a bit of fun."

"Right." She struggled with what else to say. She wasn't against the idea, but his evasion was making her wonder.

"What about you?" He changed the subject, the flash of the match highlighting his tired features for a brief second. "Have you talked to Mason yet?"

She was unable to hide her flinch at the rapid turn, avoiding his knowing look. How could she possibly explain the mess of emotions she was feeling in regard to Nees, Mason, and her daughter? "No. I haven't."

He lifted an eyebrow at her, and she crossed her arms, letting out a long exhale.

"I'm just . . . waiting for the right moment. After all this business with Nydas is over with. I don't want to trouble them until then," she argued.

"Evie," he said softly. "Otis told me Stella's powers are starting to show. He asked me to talk to her just before you got back."

She pressed her lips together, fighting the tears that were pricking the backs of her eyes. "I know. I just . . . I can't right now. I have to focus on the plan first, then I'll figure it out."

"Right." He gave her one last look, then scooted to the edge of the bed. Bending down, he rifled around for clean clothes. "So, what's the next step? Who else do we need to track down?"

She watched as he located a shirt and sniffed at it, apparently finding it suitable as he bit his cigarette between his teeth and carefully wriggled into it. "I was going to ask you about that. Who else is there? We need at least two more. Four isn't going to cut it."

"I was thinking about this last night when I was . . ." He shook his head, rerouting mid-sentence. "I was talking to Andra while we were hanging around and it struck me that she might be a good addition to the group."

"Really?" She vaguely remembered that Andra had been hired as a bouncer just before Evelaine had left, so she didn't know much about her.

"Yeah, her and I have become pretty tight over the years. She's chill and a great fighter, doesn't take any shit from anyone. I have a feeling she'd be up for it." He found a pair of unwrinkled pants and began unlacing his loose lounge pair as she clapped her hand over her eyes against the unwanted visual.

"Do you think she'd keep her cool? It's not like we're going to be fighting everyday thugs," she asked into the darkness, listening to him rustle around.

"She's seen a lot. She's got the look, you know?" Hearing the clanging of his weapons belt, she opened her eyes. He stood buckling everything in place as he thought about it. "I can talk to her, see what she thinks. She'll do it for money. She's got a debt she's working off with the Mistress."

"Alright, I'll trust you on that one, but I think we also need someone who has more . . . knowledge. Like, I know you all can handle a fight, but you're still a bunch of fuckwits. No offense."

He put his hands on his hips and narrowed his eyes. "Offense taken. I'm a genius and I need that to be respected."

She puffed out a dry laugh. "Of course, my sincerest apologies."

"Plus, you're the brains of this operation. You're the one who's done this before." He shrugged on his coat, straightening his cuffs.

Her stomach twisted at the reminder, the sensations of what had woken her in the middle of the night blooming once again. She knew they needed someone who could think on their feet. Someone who could not just react to whatever was thrown at them, but could anticipate and help them come up with some sort of strategy beyond punching and slicing their way through.

"Honestly, I have no idea what we're going to be facing in the metal temple. It seems like the wraiths are at every corrupted temple, but the fire blessed and his guard were surprised by how many there were in Talegartia. And the ooze seems to take different forms. I think they said it looked like a scorpion in Zahar, but we encountered snakes in the plant temple. We need someone who knows about the gods and how this might all be related. It's not like you can guide us through. You don't know anything even though it's technically your temple we're clearing."

"Hey, it's not my fault the bastard didn't stick around to teach me. He just left that fucking letter and was like, 'see ya!'" Corsair held up his hands. "Don't blame the messenger."

"Can't you, like, feel it or something?"

"Feel what? The temple?" He closed his eyes and turned to the window, reaching toward it and wiggling his fingers. "Ooooooooooh, great Metal God, show me the way!"

When nothing happened, he dropped his arms and shrugged, turning back to her. "I may be a genius, but I'm just a fuckwit with a useless tattoo without my blessing."

She rolled her eyes, standing and propping her hands on her hips. "Fine. You go talk to Andra, see what she says, and I'll try to figure something out for the other pieces."

"Good luck with that," he offered drily, opening the door for her with a flourish. "Meet back here this evening?"

She agreed with a huff, frustrated by their lack of progress, and gave him one last, pointed look. He went the other way down the hall while she headed for the staff entrance, nodding a brief farewell to Wexit as she passed him and descended into the streets below. She had no idea where she was going, but chose a random direction, keeping her senses on high alert as she carefully watched everything she passed from under her low hood.

Once again, it was misting and overcast, the grim atmosphere matching the haggard looks of the people who passed her on the streets below. Above, she could catch glimpses of richly draped windows and scenes of warm merriment beyond in the upper echelons of the Gildan District and it curled her lip, but she refused to get lost in her ire, focusing on the task at hand: if there was a temple to the Metal God in this damned city, where would it be?

She racked her brain for what she even knew about the god who held dominion over all things metallic. Not much, to be honest. She had watched Corsair's abilities develop over the years, his control over all forms of metal just as manipulative and creative as hers over plants. He couldn't really summon metal from himself like she could with the seeds and pollen, but a few times he had been successful in extracting miniscule amounts of iron from blood, which was impressive, she supposed.

But give him the raw material? A piece of ore, a sword or dagger, the ever-present scaffolding that loomed above them everywhere in this city? He easily could shape and control it all to his will. She had watched him turn metal stairs into slides within seconds and bend blades back on their own wielders before they could blink an eye. When he had access to those twin blades on his back, he could pop them out in an instant, swinging them around and slicing through whatever was in front of him in one smooth motion.

He had been saving up for more tattoos, smaller blades on his forearms and calves, but he also had a tendency to give his money away when the people around him needed it. He had a secret penchant for philanthropy that he had always tried to hide, but she had connected the pieces a time or two when he had turned up broke as a joke after one of the courtesans had disappeared briefly to take care of a certain operation. More reason for him to expand his duties at the Rouge, she guessed, but she doubted he would risk spending the money on tattoos now that he didn't have access to his blessing. Perhaps that was something she could help him with when all of this was said and done. He deserved to be paid for his assistance as much as Gimlet or Rikeland.

She tucked the idea away for the time being and summoned a mental map of the city. She had reasoned from Rakhmet and Hara's stories that the temples were likely to be located in areas where the elemental forces they were related to were most present or "felt," as Corsair's letter had put it. Without Corsair's ability to connect with his powers at the moment, she knew they were at a disadvantage for locating it through feeling alone. But maybe it was a puzzle she could logic her way through.

Where in or around Risten was the presence of metal most obvious? She immediately thought of the Urdian Spire, the towering clock around which the city was centered, but something about it didn't seem right. There were countless guards who patrolled the structure day and night, as well as workers who kept the mechanisms running smoothly, not to mention the wealthy who lined the square around the tower with their glittering residences. It was the one part of the city where the lower portions weren't left for the working classes to populate. Instead, expensive dining establishments and high-end florists, gift shops, and spas fit snugly beneath their rich patrons, within easy reach for them to enjoy at their leisure.

Even if she couldn't understand how a temple to the Metal God could be hidden in plain sight in a place like that, she headed in that direction just to make sure. Keeping to the shadows, she circled casually and studied the tower from ground level, its spire reaching far above even the tallest of buildings in the city. An architectural marvel that drew thousands of tourists every year, it was buzzing with activity despite the gloomy day, with pedestrians milling around its base, winding their way up the stairs that wrapped around its exterior, or paying extravagantly to experience the overpriced amenities nearby.

She couldn't help the sneer on her face and kept her hood low, using the rain as an excuse to dart underneath the overhangs and subtly examine the structure for any signs of hidden entrances or unusual markings that would indicate past use as a temple to the gods. But after a few hours of finding nothing, she had to admit that she was getting nowhere and branched off to weave her way elsewhere.

The Tirdan Republic was not a nation that held old-fashioned religious beliefs dearly, and she couldn't think of even one building dedicated to the worship of the gods in Risten, all evidence of any political past connected to the divine having been erased long ago. Capitalism, industry, and profit were the ideals that were treated with reverence and glory here, the altar at which the masses and elite alike prayed with fervor and dedication.

While the odds that the everyday worker would ever achieve financial prosperity were laughable, it would never stop some from dreaming the impossible dream and praying that one day they could feast upon lobster and cakes, wearing jewels and fine silks. They could look down at the people below and say: "That was us once, but no more. Our hard work, dedication, and superior strategies paid off, delivering us to the abundance we truly deserve."

Evelaine herself had once believed that lie, working her ass off to scrimp and save so that one day she could escape the circumstances into which she had been birthed. But she knew better now. Raised under the protective wing of the Mistress, she had seen enough of the inner workings of the upper classes and been privy to the elaborate machinations that the older woman carefully wove to maintain her elevated standing. She knew how easy it was to bolster the lie that tricked the affluent into believing that they were meant to be in power simply because they were fundamentally better than everyone else.

Heavy the head that wore the crown? More like deluded and indoctrinated into thinking they had the right to make decisions for all. That was ultimately the issue she had with the other blessed who had so readily taken up their "rightful legacies." She wasn't fooled by their noble missions, as she had seen how easy it was for Tabriara to convince Rakhmet to usurp his father and seize the Fire Crown. How quickly he had turned around and begun giving Evelaine orders to stay with them and assist them in their plan to find and purge the temples and reinstate the elemental crowns across the world. How the moon, sun, and water blessed had chosen to stay with their own families, leaving Evelaine to fight and lose.

She knew full well how power corrupted people, and she had no interest in partaking, thank you very much. All she wanted to do was take down Nydas, right the wrongs that had been done to her and hers, and get the fuck out of there. Balance the scales and be done with it. No more bending over backward, trying to fit into other people's molds of who they wanted her to be. No more compartmentalizing pieces of herself for the fulfillment of others. No more giving without taking.

Nature was the great equalizer in the end. It consumed what died, the nutrients returning to their origin. Maybe her bloody vengeance could level the field. She could devour the decay that Nydas and his ilk had spread, mulch the land, and prepare it for the propagation of something new, wild, and free. Forget the other blessed and their grand schemes. She would simply leave her corner of the world better than she had found it and move on from there. First, though, that required her to ask a lot from those that followed her into the temple, but she would make sure she compensated them with enough to make the risk worth it. Nature gave and took in equal measure, after all.

She finally admitted she was getting nowhere with her random wanderings around the city and redirected herself to the immediate plan, turning around to head back to the Rouge. She was feeling vindictive after spending the afternoon ruminating on the imbalances of power as she approached the red beacon proudly advertising decadence to anyone who could pay, and at the last moment, she chose to enter through the front, tossing back her hood and smirking at Lyle and Hangren, two doormen she knew well.

Their brows hit their hairlines when they saw her, glancing at each other in confusion as she broke protocol and walked right up to the grand double doors, something she had never done in all the years she had called the Rouge home. But she had damn well paid for her right to be there and was done submitting to the old rules.

"Gorgeous night, isn't it, boys?" she greeted them, a slight bite to her tone as they frowned.

"Evelaine." Lyle looked around as he leaned toward her. "What are you doing?"

"Does the Mistress know you're here?" Hangren asked, already reaching to guide her back to the rear of the building.

She shrugged off his hand and brandished five gold pieces, knowing that entry required only one. "Is this how you treat your patrons? Come on, I know you two are better trained than that."

Hangren drew back, looking even more confused as he turned to Lyle. "I don't—I mean . . ."

Lyle slowly put out his hand for the gold as Evelaine deposited it in his palm with a sharp smile. "Treat yourself to something nice tonight. She's aware I'm in town and I'm free to do as I like."

"Right." He drew out the word as he absently motioned for Hangren to open the door for her. "Thank you."

She gave him a wink and strolled into the lush entryway bathed in shades of vermillion, dark wine, and garnet. Passing under the silk curtains that provided privacy for patrons and workers alike, her boots clicked softly on the polished marble floor veined with gold as she approached the massive front desk carved from rich mahogany and inlaid with delicately shaped pieces of pearl. Behind it stood two stunning attendants, their kohl-lined eyes going wide as their attention landed on her, and an idea unfurled in Evelaine's mind.

Subtly stuffing one of her coin purses into her pocket, she handed her cloak and pack to Grecia, the raven-haired attendant on the right that she had often seen in passing. "You two are looking lovely as always. I hope you have been treated well."

"Evelaine . . . thank you. I-it's a pleasure to see you again," Quinn answered with a hesitant smile, waves of blonde cascading over her shoulders with artful intention.

Grecia reached for Evelaine's things, looking confused, but her training was well-ingrained, the act of service as much of a muscle memory as Evelaine's ability to slip into the shadows unseen, and Evelaine's smile grew sympathetic as she slid four gold coins across the top of the desk.

"For the both of you," she murmured, knowing that these girls were lucky if they made that amount in a week. If she was going to walk into this den of inequity as a free woman, she vowed to put her own thumb on the scales to balance things a bit. She had done nothing to earn the fortune that Rakhmet had handed over so casually, so she had never really considered it hers. From the very start, she had planned on using it as a means to an end, and she was starting to realize that a redistribution to those who had been overlooked and underserved for their entire lives aligned well with her plans. Gimlet and Rikeland were only the beginning.

Grecia nearly dropped Evelaine's things, but Quinn gave her a quick look and the other girl dipped her chin, scurrying into the coatroom behind them as Quinn slid the offering into her pocket and bowed with easy grace. "Of course, madame."

She swept to the side, opening the drapes that led to the main hall, and the muffled chattering of the crowd of patrons beyond became clearer as walls of shimmering brocade and grand chandeliers of gold illuminating them all in soft warmth came into view. Evelaine strolled in with her chin tipped in arrogance, her hand resting on the pommel of the gemmed dagger at her waist in a precise move that dared any of the eyes that slid her way with interest. The message was clearly received as she made her way around the room, whispers following in her wake.

She was done with playing her old part, no longer interested in moving in silence. She had thought that she needed to be sneaky as she tracked Nydas down and cornered him before he realized it, but why should the privileged waltz about, stepping on those they deemed below them without shame or remorse? Why couldn't she become the force of nature they feared, threatening their impermanent empires that would eventually fall prey to the test of time? She was here to right wrongs, and her old home was a perfect place to start.

Weaving her way through the cavernous space, she passed elegant card tables with comfortable chairs that encouraged their visitors to sit for a while, burbling fountains that provided calming background noise, and secluded lounge areas where deals could be bartered in secret and hands could wander wherever they liked. While

115

she didn't recognize any of the faces of those partaking in the festivities, she knew almost all of those that were working, and every time she drew near an attendant, bouncer, dealer, or courtesan, she subtly caught their attention and motioned them over.

For the ones she knew well, she whispered a brief greeting and tucked a couple of gold into their hands as she shook them with a word of encouragement. For others, she simply dropped the coins into their pockets with a nod before moving on. By the time she reached the rear of the hall, she had become the biggest power player in the room and the patrons were murmuring amongst themselves, wondering why all of the workers were suddenly treating this nobody with respect and gratitude.

That was when her attention landed on one of the alcoves tucked into a back corner, where the Mistress liked to place fortune tellers or tarot readers, and found a piercing brown stare watching her with intrigue. She stuttered to a halt as recognition hit her: Kaiseln, her old trainer. The one that had sharpened her into the blade their employer had gladly wielded against her enemies.

Her feet carried her forward, an impossible thought suddenly sprouting as she untied the curtains, letting them fall closed behind her to shield them from view and taking a seat. A knowing smile curled across Kaiseln's face and they leaned forward, setting their tarot deck in the middle of the table.

Evelaine didn't say a word, dividing the pile into three as the trainer and their protégé studied each other.

Kaiseln stayed locked on Evelaine, their hand turning over the top cards and setting them in front of her. Only then did the trainer's attention fall to the spread, their long finger tapping on the first. It showed eight cups set on the ground in front of a snow-covered range.

"You have journeyed far and climbed the tallest of mountains, forced to leave behind much. Yet it was weight that needed to be shed in order to reach the heights for which you are destined."

Their hand moved to the middle one, featuring a beast with wicked-looking horns perched on top of bodies writhing to get free.

"Now, you face a devil of your own making. Be wary of the lies that bring you false comfort."

The last was a card Evelaine knew, her lips pressing together as she eyed the figure falling from a tower. She didn't want to hear what came next, but Kaiseln slid it toward her, separating it from the previous two.

"Reality will be irreversibly changed by the decisions you make. When the time comes, do not look back."

Evelaine's heart thumped in her chest as she raised her gaze to Kaiseln's, an extended moment passing between them.

"I need your help."

The trainer leaned back, that knowing smile still in place. "Do you?"

Evelaine remembered the stories Kaiseln used to tell her, their steady voice an unwavering backdrop to their training sessions. Tales that were an interwoven tapestry of history and fantasy, where the lines between fact and fiction were blurred, as indistinct as the boundaries of shadow they had taught Evelaine to penetrate and merge with.

Kaiseln had been as unsurprised as Otis when Evelaine had accidentally revealed her innate connection to plants, an oddity that she had never forgotten. Her trainer had only smiled, an uncanny glint of delight in their brown eyes, and it had always made Evelaine wonder.

"I'm looking for an ancient temple devoted to the God of Metal." Evelaine leaned forward, her voice lowering despite the curtain that hid them from the rest of the room. "I want to infiltrate it and recover my blessing."

"By order of our dear Mistress?" Their tone was mild, but Evelaine could hear the discontent behind it.

"I have bought my freedom. This is my path, not hers." Evelaine unsheathed the dagger from her belt and set it underneath the spread of cards in front of her as Kaiseln focused on it with a look of recognition.

"You have found your dagger," they breathed in awe.

Evelaine's skin prickled at the revelation and her mind filled with a thousand questions, but only one mattered. "Will you help?"

"You will find the entrance inside a long abandoned blacksmithy in the southwestern corner of the Industrial District," her trainer revealed, their expression set with conviction. "It has been boarded up for decades, the building considered condemned. Every century or so, new 'owners' take over and open up shop for a while before closing again, but it is a ruse to fool the surrounding business community."

She inhaled in a rush, blinking rapidly as she processed the information. "H-how do you know that?"

"It is no accident that I was here to train you." Kaiseln looked at her long and hard. "There is much you do not know."

"Tell me," Evelaine urged, her knuckles turning white as she gripped the table.

"I have sworn an oath to guide and protect you, but there are secrets that must be kept at all costs. The darkness that threatens to overtake us all is pervasive and insidious, and there are eyes and ears everywhere."

"Secrets?" Evelaine pushed away from the table, but her legs refused to stand as the betrayal stole her breath. She had trusted Kaiseln as one of the few people who knew who she truly was. Had it all been a lie?

"You had to find the path on your own. My orders were clear. I was to prepare you for what you might come to face. I am one guide of many, and I only had so much I could teach you."

"Orders?" Evelaine shook her head in confusion. "From the Mistress?"

Kaiseln huffed out a deprecatory laugh. "That woman is just a pawn in the grand scheme of things, a means to an end. My true orders come from elsewhere."

Evelaine rubbed her face, trying to follow what they were saying. What the fuck did that mean, that their orders had come from elsewhere? And what was this darkness they were talking about? She dropped her hands as it hit her. "You know about the corruption."

"I do."

Visions of what they had encountered in the plant temple bloomed unbidden, and the fury that filled Evelaine finally shoved her to her feet. She threaded her fingers through her hair and pulled. Her trainer had kept so much from her, and she had been utterly unprepared for what they had found lurking deep beneath the ground in that sacred forest, but she hadn't had any of her memories either. Even if Kaiseln had told her everything, she still wouldn't have been able to save Nees from their terrible fate.

A frustrated scream built in her throat as she paced back and forth, Kaiseln's keen eyes following her. What was she supposed to do with this information? Her trainer still wasn't telling her what they knew, only bits and pieces, and Evelaine couldn't help but feel she'd be leading her friends into the metal temple with half a plan as a result. She had vowed to be better this time, smarter and faster, so she turned, planting her hands on the table and leaning forward.

"You will come with us," she gritted between clenched teeth. "To the metal temple."

Kaiseln raised an eyebrow, but their smile reappeared. "Is that an order?"

Evelaine's mind raced as she tried to read them, getting the feeling that there was more behind the question than what she fully understood. What was she not seeing here? Was this another trap? But they needed the help. Kaiseln obviously knew more than she and Corsair did about the temple, and it could be the edge that ensured everyone would get out of there in one piece.

She thought of Gimlet's request and Rikeland's family, feeling the weight of her responsibility to them on her shoulders. It was another decision where she had to either take the leap or walk away from everything. Kaiseln had guided her through so much. They had been the role model she had looked up to for so many years, which was why the revelation that they had been keeping things from her had cut so deep. Did she dare trust them still?

Kaiseln waited for her as she warred with herself, the uncertainty twining around her lungs with thorned vines. She had to stick to the plan. That was the only thing keeping her moving forward. Having her trainer come along would be a formidable weapon in her armory, and she couldn't help the eagerness that arose at the thought. They were bound to be victorious with Risten's top two assassins working together, right?

Glancing down at the tower card that sat just above her dagger, she thought back to what had been said at the beginning of this conversation: "When the time comes, do not look back." She couldn't afford to doubt herself. There was too much on the line.

She straightened, locking eyes with her old trainer, and felt the balance shift between them. Grabbing onto her destiny with both hands, she nodded once as her trainer's smile widened.

"Yes, that's an order."

DAY EIGHT

Evelaine had left the Rouge soon after finishing her conversation with Kaiseln, her head too full to seek out Corsair to see how he had fared with his own discussions, but she didn't have to wait long, as he showed up at the apothecary late the next morning with good news: Andra had agreed to come along. It would cost Evelaine a hundred gold, half up front and half when they returned. Despite herself, she swallowed her consternation at Corsair bartering away her decreasing fortune without asking first, because she was finding it hard to ignore the tiny buds of hope that were growing inside her.

Her plans were starting to come together. With six confirmed in their party and a solid location for the metal temple acquired, she kept resisting the urge to pinch herself, too afraid to question their luck. Nothing had been going right until she had enlisted Corsair's help, and she was beginning to wonder if her previous insistence on doing everything herself had been based on faulty logic. Maybe there was something to the phrase "teamwork makes the dream work." She would be paying dearly for it, but it was only money. With her larger ideas about doing something about the crooked power players that polluted Risten with their greed, she was betting she could find a way to redistribute their deep coffers while she was at it.

In light of her nascent optimism, her mind kept returning to the window a few blocks away that proudly displayed carefully crafted wooden objects, and by the time night fell, she found herself slipping out the back door of the greenhouse. The shadows welcomed her once again as she wound her way through familiar alleys, tucking into an unused doorway from which she could watch the last few customers of the day come and go with their purchases tucked securely under their arms.

Foot traffic eventually petered out, many of the city's working class retiring for the evening and sitting down to dinner, but Evelaine stayed right where she was as she caught glimpses of a tall figure bustling around the shop and getting ready to close up. Her heart pounding, she gripped the edge of the stone archway and crouched just enough to see his kind face come into view. She leaned in, studying the new creases around his trusting blue eyes and the scattering of white patches that were starting to show on his stubbled chin.

Mason had always been a handsome man, his beauty more stalwart than refined. There was a certain appeal to the cracked calluses that decorated his squared fingers and the soft outer belly that hid layers of compacted muscle underneath. Age suited him well, too. His shoulders might have seemed a bit more rounded than when last she'd seen him, but it made him look wiser. A paternal figure that could give sage advice about life's matters.

Her heart ached at the sight, the urge to burrow her face into his broad chest and breathe in his scent of sawdust and sweat impossible to ignore. She had truly loved him, and there was no doubt that part of her always would, despite the care and affection she had built with Nees. Did the return of her memories and the devotion to her long-lost husband invalidate what she had felt for her loyal guard? She didn't think so. It was as if her heart had simply expanded to hold them both, alongside her precious daughter and her deep-rooted ties to Otis and Corsair.

Falling for each of them had felt like finding a home, a place where she could rest her weary head and trust in the strong arms that held her tight. It had been easy and effortless, quieting the anxieties that circled endlessly within her, and they had both adored her in their own way. Mason had admired her strength and fortitude, understanding how rare it had been for her to crack her heart open and let him in, and he had cherished the opportunity to stroke the soft down hidden under so many layers of protective armor.

She had come to Nees, on the other hand, as a broken, confused, and lost soul. All she had been was weak and vulnerable, but they had shored her up, provided the crutches with which she could learn to walk again. They had believed in her, instantly placing their full, unbreakable dedication at her feet, and had never wavered. Unconditional, no matter what.

They had never questioned her lack of desire for physical union, accepting it as easily as the sun journeyed across the sky every day. Sure, Evelaine and Nees had shared a bed and twined their limbs together, finding comfort in one another, but her guard had never asked for more than that and neither had she. She would've been happy to give it, once she had regained her health, but it simply hadn't been requested. Their love had been as genuine and full as the one she had shared with Mason. There had never been any perceived lack.

She watched as her husband tidied up the shop, her pulse thrumming, and wondered if it was time to say something. To reveal herself. But she couldn't get her feet to move, instead basking in the image of him alive and well. Her mind had come up with all sorts of horror stories about his and her daughter's fates. She had envisioned them starving on the street, begging for food after he had injured himself in the shop one day and could no longer work. Or perhaps they had fallen to mindless violence, the all-too-common accident of simply being in the wrong place at the wrong time. The what-ifs had haunted her, making her question whether she even wanted to know the truth or live on in ignorance.

Mason's head turned toward the rear of the shop, and her breath stopped as she saw a young girl with a long blonde ponytail skip into view. The girl rushed Mason, throwing her arms around his midsection, and Evelaine pressed her shaking hand against her mouth as she struggled to hold back the tears that blurred her vision. His smile lit up the shop as his head dropped back with a laugh, and the girl beamed up at her father with joy. They spoke to each other, their mouths forming words Evelaine couldn't hear, but their shared love was clear as day.

She imagined Estella asking Mason how the day had been. Had he sold a lot today? Then he would reply in his deep voice that it had been an excellent day, despite the gloomy weather. He would then ask if she was hungry for dinner and if she wanted some stew, or perhaps some grilled meats and vegetables? She would beg for some cakes and he would laugh again, mussing her hair as he shooed her up the stairs and told her maybe this weekend they'd go to the market and pick up something nice.

Evelaine blinked several times, trying to focus on the tableau in front of her. The desperate want to wrap Estella in her arms and bury her nose in her hair had her straightening, about to step out of the shadows, as a hooded figure came around the corner and stopped in front of the shop's door. Whoever it was knocked, leaning to peek through the small window of the door and waving as Mason's and Estella's attention turned their way. They had a basket hooked over one arm and readjusted its weight as Mason smiled and moved to let them in.

Stalling, Evelaine was unsure what to do and simply watched, her foot still poised to step forward as the figure entered the shop. They dropped their hood and Evelaine's heart picked up as she spied shining auburn ringlets falling forth, scattering around the figure's shoulders as they set their basket down on a nearby table and grasped Mason's shoulder in a warm greeting. Evelaine instinctively slunk farther back into the shadows, her hand clutching at her throat as Estella ran forward and threw her arms around the figure's neck with a broad smile.

Her daughter pulled back, chattering excitedly as the figure turned to shed their cloak, and Evelaine recognized them as Frederica, the eldest daughter of the florist on the other side of the block. Mason took her cloak, his eyes lingering on her face as she glanced at him, and Evelaine instantly felt sick to her stomach. She knew that look, had seen it a thousand times. She knew exactly what it meant.

Estella was busy picking up the heavy basket and hefting it toward the rear stairs as Mason folded Frederica's cloak over his arm and gestured for her to follow his daughter. His free hand landed lightly on the small of Frederica's back as they walked, and Evelaine had to turn away, unable to watch. Her chest heaving, she pressed her hot forehead against the cool, wet stone of the archway and tried not to throw up.

Out of all the possible scenarios that she had fretted over, this had not been one of them. She was blindsided, panic blooming inside her at a rapid pace. He had loved her. He had **loved** her. They were **married**. Husband and wife. 'Til death do them part.

Maybe he thought she was dead. Maybe he thought he was free to do as he wished.

But her grandfather had said that Mason still asked about her.

Estella still visited the apothecary.

There was still hope, but her stomach suddenly dropped to her feet as she remembered Nees. Poor, dear Nees.

A sob caught in her throat and she chided herself for being a fucking hypocrite. She had moved on, so why couldn't Mason? She had found room in her heart for another. He deserved to do the same.

She felt tears begin to stream down her cheeks as she stuffed her fist in her mouth to keep quiet, the ache inside her chest becoming a bottomless pit of heartbreak. She had lost them both. She had lost Nees to the plant temple and Mason to the florist's daughter.

The florist's daughter, for gods' sake!

Of course it would be the florist. The only other people in the neighborhood beyond Otis who worked with plants, the only other shop to which Estella would be inevitably drawn. Where else could she go to help understand the strange changes in her body without her mother around to guide her?

Evelaine gulped down air, trying to calm herself as she straightened and begged her churning mind to think straight.

They still visited Otis, they still came by the apothecary from time to time, and another realization hit her as she spun in place and bolted into a sprint. She made it to the greenhouse in two minutes flat, the door rattling as she slammed it closed behind her and rushed into the cozy personal quarters. Her eyes were wild as her grandfather jerked in surprise at her sudden appearance, glancing up from a pile of papers where he was making notes.

"Lainey—" he began.

"You knew." She pointed an accusing finger at him.

"Knew? About what?" He removed his glasses, frowning.

"Frederica! You knew!"

"Ah, well." His brows creased and his mouth opened to say more, but she didn't let him.

"YOU KNEW!! AND YOU DIDN'T SAY A WORD!!" Her hands fisted at her sides, her muscles vibrating with anger. "YOU LET ME JUST WALK OVER THERE AND SEE— AND SEE—"

"I didn't know if—you know, it's hard to tell how far it has grown. I-I'm just an old man and it's been so long since I've been privy to—" He pushed himself to his feet, holding his hands out to her.

She screamed through clenched teeth, yanking on her hair as she started to pace. "Why does no one ever tell me anything?! You all have just been fucking lying to me this entire time! And I somehow think it's my fault that I can't fucking TRUST ANYONE!!"

"Lainey—" he tried again. "He still asks—"

"No!! Shut up!! I saw the look. I know that look!! I've lost him, just like I've lost everyone!!"

"Please, calm down. Let me get you some—"

"Shut the fuck up!! I don't need any of your fucking tea. I don't need any of your fucking help because all you people do is fucking lie to me! How am I supposed to trust anyone when all you do is lie?! How am I supposed to do what I need to do?! What am I even fighting for at this point?!!" Her breath caught in her throat, the air not making it to her lungs. "My child and husband are not even my own anymore. No one in this city wants me here. This isn't my home. Why the fuck am I even here?!"

Her grandfather sighed, his sad eyes following her as she stomped back and forth across the small space. "Lainey, I understand that you're hurting right now and it's completely valid. I had no idea that things had progressed so far between them, otherwise I would have said something. But there are people who love you here still. I love you, and I know Corsair cares about you deeply. He's like a brother to you, yes? He's always been by your side, as will I be, my dear. And I'm positive that if you just speak with Mason, you will see that—"

"No." Evelaine stopped, dropping her face into her hands. "I-it's not going to happen. They're better off without me. I know it."

"Estella needs you," he urged. "You must know that."

Her stomach bottomed out through the floor at the reminder and she groaned, her knees buckling as she folded into the chair behind her. She couldn't do this. There was no way she could be there for her daughter and free them from her rot at the same time. It galled her, but she knew without a doubt that Mason would be happier in the long term with Frederica, a lovely woman who could provide everything he desired. Who could give all of herself freely, without hiding dirty, unforgivable pieces away.

There were roots buried deep within Evelaine that she could never let Mason see, integral parts of her being and history that she didn't even want to reveal to Estella, even though her daughter would eventually discover it on her own one day. As much as Evelaine desperately hoped that Estella's blessing would develop into something nutritive and generous, the more wholesome aspects of nature's bounty, she was well aware that was a naive wish destined to be proven false.

Tabriara's sacred plant was the castor bean. The seeds and pollen that her blessed produce are inherently linked to a poisonous plant, and while they have the ability to shape the expression of their seeds into any form of flora they wish, like vines, trees, or flowers, each and every one they create contains ricin, a highly potent, water-soluble toxin. Yes, they could manipulate existing plant life as well, but the poison was nestled deep within each of the goddess's blessed like an intractable bur. It was an inalienable part of them, and Estella was bound to realize it sooner or later.

There was no way she was removing her daughter from Mason's protection either. He was her best chance to live a mostly normal life. He would ensure that she never had to weaponize her poison like Evelaine had in order to survive in a cruel world. She would never have to face the pity and disappointment that Evelaine had as the bastard child of a courtesan. What could she do?

"Please," her grandfather said softly from the other side of the room. "Think about it."

She moaned, the anguish inside of her multiplying until her bones ached with it, and hugged her knees to her chest, curling tightly into herself. She hadn't thought her already shredded soul could suffer much more, but these decisions she was facing were tearing it into pieces too small to see. They floated away like flakes of dust, landing on the sticky pitch of the blackness inside of her.

Gods, she had been so hopeful earlier, all of her plans had been coming together, and there had been the barest hint of sunrise on the horizon, to which she and her band of misfits confidently marched. But she should have known better.

Her whole life had been mistake after mistake.

She should have never worked for the Mistress. Never fallen for a kind man, given him a child, and propagated her curse in an innocent babe.

She should have prepared better for the fight with Nydas. Should've resisted the innate call to find the plant village. Should've never let herself care for someone who would fall on a blade to save her.

Returning to the Tirdan Republic had only doomed her further, leaving her revenge unrequited and then adding insult to injury by stealing her blessing once again. Who was she to think she could right her path and achieve the impossible? Now, she was powerless, had more people counting on her, pined for an estranged husband who had his hopes pinned on someone else, and was fumbling her duties to a daughter who was a walking time bomb.

What could she possibly do? Run away from it all? She was stuck, an insignificant insect trapped in the unforgiving clutch of a carnivorous flytrap. She gritted her teeth, nails digging into the sides of her legs, and she wished she could simply explode. Take the whole damned city with her. Scorch the field and start over. But she was effectively neutralized without her blessing and couldn't do jack shit about it.

What was the phrase? "There's only one way out: through?"

She could either run away, get the hell out of Risten, and leave a host of devastated loved ones in her wake, or she could continue with the plan: go into the temple, get her blessing back, and leave a host of devastated enemies in her wake. Either way, she would be the means to someone's destruction.

Taking a few deep breaths, she forced her body to unfold and planted her feet firmly on the floor. It was her true purpose, after all. The need to consume and conquer a ravenous urge. She reviewed the plan, staring at the wall in front of her until the overwhelming ache ebbed: temple, blessing, devastation. Temple, blessing, devastation.

Temple.

Blessing.

Devastation.

After Evelaine enacted her revenge, she would devour the rot of the city and fertilize the land for her daughter. She would ensure that Estella's blessing was cultivated into something better. Something worthwhile. Something new, wild, and free.

How exactly she planned to do that was a bridge she would cross later. For now, she held tight to the vow blooming inside her: Her daughter would never give without taking. She would never sacrifice pieces of herself for someone else's fulfillment.

Estella would bend to no one.

DAY NINE

There was no way to tell what time it was inside the darkened tavern, its dirty windows streaked with rain that had been falling since the early hours, when Evelaine had finally given up on sleeping and had found her way to one of her old hiding spots sandwiched between the docks and the Skidden District. Patrons had come and gone as she had sat hunched at the corner table, staring at the scarred wood underneath her tankard.

Her hood up, she drank just enough to keep the bartenders satisfied with her continued presence, tossing a silver whenever they cleared their throats in her general vicinity. Some logical part of her brain knew that everyone was giving her a wide berth, but she honestly preferred it that way. The muffled silence that surrounded her had been a necessity, a much-needed relief from the throbbing in her temples that had kept her tossing and turning until she couldn't stand it anymore. She had needed space, not to think—no, thinking wasn't doing her any favors at the moment—but to escape the questions clogging her throat.

She spent the hours repeating her vow and building an impassable barrier inside her to block out the doubts and uncertainties that threatened her plan. Stone by stone, she mortared them in place and reinforced it with layers and layers of vines. A thick casement of green that kept her confused unease at bay, the disquiet that would only distract her from what she needed to do. Temple. Blessing. Devastation. Vow.

Sure, things hadn't gone exactly as anticipated, but she could adapt. Pivot a few wheels here and there, reinforce a lever, shore up the retaining wall. To reduce further complications, she buried her heart deep under the overgrowth, never to be pierced again by betrayals born of the mortal condition. She was the vessel of eternal nature, the force that would outlast all. Who needed humanity when perpetuity was seeded within?

As she slipped the stones into place, she began to hear the soft murmur of Kaiseln's voice from a dust-covered memory. It had been another long training session and Kaiseln had been particularly unforgiving after Evelaine had shown up hungover thanks to a long night of making sure Corsair hadn't gotten into too much trouble. Evelaine had been weaving on her feet after hours of sparring, her sweat making the floor slick as Kaiseln had circled her with a bored expression.

"You know of Talegartia, yes?" her trainer had asked.

Evelaine had squinted at them, wondering where exactly this line of questioning was going. It hadn't been

unusual for Kaiseln to bring up seemingly unrelated
questions during their sessions, and Evelaine had learned
the hard way that her time was wasted if she remarked on
the apparent randomness of the topic instead of following
her trainer's lead.

"The westernmost country on South Endrian. Known
for their obsession with inventions, efficiency, and
productivity, especially in regard to the raw minerals, ore,
and agricultural resources found in their rainforests and
mountains," she had recited, wiping the back of her hand
across her swollen lip.

"The council. How did they come to power?" her
trainer had continued.

"They were formed about 800 years ago to . . ."
Evelaine had paused, uncertain how to continue. It had
been a year since she had inadvertently revealed her
blessing to Kaiseln and they hadn't really talked about it
beyond the enhancements it brought to her fighting style.
Even though Otis had told her some of the tales passed
down through the bloodline regarding why her ancestors
had fled South Endrian, she had had no idea how much
Kaislen knew about it all.

"To modernize the country," she had finally said,
gauging her trainer's reaction.

Kaiseln hadn't given anything away, their uninterested
gaze watching Evelaine's foot placement as she stayed
out of reach of their slow pace around the training room.
An extended breath had passed between the two of them
before her trainer had struck, moving before Evelaine
could react and kicking out a foot that had caught the plant
blessed right behind her knee. She'd gone down hard, her

tired muscles burning as they'd attempted to steady her and failed.

"What will be their downfall?" Kaiseln had calmly resumed their line of questioning, stepping back once more.

Evelaine had grunted, muttering as she'd pushed herself back up and found her footing. "Fuck if I know. They haven't had a war since the ECR treaty."

Her trainer hadn't responded, just kept up their slow, revolving progress as they'd eyed her increasingly sloppy movements, and the silence had stretched on. Kaislen had eventually darted in for another hit, and this time, Evelaine had just barely managed to swerve out of the way, but it had cost her as something had torn in her side.

"They will fail because they have not invested in endurance," Kaiseln had stated, coming to a stop in front of the door as Evelaine had panted through the pain. "They will fail because they believe their privilege to be intransient.

"All who dare to rule others must realize the truth in order to persist. True endurance is only available to those who honor the material world from which we are all birthed, for perpetuity existed before mortals graced these lands and will remain after we are all gone." Kaiseln had grabbed one of the towels folded on the bench against the wall and tossed it to Evelaine. "Unless you trust the roots within, you will fall."

"There you are!" Evelaine flinched as a thump hit her table, her stumble down memory lane interrupted as she glanced up to find Corsair plopping down in the chair next to her with Gimlet, Rikeland, and Andra in tow. Her irritation doubled and she narrowed her eyes as he spread his arms wide with a smile. "Our fearless leader!"

"What do you want?" The question was asked through bared teeth before she was able to shut down her expression, the glint of challenge lighting in Corsair's eye as he smirked at her snarl.

"I've brought the gang! You know, the group of friends who have agreed to stand by you in the coming fight?" He leaned toward her, his jaw firming. "The friends who care about your well-being?"

Evelaine took a deep breath, counting down from ten before she answered.

"Right." She jerked her chin in the direction of the others. "Hey, guys."

Gimlet exchanged a look with Rikeland then flagged down the bartender as they all settled around the table, Andra nodding in greeting as Corsair draped an arm over the back of Evelaine's chair. She attempted a thin smile at the group as tankards soon arrived for each of them, the awkward silence lingering.

"Now, I brought them because you said you wanted to go over the plans with everyone. Isn't that right?" Corsair gave her a weighty look. She had said no such thing and they both knew it. Corsair was simply rubbing her face in the fact that she was supposed to be the brains of this operation—not a grumpy ass mope in the corner.

"Sure, yeah." She took a swig of her room-temperature ale, wrestling her attention away from the verdant wall. "I've gotten Kaiseln to agree to join us, so that makes a total of six. That significantly increases the odds. I'm hoping that means we can get in and out of there quickly."

"Where are we going again?" Rikeland asked, pulling out the notebook he had started carrying since his head injury, jotting down notes of whatever happened so that he had a record he could reference.

"Word is the temple is underneath a blacksmithy in the Industrial District."

"A temple? In the Industrial?" Gimlet frowned. "But this is Risten we're talking about here."

"I know. I have no idea what kind of state it's going to be in. It obviously hasn't been used for a long time."

"And you said something about fighting things? Like, unnatural things?" Andra's brows knit together as she glanced at Corsair.

Corsair shrugged, hitching a thumb at Evelaine. "That's what she said."

Evelaine lowered her voice. "Yeah, it's not going to be like anything you've fought before. How much did he tell you?"

"Enough to know that I'm wondering if I even want to know." Andra grimaced.

"The wraiths are easier to take down. Just a bit of slash and slice will work. It's the ooze you need to stay away from. It burns like hell and is highly unpredictable. Don't underestimate it." The reminder of the thick snake body squeezing Nees was hard to ignore as Evelaine shook her head to clear it. "It's vulnerable to flame, so we can clear a path. I'll make sure to go first, of course."

"Flame? Like torches?" Gimlet asked.

"You can use them, sure. I've asked Otis if he can prepare something stronger, though."

Gimlet nodded and Evelaine turned to Andra. "Also, thank you. I haven't said that yet."

Andra took a sip of her ale. "Of course. I know we haven't had much of a chance to get to know each other, but I've been impressed by the stories Corsair has shared over the years. I'm looking forward to fighting alongside the Mistress's favorite blade."

Evelaine winced, uncomfortable with the praise, and frowned at Corsair. "Oh yeah? I'm sure he exaggerated."

"I'm more than honored to help out those responsible for taking down the Aldaran pirates." Andra clapped Evelaine on her shoulder with a dark look passing across her expression.

Evelaine pressed her lips together, remembering when a band of pirates had been hired by a new brothel owner in Risten to, one by one, abduct the Rouge's best courtesans. They had been smart about it, carrying out their plan over several months by pretending to be well-paying clientele. They would visit with the courtesans in-house for a few nights, then request to take them out for a night on the town as an escort, but failed to return them by the next morning.

A pattern had soon emerged, but they'd been intentionally random, with a different pirate masquerading as a client each time. Sometimes, they'd taken two courtesans in a weekend, sometimes it had been once a month, and it had infuriated the Mistress, not being able to distinguish between the clientele she could trust and those she had to keep an eye on. She couldn't simply halt all courtesan business activities, that would've hurt her bottom line too much, but all of the preventative measures she had attempted to implement had failed as well.

Finally, it had been decided that every single courtesan would have two assigned guards to watch over them during all client interactions. That had been an interesting month for all involved, the guards getting free shows while the courtesans and clients had been forced to deal with an audience in their intimate moments. (It had soon become clear that there were some who enjoyed the extra sets of eyes and it had unexpectedly given the Mistress some ideas for future services.)

It had just so happened that Evelaine and Corsair had been assigned to a certain courtesan on one of their escort nights when the pirates had launched a coordinated ambush against them. Twelve pirates against the two of them in a deserted alleyway while the courtesan had had a complete meltdown as two additional pirates had attempted to subdue her. It had been a brutal fight, but Evelaine and Corsair had returned to the Rouge, bloodied and limping, with the sobbing courtesan and an unconscious, captured pirate in tow.

After two days of interrogation, the pirate had eventually broken and revealed the details of their deal with the brothel owner, and Evelaine and Corsair had been dispatched to take care of the issue with their particular skill sets. The whole matter had been settled within the week, all stolen courtesans returned and given a few days off to recover from the ordeal. They had not been treated all that well during their captivity, and a few of them had needed to spend some time at the doctor's to take care of the resulting injuries. But life had quickly moved on at the Rouge, most of the staff choosing to pretend it was business as usual.

Evelaine wondered if Corsair had included that particular detail in his recount, knowing that his stories typically centered around the slashing and stabbing to highlight his heroics, but her stomach still turned at the reminder and she simply nodded at Andra.

"Yeah, I remember us having quite the celebration after that fight, right, Gim?" Corsair slung his arm over the man in question's shoulders as Gimlet rolled his eyes.

"That's old history," he insisted, shrugging off Corsair.

"Oh, come on. I've seen the way you still look at this ass." Corsair winked.

Gimlet huffed, the barest of blushes staining his cheeks as he glanced at Evelaine with a pointed look. "Shut him up or he'll find a dagger in his gut before we even get to the temple."

Evelaine sighed, well aware of the affair Corsair and Gimlet had had years ago. As far as she could tell, it had been a flash in the pan like all of Corsair's attractions, and she still regretted the moment she had accidentally walked in on them fucking furiously in one of the Rouge's weapon storage closets. It was one of the memories she wished Tabriara hadn't restored.

She frowned at Corsair, and he shrugged with a grin, clinking his tankard against Rikeland's as the baker puffed out a laugh. He was writing in his notebook, and she grimaced again, wondering exactly how much of Corsair's bullshit was scrawled into its pages.

"So what happens when you do get your . . ." Rikeland's eyes darted around as he lowered his voice. ". . . blessings back? That's the reason we're going to the temple, right?"

"You said you wanted to go after Nydas." Gimlet jerked his chin in her direction, also leaning in. "How the fuck do you plan on accomplishing that?"

"What exactly do you know about him?" Evelaine asked instead.

"I know that he's a right asshole. Scum of the fucking dirt." He scoffed, hitching his thumb over his shoulder toward the front of the tavern. "You hear about the Waltzins buying Stephenson's chemical factory?"

"No?" She looked to Corsair for confirmation, and he paled like he knew how this story ended.

"They wanted to get rid of the middleman, you know? Manufacture the dyes and cleaning supplies and whatever the fuck they sell in their stores for cheap, so they bought the factory and changed shit up. But the workers started getting sick, you feel me?" His brown eyes grew sharp, his voice a soft murmur. "Coming home with boils on their hands and arms, coughing up blood, nasty migraines. It got people talking. Soon there were whispers of organizing. Fighting back, you know? That U-word those fuckwads are so triggered by."

Evelaine deepened her frown, knowing exactly what he was referring to: unionization. Of course, there had been countless attempts to do something about the deplorable working conditions that existed in this great country of theirs, but every time the ants had dared to consider it, there had always been someone to step in and squash everything.

"So the Waltzins hired Nydas and his crew on the sly. Had them infiltrate the factory, pretending to be workers. Before we knew it, folks were showing up dead. 'Unfortunate accidents,' they called them. A certain outspoken leader tripping into a boiling vat, another finding himself locked inside the furnace, one woman scheduled for a late shift, never to be seen again." He curled his lip in disgust.

"They never copped up to it publicly, of course. The official word was that there was an unusual infection going around the factory and they brought in 'doctors' to clear it all up. Afterwards, the injuries and mishaps were a lot less frequent, but they lowered everyone's wages to pay for the safety upgrades. Only fifty gold a year, even for the tenured who'd kept their mouths shut the entire time. Anyone who complains gets a visit from one of Nydas's people."

Evelaine couldn't help but remember the conversation she'd had with Otis about how exactly Nydas had gotten his hands on a sedative powerful enough to erase memories. "Do they . . . Have they gotten into the trade of medicines?"

Gimlet shook his head. "Not that I've heard of, why?"

"No reason." She took another sip of ale.

"So you're really going after him?" Andra asked, her expression drawn.

Evelaine didn't say anything, conscious of the ears in the room, but the look she gave the bouncer was more than enough. Andra's eyes dropped to her tankard, her throat bobbing with a swallow.

They sat uncomfortably for a moment and Evelaine could sense it, the moment each of their focuses turned internal. The moment they pulled their answer from within and became lost in their individual reasons for why they were embarking on this journey of peril. Rikeland looked toward the windows, the hope of a new home for his growing family shining from his eyes, but Gimlet's attention darted to Corsair before slipping away, the expression of finality shadowing his brow while Corsair absently stretched to rub at his own shoulder.

Evelaine comforted herself with the knowledge that she had found Kaiseln at just the right time. It had to be a sure sign of their success, right? They had to be the missing puzzle piece she had been looking for, even if she was still unsure why they had agreed in the first place. Was it somehow a lingering remnant of the bond they had formed as trainer and trainee over the years? But what about everything else they had said at the Rouge about their orders? What had it all meant?

What would it all mean in the end?

She could only hope that time would favor them for once in her life.

Day Ten

Evelaine had spent the night before their infiltration preparing the bundles of explosives and fire starters that Otis had cooked up for them. He had been grim but determined, watching her from the corner of his eye as they'd poured his concoctions into bottles and mixed flammable powders with care, but she had promised to speak with Mason and Estella once she returned from the temple, so he hadn't prodded further.

The day of, everyone arrived at the apothecary before dawn as instructed, their heavy cloaks covering the leather breastplates and dozen or so blades strapped to their bodies. Corsair, Gimlet, and Kaiseln all had their weapons well-concealed, but Evelaine could see the top of Rikeland's preferred battle axe peeking out from behind his back and was pleased to see Andra with two wicked-looking swords hanging from her hips.

"Right." Kaislen drew out the word as they surveyed the group with their arms crossed. "Are we ready, then?"

"I am." Andra smiled, seeming eager to stretch her muscles with a real challenge beyond guarding overindulgent patrons at the Rouge.

Rikeland nodded, stashing his notebook away, and Gimlet went to stand by the door, refusing to look at Corsair as the metal blessed wiggled his brows and secured the clasp on his cloak.

Otis pulled Evelaine aside for one last hug. "Please take care of yourself."

"I will, I promise," she murmured, glancing at her allies chatting amongst themselves. Could she even make a promise like that? Tendrils of apprehension were squeezing through the cracks in her stone wall, but she pushed them back, resolutely sealing them over. Her plan would work.

Temple, blessing, devastation, vow.

She would make sure that they all made it out in one piece, and then she could finally get on with the real reason that had brought her back to this damned city. She would enact her revenge, do some good while she was at it, then figure out how she could be the mother Estella needed. With that insistent reminder, she gave her grandfather's shoulder one last squeeze and nodded for Kaiseln to lead the way.

Pensive silence followed them in the dark streets, a touch of light just beginning to appear above the Dock District as they headed toward the southeast corner of the city. Even Corsair was uncharacteristically quiet, puffing at a cigarette as they swiftly moved from shadow to shadow underneath scaffolding that provided the cover they needed, and before long they found themselves in front of a decrepit blacksmithy shop. Its long-peeled wooden sign hung crooked off the front post, dangling carelessly in the wind, and its windows were boarded up from the inside, a few panes of glass broken from thrown rocks and cracked from years of disuse, but Kaiseln led them down the side alley to a rear cellar door made of two thick slabs of iron.

Corsair sighed, looking at the mess of chains and locks that secured it, and Evelaine could tell he was thinking of how easy it would be to open it all if only he had access to his blessing, but they were forced to do it the hard way. Kaiseln and Evelaine quickly dropped to a knee and started working on picking the heavy locks. Her trainer finished with hers first, having been the one to teach Evelaine the skill after all, but the plant blessed was not far behind her, Corsair catching the chains as they fell to keep them from clattering and attracting unwanted attention.

Rikeland and Corsair then worked together to muscle one of the rusted doors open, the baker holding it in place as Kaiseln crept into the darkness first, with the rest of them following close behind. Kaislen lit a torch, then Rikeland pulled the chains inside, quietly closing them in as the group stayed bunched in the dank stairwell, and he did his best to lock it back up from the other side.

As Evelaine took the opportunity to study their surroundings, she found evidence of thin branches of ichor reaching up the stone walls and stairs and pointed them out, cautioning the others to avoid touching it if possible. She warned them that it was only going to get worse from there, reminding them to stay silent and listen for the wraiths that were bound to find them. The group eyed her warily but nodded, trusting that she knew what she was saying even as she reinforced her wall to keep her doubts from rearing their ugly heads.

Her teeth gritted against the indistinct images that turned her stomach, almost as if she were remembering them through someone else's eyes. A gauzy film laid over the scene in front of her. She supposed that was accurate, for it had been Esia who had gazed upon the sprawling tendrils of black that had reached across the land, strangling fish, rodents, and other creatures. The massive bodies of monstrous worms, constricted and contorted. The thick limbs encircling Nees and squeezing until bones had popped and cracked. Hand flying to her throat, she shook her head and ordered them away. It hadn't been her. It had been Esia. Another person. Another life. It would be different this time, she swore it.

Kaiseln unsheathed one of her blades and motioned forward with the torch as everyone followed suit, the soft sound of metal on leather echoing off the stairwell. It descended much farther than one would guess based on the exterior of the building, going at least two stories underground, and despite her best efforts, Evelaine's unease only kept increasing as they slowly progressed. Fighting the memories that bombarded her, she forced her breaths to be even in order to keep the group calm, but Corsair kept glancing at her, his lips in a thin line.

Finally, they reached a small platform at the end of the stairs where another metal door blocked their way. The ichor had thickened, strands of it pushing its way out of the thin seams and spreading across the surrounding stone, and Evelaine eyed it suspiciously. Gimlet leaned forward and sniffed one of them, his nose wrinkling at the acrid scent, while Corsair poked the tip of his dagger into another. The blackness stuck to the end of his blade in a tiny glob and he frowned, rubbing it off on the side of his pants, but he jerked with a small yelp as the substance burned a hole through the fabric to his skin.

Evelaine snatched the dagger out of his hand. "I fucking told you not to touch it."

"I didn't!" he insisted as she scraped the tip against a bare patch of stone to remove the ichor. "I thought the dagger—"

"Don't. Touch. It," she gritted and held out the pommel end for him to take. His hand closed around it as distant moans filtered to them through the stone walls, and he froze, his eyes going wide.

"What is—" he began, but Evelaine didn't give him a chance to finish the thought.

"Back-to-back!" She tried not to let her panic bleed into her voice, the words rushed. "Wraiths, slash and stab!"

She barely got the message out as shadowy black forms suddenly surrounded them, half of them clustered on the platform and half still in the stairwell, and a muttering of swear words sounded as the group sprang into action. Kaiseln dropped the torch, the light flickering as their weapons started slicing through the air, but Evelaine almost lost the grip on her own as she spun, dodging a swipe.

She couldn't see any of her allies as she refocused on the wraiths that circled her, wincing from the claw swipes that made purchase, but muscle memory soon took over, her body moving without her conscious instruction.

Something cracked open inside her, a meditative ease that suddenly bloomed in the midst of chaos. It was as if she could finally breathe again. As if she were watching from a distance as her blades arced and danced, her torso twisted, and legs held her steady. Rooted, grounded, and secure.

For the first time in years and years, her mind went blank and all of her anxieties quieted as she was finally given an outlet for the fury that had built up within her. An expulsion of the poison that had been crowding her lungs. The feeling of release calmed her system, and she felt a smile begin to curl her lips. It felt wonderful, giving in to the fight and letting her anger bloom unrestricted. Even though she had had the chance to fight at the plant temple, it hadn't been like this. Now, every fiber of her was humming. It made her feel clear and crisp and whole. It wasn't Esia fighting. It was pure Evelaine, through and through. The grin widened and a chuckle crawled up her throat, her blade plunging into wraith after wraith. She had hungered for this. Starved for it.

As they fell away like leaves in the wind, the space cleared and she found herself laughing as she beamed at her companions. The last few wraiths were finished off, and she watched as the group turned to her with confused frowns, breathing heavily from the exertion. They had some minor injuries, scrapes and cuts here and there, but they were all standing as they glanced amongst each other.

"Fun, right?" She smiled at Andra, whose brows furrowed.

"Sure," the bouncer answered slowly.

Kaiseln sheathed one of her blades and picked up the torch, watching Evelaine carefully as the rest of the group dusted themselves off.

"Great fun," Corsair added, an attempt at being supportive as he gave her an uncertain smile. "Was that . . . Those were the wraiths?"

"Yep," Evelaine answered cheerfully, moving to the door to examine it. "The first wave, at least. There'll be more through here."

There were two handprints embedded in the metal, and she glanced over at Corsair. "I'll need your help with these."

He squeezed his way past the others in the stairwell to join her, and she grabbed his hand, placing it against one of the handprints as she positioned her free one on the other. She felt the same pull she had at the plant temple, the door drawing a single grain of leftover pollen from her depleted stores as Corsair gasped next to her.

"Good gods," he murmured as there was a loud shifting sound and the door started lowering into a gap in the stone below. Perfect. As soon as the way was cleared, Evelaine confidently strode forward into the long metal hallway that was revealed but was yanked back as Kaiseln grabbed her arm.

"Are you stupid, girl?" They glared at her. "I've taught you better than that."

She chuckled, rolling her eyes at the misstep. "Right, of course. After you, master."

Kaiseln's frown deepened, but they chose not to respond as they took the lead and began studying the patterns etched into the walls, ceiling, and floor. Corsair's hand landed on Evelaine's shoulder as they waited, and he leaned toward her.

"Are you alright?" he asked, low enough not to be heard by the others.

"Yeah." She glanced at him. "Why wouldn't I be?"

A crease formed between his brows. "You're . . . You just seem . . . excited."

"Well, sure. Aren't you? We'll have our blessings back soon enough."

He glanced over his shoulder at the others. "Yeah, I guess. Just . . . be careful."

"I will, don't worry." She smiled at him. He looked unnerved but accepted it, dropping back a bit to give her some room in the tight space.

They had to enter the hallway in a single line, the walls closer than they had been in the plant temple, and Kaislen soon stopped a few feet in front of Evelaine and raised a hand. They were looking at the carvings above their head, another bunch of geometric shapes that seemed more or less random. Circles, squares, lines, rectangles, and triangles were grouped here and there throughout the tunnel, winding under the group's feet and arcing across the walls and ceiling.

"We're going to have to follow a certain path through this portion," they warned, locking eyes with each of them for emphasis. "Follow my footsteps exactly."

The group nodded and the trainer carefully moved forward, tiptoeing around shapes that Evelaine didn't understand. Sometimes their foot would settle inside a large circle, sometimes on the edge of a square, and other times on completely blank spaces, but she followed the route without question. This was exactly why she had asked them to come. They would be the advantage that helped Evelaine get everyone out safely.

Kaiseln even crouched at one point, shuffling underneath two long lines of triangles on either side of the walls, and the rest of them followed suit, but Rikeland was too big. His bulk prevented him from clearing the bottom of the design entirely, and there was a sudden grinding sound. Everyone jerked, reaching for him just as a handful of darts shot from the wall and embedded into his shoulder.

He yelped, his hand going to the wounds as he slumped forward and fell to the floor in a heap. His eyes were wide as he groaned, his limbs going limp. Gimlet swore next to him, plucking the darts out of the baker's flesh as quickly as possible and sniffing the end of one.

"Smells like Cestrum serum," he told them. "It's sometimes sold in low concentrations as a mild hallucinogen."

"Is he going to start tripping?" Corsair asked, looking worried.

"I mean, he probably already is, but it seems like it's a higher dosage, which causes fever and paralysis." Gimlet frowned down at Rikeland, who had begun to drool.

"Shit," Corsair muttered, looking between Kaiseln and Evelaine for guidance. The two assassins had already made it to the end of the dangerous design, waiting for the others to join them.

"Gimlet, you can squeeze by Corsair and get to us to clear the way," Kaiseln ordered him. "Andra, sling Rikeland's legs over your shoulders, and Corsair, you grab his arms. You will need to maneuver him through it. Just make sure you stay close to the right wall through the last section."

They moved to follow the directions as Kaiseln slung their pack to the floor and started rifling through it. They located a brown bottle, and Evelaine recognized it as the antitoxin Otis had made them take before leaving.

"You think that'll work?" she asked her trainer. It was typically used for ingested toxins, not those that had been directly injected into the bloodstream.

"It's our best bet, unless you have any other ideas," they answered as the rest of the group made it to them and deposited Rikeland at their feet with a huff. The baker giggled, the sound gurgling in the back of his throat. Andra and Corsair were out of breath from hauling his considerable weight, and they were bracing their hands on their knees when Evelaine heard a distant sound that made her skin prickle.

Kaislen's head spun toward the direction they were heading and they frowned as the sound got louder, Gimlet popping up from where he had been kneeling next to Rikeland with a sneer.

A cloud of shadow came barreling into view and Evelaine smiled, eagerly pushing past her trainer and placing herself in front. "Surround Rikeland. Protect him."

She unsheathed a sword and her blessed dagger, the familiar weight of it comforting as the mass reached them, and she threw herself into it with a laugh. Buffeted by countless forms, she grinned and let instinct take over. Gods, this was fun. Her anger burst from her, causing her breath to catch in ecstasy as her pulse quickened.

This was what she had been craving ever since she had woken up to find Nees's cold form beside her in the sacred forest. She had just wanted a target, a recipient for her fury, but there had been so many reasons to resist the urge to force her pain onto something or someone else. She had barely been able to restrain herself when she had blown up at Hara once they had returned to the village, well aware it was a bad idea to pick a fight with her.

Running after Nydas had been the best option, but he had evaded her and left her even more frustrated than before. Then she had been faced with obstacle after obstacle since, but here, she could give in to her baser hungers. The driving need to dispense the festering pitch that coated her insides, administering the agony that plagued her day and night. She could be the one to deliver the destruction that waged its war in her chest, spreading its rot.

She lost track of time as she fought her way through the horde, only vaguely aware of how her allies might be faring behind her, but eventually, the last of the wraiths were cut down and she glanced back to check on them. Andra was holding her cheek, blood running through her fingers from some claw marks, and Gimlet was standing over Rikeland's prone form protectively, breathing heavily with a bloodied arm. Corsair and Kaiseln had stood together in front of them, forming a second line of defense, but looked relatively unscathed as Evelaine rejoined them.

"Good work," she complimented them with a smile, patting Corsair on the shoulder and looking her group over.

"Thanks," Corsair grumbled, wiping his blades off as he caught his breath.

Evelaine reached over and plucked the bottle of antitoxin from Kaiseln's belt, where they had quickly secured it before the wraiths had reached them, then knelt next to Rikeland. "Gimlet, patch everyone up before we move on. Here goes nothing."

Propping open the baker's mouth, she poured in half of the bottle and closed her hand over his lips to force him to swallow it as his huge pupils wandered around aimlessly. His throat worked as the antitoxin went down, and he began coughing, curling in on himself as he twitched, and Evelaine helped him onto his side, where he began vomiting in great heaves.

She held him there as the spewed liquid changed from mostly foam to a lumpy mix of what had been his breakfast and his limbs began moving, his hands attempting to find purchase on the floor. It seemed like a good sign, and she helped him into a kneeling position, patting his back as he finished with a groan. His eyes were still blown wide, but at least he was holding himself in place, only a slight tremor in his muscles, and Evelaine grinned, happy with the progress.

"Ready?" She glanced up at the rest of them.

"Are you serious?" Gimlet griped, tying off the bandage around his arm. "We can't just carry on like this. What are we going to do with him?"

He pointed to where Rikeland held himself on all fours, staring up at them with dazed amazement and muttering something about rainbows.

"It'll wear off soon, right?" Evelaine assured them. "Andra can help support him until he can walk on his own again."

"That's insane. He has another hour of that, if not longer since we don't even know for sure what was on the darts," Gimlet insisted.

"How about we rest for a bit?" Corsair held up his hands between them. "Catch our breath?"

"We don't have time for that. The next group of wraiths will find us soon," she argued. "We have to keep moving."

"We're out of the trapped portion of the tunnel now. We can fight them here." Gimlet crossed his arms and squinted down the dark tunnel. "We have no idea what's down there."

Evelaine looked to Kaiseln for help, but her trainer just lifted a shoulder. "He's right."

"Fine." Rolling her eyes, Evelaine relented. They were being obstinate, but she supposed she couldn't blame them. It was probably terrifying for them to experience these nightmares for the first time. They didn't know how well they were doing. She had to keep morale high. Show her confidence in their abilities. "You all are doing great. Take a break, I'll stand watch."

She moved farther down the tunnel again, lighting her own torch so that she could see while Gimlet grumbled to himself. He got Rikeland to sit up and reached into the baker's pocket for the notebook and started scribbling in it himself to record what had happened. Andra sat down next to him, glancing at Evelaine warily, then started cleaning her blades as Kaiseln continued studying the patterns around them.

Corsair joined Evelaine where she stood, staring into the darkness ahead of them, and placed his hand on her shoulder, leaning in. "Hey, what's going on, dude?"

"What do you mean?" she asked, matching his tone.

"You're not acting like yourself. Your whole vibe is off."

"My vibe?" She frowned. "What would you know about what I'm supposed to be acting like?"

He drew back slightly. "Are you kidding me? I've known you since you were born, for fuck's sake."

"You all haven't been in a temple before. It's understandable. You don't know what it's like. This is going well. We should be happy with our progress." There actually seemed to be fewer wraiths than at Curacu, and she wondered if it was because it'd only been four months since the corruption had taken over. It hadn't had as much time.

"Waiting until Rikeland isn't tripping his balls off is the smart move, Evie. It's making sure we're prepared for whatever is coming next." He nudged his chin down the tunnel.

"I agreed, didn't I?" She huffed.

He studied her face, his lips set in a grim line. "This isn't a suicide mission. Stop acting like it is."

Her fist clenched at her side. How dare he suggest that was what she was doing. She knew the risks more than anyone there. She knew what they were facing, and she was doing her best to make sure they all got out of there alive. And the plan was working! Suicide mission? This was the furthest thing from it. He had no idea what he was talking about.

"Whatever," she muttered, turning away from him. It wasn't worth arguing. He couldn't understand.

He didn't respond, just gave her a pointed look then returned to the others. They talked quietly amongst themselves as she stewed in silence. They had no idea what she was feeling, no idea why she was pouring every ounce of herself into the fight. She had to unleash the devastation inside of her. It was what she'd been made to do. It was the only way forward.

About half an hour went by before she heard oncoming moans and alerted the group, bracing herself for impact as she spied the whirling shadows headed in their direction once again. They sprang into action and another blinding clash ensued, the smile returning to her lips as she slashed and parried.

It was exhilarating, seeing her opponents fall before her one after another. She had almost forgotten how satisfying it was to slay something, and the wraiths were perfect targets. She didn't have to worry about the moral implications of what she was doing, wondering if they had a family at home that she was stealing them from or if their broken body would lead the authorities back to her somehow. They simply dissipated into a puff of smoke and then another took their place until she had worked her way through them all.

She came out with a few more scrapes and bruises that time around, but she barely felt them as she glanced her team over. She was proud of them. They were a scrappy bunch and looked like they had adapted well, learning the patterns of the wraiths and doing their best to dodge out of the range of their teeth and claws. They knew how to fight for survival and it showed. Surface-level gouges decorated them here and there, but they were quickly cleaned and wrapped up, and before long, Rikeland started coming to, shaking his head and glancing around with a clearer gaze.

161

He wondered what the hell had happened, and Gimlet showed him the notebook, filling in the gaps to his memory as best he could. Then Rikeland was moving to stand, his legs finally stable enough to hold his weight as he tested his reflexes and swung his axe a bit to limber up again. When he nodded, only tilting to the side slightly, Evelaine motioned for Kaiseln to continue leading the charge, and the trainer began moving forward with a frown on their face.

Evelaine couldn't bring herself to worry about the tension that bracketed the group. She had to be the confident leader here. She knew what was waiting for them at the end of this, and there was no room for her to doubt or question. The plan was working. She would not bend. She would not break. She would prevail. There was no other choice.

Eventually, the tunnel came to a dead end, the only exit a dark, square hole that was lined with a long metal ladder, thick strips of ichor snaking out of it. It was just wide enough to fit one person at a time, and they all stared at it for a moment, realizing that they would have to simply trust that it would lead them to where they needed to go. Rikeland groaned, already dreading the tight fit with his bulk, but Evelaine simply took out some fire starter and started pouring it around the edges. Gimlet emptied one of his bottles as well, aiming deeper down the hole, then everyone backed up as Corsair lit a match and threw it in.

They all cringed back from the rush of heat and covered their noses and mouths with their cloaks as smoke began filling the space, but it soon cleared, and Evelaine nodded for Kaiseln to start them off, eager to continue their forward progression. The trainer gave her a side-long glance but gripped the end of the torch in their teeth and began the descent. Evelaine knew she could count on them as the others shuffled their feet. It would do them no good to worry, she wanted to tell them. They'd get through it, and it would be fine. She would make sure of it.

A Sentence

Kaiseln called up to the rest of the group after a few minutes, letting them know that there was no end in sight yet, and Evelaine only hesitated for a moment. There was no way she was going to let Kaiseln continue on their own. She had sworn to herself that they wouldn't split the group, so she motioned for them all to follow, despite the frowns that were reflected back at her. They would just have to trust that she knew what she was doing.

It seemed like solid logic until there was a shift of metal on metal as small holes appeared in the walls surrounding them. Evelaine swallowed the immediate bloom of regret, fighting to gird herself against the doubt that began to peek through, but a chorus of curse words echoed her unease as the group realized they were trapped with allies above and below them on the ladder. Gimlet's voice raised to yell something, swept away by a distant howl of wind that began rushing toward them from somewhere. It got louder and louder until it hit them with gale force, intense streams of air buffeting them from all sides as they clung to the ladder in order to not be thrown off it.

Corsair shouted something, but Evelaine didn't catch it, watching as Andra slipped above her. There was a precarious moment as the bouncer found her footing again and Evelaine implored her heartbeat to slow, trying to think of a plan. There were a few more attempts at communication, but the wind was too loud, stealing their words and carrying them away as they fought to hold onto the metal rungs.

Evelaine's hair whipped around her face, but after several minutes of nothing but air, she looked below her and indicated that Kaiseln should try to continue on. Still frowning, her trainer deliberated for a moment but came to the same conclusion, their knuckles white as they slowly moved to the next rung. Evelaine then reached up and tugged on Andra's pant leg to get her attention, the bouncer's eyes finding hers over her shoulder. She pointed downward, encouraging her to pass the message on, and saw, more than heard, Andra's grunt of disapproval as her jaw clenched.

Soon enough, though, they were all descending again, foot by agonizing foot. Andra slipped a few more times and Evelaine had to reach up, catching the bottom of her boot to stabilize her, but the rungs were found and their progress continued. It felt like hours, Evelaine's shoulders and thighs protesting, but she gritted her teeth and repeated her plan in her head. She couldn't let her doubts squeeze their way in now, knowing they were getting close to wherever they were going. Their success was inevitable, she kept telling herself.

Finally, Kaiseln shouted something to her, and Evelaine glanced down to see that the trainer had emerged from the hole they were climbing, the ladder leading them to some sort of floor below. Hope budded within her, but she jerked as she heard a shout from above and saw Andra take the impact of someone falling, the bouncer losing her grip on the ladder as she also began plummeting toward Evelaine.

"Fuck!" Evelaine grunted as they hit her, her head banging against the metal wall as she also lost her footing, and the group of them fell in a tangled mess of limbs the rest of the way. They landed with a jarring thud in a pile of sticky ichor, blood spilling in her mouth as she felt a tooth pop loose.

Kaiseln rushed over from where they had leapt out of the way and began checking for injuries. Spitting out the tooth and hissing at the sting of the ichor, Evelaine pushed Andra off her and realized it was Gimlet who had fallen, his face covered in blood from where his brow had burst open. Both of them were fortunately still conscious, but Andra's left wrist looked to be broken, her hand hanging awkwardly as Kaiseln inspected it.

Evelaine did her best to clear them of the blackness with the dropped torch as Rikeland and Corsair joined them, the rush of wind immediately dying the second they both exited the hole. She cursed the design of this temple, knowing full well that it had been intentional to keep intruders out. It was only made worse by the ichor that spread out around them in thick branches, irritated welts beginning to form where it had burned through her clothes. But they were close. She could feel it.

Wiping the blood from her mouth with the back of her hand, she studied the space that opened beyond them as the others worked on wrapping Andra's and Gimlet's injuries. It was enormous, the echo of their movements going far beyond the reach of the torch as she tried to peer into the darkness. She couldn't even see any walls to the left or right of her, the only reference point the metal wall to their rear with the ladder rungs they had entered on.

It looked like the hole disappeared above them into a metal overhang, but the wall beyond that showed no ceiling in sight. It was eerie, not knowing how big the space was or what it contained, so she instructed Rikeland to light another torch for the group working on injuries and called over Corsair to join her as she tentatively followed where the ichor branched from. They walked for a small distance, a stretch of dark space now between them and the light of the other group, before they began to see a sharp drop-off.

Coming upon a thin metal bridge that extended out in front of them, they could just see another metal wall on the other side of it. The bridge ended about half a foot before the wall, where a door stood closed. Evelaine peeked over the edge of the floor, but it was pure darkness below, no sign of how far it went, and she repressed a shiver. Nope, no need to look down there. Instead, she focused on the ichor that was completely wrapped around the bridge, spreading out again once it reached where she and Corsair were standing.

"We need to clear it away," she said, turning to Corsair and handing him the torch. He took it, eyeing the bridge with mistrust, but nodded, and she took out one of her bottles of fire starter. Throwing her arm outward, she tried to sprinkle it on as much of the bridge as she could reach, then retrieved the torch from Corsair and touched it to the edge.

It went up in a flash, the burst of fire illuminating the wall, and Evelaine got a quick glimpse of the black veins that seemed to climb down it from farther up. There was a horizontal seam in the metal maybe ten feet above their heads and another twenty or so feet above that. The ichor was seeping out from those, spreading across the rest of the wall from there. To the right, there was a vertical seam about ten feet away that ran from the bottom upward. To the left, another at the same distance. The wall eventually ended on either side with another gap of dark space beyond.

As the light died away, she was just about to ask Corsair if he had brought the letter from his father when moans began echoing from all sides, and her head whipped around to the group on the other side of the room. Her stomach bottomed out as she suddenly realized her mistake. The flaw in her reasoning was a slap to the face. She quickly gauged the distance between her and the others but could only watch as they grabbed for their weapons and instinctively surrounded Andra as the weak link now. She began to run for them but didn't get far as the wraiths attacked both groups simultaneously.

Swinging the torch wide, she slammed one of them in the face as she heard Corsair grunt behind her, going down and grappling with another. She kept pushing forward, though, letting anger take over. Her muscles vibrated with fury as she threw herself upon them, eagerness mixing with ire at her misstep. They were so close to their destination. She couldn't get sidetracked now.

It didn't matter when she got knocked to the side, losing grip on the torch and dropping to a knee as one pummeled her. She simply tackled its form and took it down with her, grinning predatorily. She had to trust her teammates' skills as she sliced and kicked and punched the crowd around her—her nightmares come alive. She had spent so many restless nights haunted by the images of what they had faced in the plant temple, but now she was being given the chance to punish them as they had her. There was no reason to hold back. She knew exactly where to aim the pain inside of her here. She was in control.

It was time for payback.

The fight ended sooner than she wished, her wild eyes darting around for another target as the last one puffed away, but Corsair was right there, offering his hand to her as he breathed heavily and helped her to stand with a concerned frown at her expression. She spit out some of the blood that had pooled in her mouth and shrugged him off, glancing over to the other group.

Relief sagged her shoulders when she saw that they were still standing. Well, mostly. Gimlet was struggling to his feet and coughing, holding his throat where it seemed like he had been strangled by one of the wraiths. But he looked like he was recovering, so Evelaine turned back to Corsair.

"Do you have the letter?" she asked, holding her hand out.

"Well, yeah." His brows creased, but he twisted to reach into his pack. "Here."

She flipped to the drawing of the object, then retrieved her torch again to study the wall in front of her. Holding up the page, she retreated a few steps to get a clearer view. Although she could barely see the entirety of the metal expanse, it seemed like it was just as the sketch depicted: three rows of squares stacked on top of each other with nine in total. An enormous geometric shape, floating in the cavernous space somehow. Strangely, there was an identical door embedded in each one, but the middle square was where the ichor was branching from, and the letter suggested that the crystal would likely be somewhere inside it.

Stuffing the letter in her pocket, she headed to the right and studied the doors she could see. They all looked the same, with no markings or anything to distinguish them, but once she reached the end of the wall, she realized that the enormous object was a cube that extended deep beyond them. It wasn't nine squares in total, but twenty-seven. Three layers of nine, and she was betting that the crystal would be in the very center.

She groaned, realizing that it meant they would have to head into one of the doors and navigate their way to the middle somehow. Clever. Any metal blessed would be able to do so easily, but anyone else? It would be one hell of a puzzle, and without Corsair's abilities, they were unfortunately in the latter category. She rubbed her brow for a moment, fighting back the headache that was forming, then returned to Corsair, seeing that the rest of the group had joined him at the end of the bridge. They

171

didn't look happy, but she honestly didn't care. They had come this far, they were going to continue, and that was that.

Turning to Kaiseln, she motioned to the door at the end of the bridge. "Take a look, see what we're up against."

"Come on, Evelaine." Gimlet coughed, still rubbing at his throat where bruises were starting to form. "This is insane."

"What? We're here. We have to finish it," she insisted.

"Andra's injured, Rikeland's still weaving on his feet, you're dribbling blood down your chin, and you want us to go into that thing?" He waved at the cube. "No fucking way."

"I told you it was going to be a hard fight. This is what you signed up for."

"I signed up for what I thought was a temple. This?" He eyed the dark space below. "This is a death trap."

"I said it was going to be bad. What do you want from me? More money? I'll give you more. I don't care. But we have to go in there." Her muscles were beginning to twitch, and she was unable to understand why they were stalling now.

"I mean, he's got a point, Evelaine." Andra spoke up, holding out her hastily splinted wrist. "How am I supposed to fight with this?"

"Just use your right hand. We'll put you in the middle. You'll be fine." Evelaine threw up her hands, frustrated. She looked to Corsair for help. "You want your blessing back, don't you?"

"Well, yeah . . . ," he agreed, sounding uncertain. He rubbed the back of his neck, glancing up at the cube.

Rikeland stepped forward, placing a hand on Gimlet's shoulder. "We can do this. Evelaine got through the other one and made it out. We can trust her."

Evelaine's stomach turned, but she refused to acknowledge the sensation, gritting her teeth. "See? Nothing to worry about."

Kaiseln was studying her keenly. "What are we to expect in there exactly?"

Evelaine sighed, waving a hand vaguely. "More wraiths, probably. At the center will be the crystal we're looking for. It will be guarded by some sort of ichor creature. We just need to defeat it and then we can leave."

Her trainer hummed, looking back at the cube. "We are aiming for the center?"

"Yeah, it should just be, like, two squares and then we're there. That's two, maybe three more fights tops."

Gimlet crossed his arms, eyeing the sections. "Only a couple more fights?"

"And you'll pay us more?" Andra asked.

"Sure," Evelaine answered quickly, their questions giving fertilizer to the doubts fighting to break past the barrier. She reached into her pack and took out more coins. "Here, how about . . . ?"

She counted out five platinum coins for each of them, even Corsair, and pushed them into their hands. Out of the corner of her eye, she saw Corsair pass a coin to the other four, only keeping one for himself as their expressions cleared a bit, the weight of the additional payment seeming to assuage some of their fears.

"Fine," Gimlet relented, "then we're out of here."

"Absolutely," Evelaine agreed, itching to hurry them along. Too many emotions were vying for control, but she kept a tight grip on her anger. It was driving her forward, the need to consume and conquer becoming unbearable. If she stopped to entertain any of the other feelings crowding like weeds, she would start second-guessing everything. There had been too many obstacles delaying her plan and she was growing desperate.

Temple, blessing, devastation, vow, she told herself.

It was so close.

Kaiseln was the only one who seemed unswayed by the amount, but tucked it into their pocket anyway, turning to the bridge. "I'll check the door."

They proceeded carefully onto the thin metal walkway, a slight creak echoing with each step as the rest of the group waited. Evelaine shifted impatiently, but her trainer took their time examining the door, first by sight alone then running their fingertips across the frame.

"It's not even locked," they announced, glancing back at them with a crease between their brows. "We should be able to go right in."

"That's disconcerting," Gimlet mumbled, but Rikeland elbowed him and he fell quiet, frowning.

"See? Good news," Evelaine insisted, the words feeling wooden in her mouth. "Open it up."

Kaiseln reached forward and hooked a finger into the indentation that served as a handle, tugging the door to the side as the metal panel slid into a compartment in the wall. Beyond seemed to be a bare metal room with more engravings on the interior panels, and they peeked inside, glancing around before waving the group forward.

Evelaine went first, following her trainer as they gingerly stepped across the gap at the end of the bridge and into the room. She then held the door open as Andra, Corsair, Gimlet, and Rikeland crossed over one by one. Closing them in, she found no ichor present but ignored the tiny twinge of warning in her gut at the discovery. It hadn't had time to spread, she told herself as she turned to join Kaiseln, who was inspecting the next door that sat in the middle of the wall on the other side, but just as the entry slid closed, the whole room shook, throwing them all to the floor as it started moving. There was a great heaving sensation and the sound of metal on metal, then it stopped as suddenly as it had begun.

"What the fuck was that?" Gimlet asked, scrambling to his feet from where he had fallen to the right side of the room.

"I-I don't—" Evelaine's eyes darted around as a loud buzzing sound filled the space and a recessed track in the ceiling slid open to reveal a wickedly sharp revolving blade.

"Holy shit!" Corsair exclaimed, ducking just as it shot across the room and disappeared into the opposite wall.

Rikeland lunged for the first door, having been the last one in, and threw his weight into opening it as the buzzing sound continued, but it had locked, shutting them in completely.

"Look at the tracks!" Kaiseln yelled, pointing them out in the walls, floors, and ceiling as one in the right wall opened and the blade reappeared. It darted from the floor to the ceiling, then vanished again.

Everyone raced to get away from the lines that scored the metal paneling, but a blade popped up from one in the floor this time, just barely missing Andra as she threw herself out of the way.

"How do we stop it?!" Corsair shouted, pulling at the second door frantically.

Kaiseln's attention flew around as they tried to figure out what the etched markings were telling them as a blade returned. It sliced across the left wall, nicking Gimlet in the arm as blood sprayed, then tucked into the wall again.

"Fuck!" Gimlet screamed, holding his arm as blood seeped between his fingers. Corsair threw his pack to the floor and tore through it, locating his med kit and grabbing Gimlet to start patching him up.

A blade emerged from the ceiling next, shooting across the room as Rikeland was forced to duck. He stumbled and fell against the wall as Kaiseln located a small metal panel next to the second door and began prying it open with their dagger. They had just popped it open, their hand reaching inside to grab something, when a track opened at Rikeland's back and a blade cut through the middle of his torso.

Wedged under his rib cage, it started lifting him as he shouted in agony and had raised him a couple feet off the floor by the time Kaiseln managed to do whatever it was behind the metal panel. The buzzing abruptly stopped and there was a sequence of clicks, the blade sinking back into the wall and releasing Rikeland as he slumped to the floor, coughing up blood.

Time slowed as Evelaine fell forward, pressing her hands to the huge slice that nearly bisected him. "No, no, no, no, no, no, no—"

But there was nothing to be done as he spasmed, great pools of red draining from him. Andra started screaming as Gimlet and Corsair looked on, frozen in horror. Rikeland's pained gaze met Evelaine's, his mouth opening to say something, but the words never got anywhere as he fell still, the life leaving him.

Andra's meltdown continued as Evelaine backed away in sheer panic. Her chest was heaving as she tried to understand the sight in front of her. This couldn't be happening. This wasn't part of the plan.

Flashes of Nees's broken body danced across her vision and she twisted to the side, vomiting in a rush. The acrid bile mixed with Rikeland's blood on the floor, soaking into her pants where she kneeled and fought to control the clench of her diaphragm.

What the fuck was going on? Pushing herself to a stand, she had to stagger away from the mess, her heartbeat loud in her ears.

"Oh gods," she moaned. Not Rikeland. His family . . . He . . . He . . .

"Shut the fuck up!" Gimlet shouted at Andra, her mouth snapping shut.

"Rikeland," Evelaine choked in the ringing silence. "Oh gods . . ."

"This is insane!" Gimlet pushed off Corsair, who had stalled in the middle of wrapping a bandage around the dealer's arm, his eyes the widest she had ever seen them. "What are we even doing?!"

The pool of liquid inched closer to Evelaine's boots, and she had to back up again, bumping into Kaiseln as her trainer caught her arm.

"I-I have to get out of here." Andra was deathly pale, her eyes glued to Rikeland's slumped body as she rushed to the first door and yanked on it. It opened easily, sliding to the side to reveal the dark abyss beneath the cube. She pulled herself back at the last second, her boot slipping on the edge as they all realized that the bridge was not where it had been. There was nothing between the door and the ledge they had started on, a good twenty feet of space separating them. "What the—"

Her head turned to the left and a sob left her, her fingers tightening on the frame of the door as she held it open. Gimlet joined her, stumbling over his own feet, and also looked out.

"Fucking shit." He spun around, his expression wild, and threw his hands up. "This is insane!"

"W-what?" Evelaine stuttered, forcing her legs to move toward them. Glancing out, she noticed two things. First, the bridge was in front of the door that was in the square to the left of them. Second, their square was now at the end of the bottom row. She couldn't grasp what she was seeing. What was going on?

Kaiseln moved her out of the way and stuck their head out, examining their predicament. "The square moved."

"What?" Corsair finally spoke up, looking dazed as the incomplete bandage dangled from his hanging hand.

"That movement in the beginning, when we all fell to the floor? It was this square sliding to the left. Or right, depending on how you look at it."

"How are we going to get out of here?" Andra asked, looking horrified.

"Maybe we can use some rope? We have pitons, right?" Gimlet suggested, staring out over the gap with wide eyes.

"What about Rikeland?" Evelaine felt like she was going to vomit again. "We can't just leave him!"

"What are we going to do? Take him with us?" Gimlet spun on her, gesturing toward the body. "He's dead weight! Literally!"

Evelaine's jaw dropped open. "He's— He's not—"

"Even if we were able to embed the pitons in the solid metal floor, Andra can't climb across with her wrist," Kaiseln interjected, the tone soft but firm. "Gimlet's arm won't hold him either."

"But . . . but . . . we can't stay here," Andra argued, her voice rising with panic.

Kaiseln didn't answer, crossing the room and reaching for the second door. It slid to the side with little effort and beyond was another metal room, a variety of circles decorating its walls. They turned, holding a hand out in an invitation for the others to go through.

Gimlet pressed his hands to either side of his head as he stared at Kaiseln. "This is insane."

"But . . ." Andra glanced over her shoulder at the abyss behind her.

Evelaine's attention dropped to Rikeland's body, the eyes blank and fixed on nothing, and her stomach protested again. This wasn't supposed to happen. What about the plan? They hadn't even gotten to the crystal room yet, but they had already failed.

She had already failed.

Patia's round belly swam before her and she groaned. Rikeland was never going to return home to her. Sorlene and Orlah were never going to see their father again. The new babe would never even know him. The whole family was going to have to find a way to support themselves without him. Because of her selfishness, a family was broken irreparably.

She staggered toward him, dropping to her knees, completely unaware of the liquids that bled into her pants as she fished through his pockets and found the notebook. Her fingerprints left red smears as she flipped through it and randomly came across a page that listed possible baby names he and Patia had apparently discussed. One column for a boy, another for a girl. The name Evie was listed under the latter, and she shivered under the assault. Sucking in a desperate breath, she snapped the book closed and stuffed down the riot of emotions that bloomed inside of her.

Nope. Absolutely not.

She couldn't let herself fall apart now.

Rikeland would've wanted them to continue. He had been the one to come to her defense before they'd crossed the bridge, and she vowed to do everything within her power to repay him for the confidence and trust he had placed in her. It was imperative. They had to get out of this damned temple alive, she realized as the plan shifted beneath her, because she now had more reparations to dole out. Another mark against her shredded soul, another crack in her blackened heart. There was no chance of forgiveness for her poisonous sins, but she had to at least pay the tithe.

Temple, blessing, reparations, devastation, vow.

Closing his eyelids with shaking hands, she said a brief prayer then emptied his pockets and rifled through his pack, taking out the necessary items. She absently distributed the fire supplies and med kit amongst the rest of them, her limbs feeling detached from her body. They had to keep going. Everyone took their portion without saying anything, but Evelaine kept whatever coins he had had on him, putting them in a separate pocket to give back to Patia when she got the chance. She swiped the back of her hand across her forehead, smearing blood, but she didn't even notice as she forced herself to move on with the next step in the plan.

As she turned to tell Kaiseln to continue into the next room, an echo of moans filtered in to them through the open doorway leading to the enormous chamber beyond. Gimlet and Andra stumbled back from where they had been standing and looking out, and Evelaine cursed, pulling a sword and her dagger as she pushed them behind her. Her body rose to the fight without her telling it to, and she braced herself for the coming onslaught, seeing a swarm of wraiths heading toward them, but Corsair dodged in front of her, slamming the door closed.

He held it in place, gritting his teeth as the mass on the other side collided with the metal panel. "Go! Into the next room!"

"But—" Evelaine started, yanked away as Andra pulled her toward the second door. She having trouble wrapping her head around what she was seeing. The wraiths had been able to materialize through stone, soil, and wood before, but it seemed like the metal was holding them back for some reason. Her brain lost track of the thought as she was pushed into the second room, Andra and Gimlet close behind. Kaiseln was already in there, rapidly studying the new engravings, but Corsair was still holding the first door closed.

"Corsair!" she yelled, beginning to panic, but he suddenly spun and bolted as fast as he could across the space. The wraiths burst through behind him just as he fell into the next room, Gimlet lunging forward to close the second door. There was a loud rumble and another sequence of clicks echoed around them as the entire room shifted, throwing them to the floor as the square moved sideways again. They landed on the side of the room that held the door they had just entered, and Evelaine wondered what exactly that meant, but then the floor started to vibrate with warning.

"Oh fuck!" Gimlet glanced down. "I forgot about the—"

He didn't get a chance to finish as one panel in the floor fell open like a trap door, leading to the abyss below the cube, and everyone's eyes widened. Luckily, none of them had landed on that particular panel, but it quickly dawned on them what was coming next.

"*Oh no,*" Evelaine whispered as another panel opened in the opposite corner from the first and the group scrambled to their feet.

There were thin strips of metal surrounding each of the panels in the floor, just a couple of inches wide, like an intersecting lattice, and if they could manage it, Evelaine guessed in that split second that it might be possible to balance on them if the panel next to it opened. It was the best option she could come up with, so she chose a corner of the room and wedged herself in, her feet braced on top of the two pieces that met at a right angle.

The very next moment, her half-baked theory was tested when the panel right below her dropped open. Her lungs emptied in a rush and she trembled, the darkness below her stretching on and on with no end in sight. She almost lost her grip as she pressed as far back into the corner as possible, her hands leaving red smears on the walls where she held herself, but it was soon over as the panel closed again and she gulped down air, dizzy from the pounding beat of her heart.

"This is insane!" Gimlet yelled again, pushing himself into a corner as he, Corsair, and Andra followed Evelaine's lead.

"There has to be a pattern." Kaiseln announced, turning back to the walls and pushing on the various circles, each of them depressing and holding in place. If they pressed the same circle twice, it would pop back out to be flush with the wall once again. Balancing their weight on the lattice, they muttered under their breath and tried different sequences.

Another panel opened to the right of Corsair and he cursed, squeezing his eyes shut as Kaiseln tried all the larger circles on one wall, then all the smaller ones. But it didn't work and another panel fell, this time a few squares away from Andra, and she began pleading, an unending prayer. "Please, please, please, please, please . . ."

Evelaine wasn't sure if Andra was a religious woman or whether it was simply desperation, but Evelaine could understand the need as she watched Kaiseln carefully move to another wall and try more circles. Nothing was working, though, and another panel released in the center of the room. The trainer cursed, perhaps the first time Evelaine had ever heard them do so, and turned their attention back to the engravings, their eyes darting from side to side as they tried to decipher the clues.

The group was fracturing. Evelaine could feel it. But what could she do? Her muscles quivered from holding herself in place, her mind racing for an answer. There had to be something they were missing. A tense moment passed as a panel opened a few feet over from Evelaine, and then an exclamation erupted from Kaiseln. "Of course!"

The trainer selected a few circles on the wall in front of them and, much to Evelaine's surprise, used them as hand and foot holds, climbing the wall like a ladder. They pressed more as they went, the top of the room a good ten feet above the rest of the group's heads, and then started depressing the large circles that covered the ceiling. Evelaine inhaled sharply, noticing that there was a door up there, the only other in the room besides the one they had already used. That was their way out, she realized.

Another panel opened, this time next to Andra, and Evelaine twisted to her own wall, following Kaiseln's lead. She used the circles to climb upward, their round edges slightly raised to give her fingers something to grip, and joined Kaiseln up high to help them reach all of the ceiling's large ones.

"Come on, come on . . . ," Evelaine murmured, smacking at as many as she could reach, and, together, she and Kaiseln had almost reached the final section when the panel right underneath Gimlet opened. He yelped, caught off guard since he had been watching Evelaine and her trainer's progress across the ceiling, and his foot slipped off the lattice.

Evelaine instinctively reached for him despite the distance between them, and he met her startled look as his arms windmilled to find his balance, but it was too late. His weight tipped to the side and his leg slipped through the hole. Corsair shouted his name, lunging to grab him. He had been on the other side of the room, though, and got there just as Gimlet's torso hit the floor, the bottom half of his body now swinging free above the abyss. Corsair squeezed Gimlet's hands, but was being dragged with the dealer, closer and closer to the hole.

Bracing his feet against the wall, Corsair tried to pull Gimlet back, but the panel was beginning to close again and there was no time. Andra's screams mixed with Gimlet's as he tried to brace his elbows on the panel at the awkward angle.

"No! Gim!" Corsair shouted, his voice thick with emotion. "NO!!"

He was making it worse, though, his grip causing Gimlet's arms to bend unnaturally as the panel continued its ascent, and tears began running down his cheeks. As he shook his head, Evelaine could see that he was fighting the inevitable and was torn apart by the pain that was creasing his features.

"Fuck!" Gimlet yelled as his hands slipped from Corsair's, his fingers barely gripping onto the edge of the panel. "Corsair—"

That was the last thing Evelaine heard as the panel shut completely, cutting off both Gimlet's voice and three of his fingers. The red stubs rolled for a second before settling as Corsair stared at them in horror, a choked sob leaving him. He braced himself on the floor, his chest heaving, and Evelaine was about to yell at him to move back to his corner, but a sequence of clicks sounded, indicating that Kaiseln had managed to finish the pattern on the ceiling, and stunned silence descended on them.

AN ENTRY

Evelaine couldn't even feel relief as she dropped to the floor. She grunted as she hit, rolling with the momentum, but didn't care as she rushed to Corsair and wrapped her arms around him. He was shaking, and she squeezed harder, pressing him to her.

Andra's screams had morphed into a mumbled monologue, her words falling in disjointed phrases as she panicked in her corner: "—just wanted to pay off my debt. I didn't know—it's insane—this is—what did I—but my sister, she—oh gods, sister—we're going to die—it's a death trap—I can't—what are we—"

But Corsair picked up her meaning, another sob racking his chest. "Wh-what are we doing?"

"We're getting our blessings back. We're—" Evelaine tried, gripping his face with her hands.

"At what cost?!" he shouted, pushing back from her and struggling to his feet. "Are our blessings worth this?!"

He waved his hand at Gimlet's leftover fingers and glared at her through his tears. "We've lost both of them and we're not even at the center yet! How much more are we going to have to sacrifice?! It's not worth it if we all DIE!!"

"We have to try!" Evelaine yelled back. "We can't go back now! We're too far in! You want to face the wraiths out there instead?! You want to be powerless for the rest of your life?!"

"We can get out of Risten! We don't have to stay here!"

"What about your mother?! Otis?! Patia and Orlah and Sorlene?!" she screamed. "Wh-what about Estella?! We have to PROTECT them!!"

"**Protect** them?" Corsair scoffed, the sound watery. "This is protecting them?"

"I-I can't save everyone." She choked on the admission. Reality hit her with a punch as Rikeland's and Gimlet's cold bodies joined Nees's in the overgrown cemetery of her heart. It was already tarred and blackened. What was another life to add to the weight on her shredded soul? "I tried to warn you."

His face crumpled at the reminder and his shaking hands gripped the sides of his head, but the tension was broken by the sound of chains falling, and Evelaine glanced over her shoulder to find that Kaiseln had released a chain ladder that had been embedded in the frame surrounding the door in the ceiling. It now dangled in the center of the room, ready for the rest of the group to use while the trainer waited for them at the top.

Evelaine turned back to Corsair, who was scrubbing his face, trying to get rid of the tears, but when she reached for him, he shrugged her off again. It pierced her heart, but the sensation was muffled under layers and layers of cracked bark. Instead of acknowledging it, she turned to Andra and helped her to her feet. Numb, she leaned into the detachment that provided her with a small measure of solace in the face of the overwhelming emotions vining around her lungs.

"I-I don't know if I can do this," Andra admitted softly.

Evelaine could feel the tremor in the bouncer's hands where they gripped her arms and she tried her best to reassure her, the words wooden on her tongue. "We're so close. You're strong, I know you can do it. I'll give you whatever you want once we get out of here. I'll convince the Mistress to clear your debt, I promise."

"My sister, she's been paying off a favor from the Mistress and I-I've been doing as much as I can to help. I-if I don't make it out of here . . ."

Evelaine's gut twisted, but she couldn't deny the request. "I'll take care of it."

Andra nodded, absently moving toward the chain ladder, but Evelaine held onto her for a moment longer.

"Remember who you're fighting for. I need you to focus, okay?" She waited until she felt the tremors leave Andra's hands, the bouncer's expression clearing a fraction, then let her go and turned to Corsair. "We good?"

Corsair didn't look at her, his mouth pressed into a grim line and his cheeks a splotchy red as he stared at the door in the ceiling, and Evelaine's anger rose to the forefront. She gripped it tight until it blocked out the pain.

189

She was sick of making these impossible fucking decisions but knew she had to be the one to push them forward, otherwise they would fracture further. She couldn't let the plan fall to pieces. They might now be down to just four of them, but they had come so far.

A perfect target for her clamoring jungle of emotions was waiting for them and she was itching to unleash it. They were so close. She couldn't look back.

Temple, blessing, reparations, devastation, vow.

One by one, they made their way into the next room in tense silence, Kaiseln insisting that they get a chance to look it over before they close the door and lock themselves in. Evelaine easily agreed, eyeing the horizontal slits in the metal walls with mistrust. There were far too many of them for comfort, and she could only guess what danger they would pose once they were activated.

Kaiseln even attempted to open the next door without closing the one in the floor, this one placed in the wall that seemed like it would lead them farther into the cube, but, after several tries, decided it couldn't be done. Their only option was to lock up and deal with whatever the square had in store for them, then progress to the next one. Having climbed upward, Evelaine now guessed they were on the same layer as the center square. The key was figuring out how to get there without any more casualties.

They couldn't afford to lose anyone else if they were going to have even a modicum of a chance against the ichor creature she knew was waiting for them. What was suspicious, though, was the fact that they hadn't encountered any of the veins inside the cube yet, and she wondered if that had something to do with the wraiths not being able to materialize through the metal. Was the material somehow resistant to the corruption's spread?

From the outside, it had looked like the tendrils had squeezed their way through the cracks between the squares, but maybe they had been unable to penetrate the interiors themselves. Evelaine remembered that the crystal in the plant temple had been entirely covered by the stuff and was betting that it was the same here, but then how had it escaped the central square? And how had it gotten here in the first place?

The questions were exacerbating the headache that pounded in her temples, and she shook her head to try and clear it, focusing on Kaiseln as the trainer walked their way slowly around the square and examined it as closely as possible. Corsair was propped in one of the corners with his arms crossed and Andra was squatting next to him, awkwardly cleaning her blades with her wrapped wrist. But every time Evelaine met either of their gazes, their eyes would slide away quickly, both unable to maintain eye contact with her.

Corsair was pissed, but Andra looked scared, and honestly, Evelaine couldn't decide which one was worse. Her muscles were twitching with impatience, needing an outlet for the restless anger that was winding its way through her limbs. This had been an utter shit show, going far worse than she had thought, and that was saying something. It wasn't like she had been expecting puppies and kittens. She had known it was going to be a brutal slog, but the fact that her teammates were getting taken out by the mechanisms of the temple itself instead of the corruption that polluted it was galling.

It shouldn't have happened this way. She had thought she'd known what they'd been walking into, but she had had no idea. There had been no way she could've prepared for this. There had been no one to warn them, except maybe Corsair's father. The fact that he was nowhere to be found was infuriating. The fucking deadbeat had left them to figure it out for themselves and now two of her friends were dead because of it.

Gods, she really needed to punch something.

"I think I've got it," Kaiseln announced, interrupting Evelaine's pacing. "Or, at least I know what to keep an eye on in here."

"Tell us," Evelaine ordered, her tone a touch on the harsh side, and Kaiseln side-eyed her but didn't comment on it.

"There will be some sort of metal that comes out of these slits." The trainer pointed to the horizontal lines in the walls. "I think it'll be a wire, sharp enough to cut if you let it. The pattern will likely be random, as it was in the other rooms, so stay alert and be ready to either duck or jump depending on the height of it."

"Everyone understand?" Evelaine asked, looking to Corsair and Andra. They nodded and straightened, joining her and Kaiseln in the center of the room. Their expressions were hard, but at least they were still following directions.

The only wall that didn't have horizontal lines was the one that held the other door, and Kaiseln pointed at it. "I will work on getting the door unlocked, but it's not guaranteed to be a safe space since all other walls will be deploying wires. I'm guessing those that come from the wall across from the door will bounce back once they reach the other side of the room, so remember that one jump or duck may not be enough. Keep your eyes peeled, no matter what."

They all took their positions, and at Kaiseln's signal, Evelaine slid the floor door closed. The expected sequence of clicks sounded around them and then the whole room shuddered, shifting to the side as they braced themselves. It seemed to move toward the front of the cube, and Evelaine smiled because it meant that they were now level with the central square. All they had to do was open the door and they'd be able to get on with the real fight. The realization gave her the boost she needed as a whirling sound filled the space and the first wire shot out above their heads.

Watching it sink into the opposite wall, they prepared for the next one as Kaiseln began fiddling with the knobs surrounding the door. There was a row of circles with intersecting lines on each side of the frame, and the trainer was turning them all, trying to find the correct pattern, when the next wire appeared near the bottom of the room next to Corsair.

"Jump!" he yelled, warning everyone as they followed suit.

"Duck!" Evelaine announced the next one, seeing it emerge next to her. When she realized it was one of the rebounding ones, she shouted the word a second time.

It went on like that for several minutes, each of them alerting the others whenever they noticed a new wire as Kaislen worked on the puzzle. The trainer kept having to pause, ducking and jumping when appropriate, but focused on the door as the directions were shouted out. As time went on, Evelaine could feel the burn in her thighs, the jumping and squatting becoming repetitive as her eyes darted around, but they were working as a team and the rhythm was easy to follow.

At one point, they were all forced to fall to the floor, flattening themselves to avoid the wire that was roughly at the height of their thighs, and Evelaine watched as one of Corsair's long hairs got clipped, the wire slicing through it like scissors. He cursed, the moment too close for comfort, but popped back to his feet, ready for the next one that was by their shins. It was a rebounding one, so they jumped a second time, and Evelaine's mouth dropped open in warning as she watched Andra land painfully, her ankle rolling to the side.

"Fuck," she complained, forced to shift her weight as they ducked the next wire.

"You good?" Evelaine asked, huffing as they all jumped together, but Andra was wincing, her ankle unable to hold her weight.

"Yeah, I just gotta—" It was another jump, and Andra had to use one foot to do it, barely clearing the wire.

Evelaine's heart beat faster as she watched what was happening, and she turned to her trainer. "Kaiseln, you need to—"

Corsair called out another duck and they all dropped to the floor again, but Andra was too slow in getting back to her feet as a wire appeared roughly at the height of their waists. The bouncer had managed to stand, but the delay in her movements prevented her from ducking soon enough and she was only partially down when it came hurtling toward her.

Evelaine shouted, reaching for Andra as her eyes widened and the bouncer bent backward in a desperate attempt to avoid it at the last second, but it was too late. The wire sliced across her forehead at an angle, shearing off the front of her skull in one go, and her body went loose, a bloodcurdling scream coming from her as she fell to her knees. Her body twitched and Evelaine shouted again, stunned at what she was seeing as Kaiseln yelled out another jump and she was forced to move her legs.

"Oh fuck, oh fuck, oh fuck." Corsair was sobbing but still standing, the both of them blindly following Kaiseln's instructions as they watched Andra bleed out before them.

Evelaine was going to throw up again, she could feel the bile rising, and the next duck forced it out of her as she squatted, the vomit making the floor slippery as she tried to move away from it. She staggered, out of breath, and just barely missed the next one as she jumped again, but all of a sudden, Kaiseln shouted.

"Finally!"

A sequence of clicks followed the announcement and Evelaine fell to the floor, panting as her stomach churned in anguish. But she didn't even have a chance to catch her breath as the door Kaiseln was in front of burst open, a swarm of wraiths rushing into the room as her trainer yelled out a warning.

Evelaine was pushed down, wraiths slicing at her with their claws, and all she could do was fight back. Swinging out with her fists, she gritted her teeth and transformed her grief into howling rage as she let it overtake her. She thrashed, tearing at them with her bare hands and plunging her nails into their amorphous, shadowed faces. She didn't even need her blades, the sheer force of her anger cutting through them as she shoved to her knees, and then to her feet. Throwing herself at them, she unleashed everything she had and sank her teeth into their necks, ripping them asunder.

She had thought there was nothing holding her back before?

She had been so wrong.

Now, she was destruction incarnate.

The whole room around her was a blur as she drove forward, cleaving a path through the horde and finding herself at the open door. Inside, ichor writhed on every surface, the smooth metal panels almost entirely covered, but her attention homed in on the horrendous creatures that awaited her.

There were two of them, their sharp, curving beaks dripping with corruption as they stretched their enormous wings and hunched their shoulders forward threateningly. Vultures. Birds of prey. Their beady eyes latched onto Evelaine as she entered, her cheeks wet with tears but her strides undeterred as she finally reached for her blades and unsheathed them.

Their knifelike talons cut through the mass on the floor as they pranced forward, snapping at her as she met them with a wide swing of her sword. One of them dodged and she plunged her dagger into its oozing eye as it came to her level, their heads a good five feet above her. Screeching in pain, it swiped at her with its claw, and the other circled to flank her, but the previous square had limbered her up, the ducking and jumping a natural movement for her as she wove through their attempts.

She soon lost all sense of what was happening around her, her blades and the vultures the entirety of her awareness as they fought. There were slight twinges of pain around her ankles and shins, lashes of burning sensations, but she ignored them, laying her full wrath upon the large birds. The song of it flowered unrestrained. A riot of consuming greed that gnashed its toothy maw and relished in the feast.

She was the predator they should fear.

Unleashing everything she had, she cut and slashed and pierced as they buffeted her with their wings and bit at her with their beaks. At one point, she managed to mount one of them, climbing her way up its hunched shoulder as it bent to attack her, and it flailed, trying to unseat her. She snarled and buried her sword deep within its neck, dropping her weight to slice down its back, and it crumpled beneath her as she yowled in triumph.

In retaliation, the remaining one swiped its wing at her and threw her across the room, where she hit the wall with a jarring thud, slumping into a pile of ichor and incurring searing welts across her skin. There was blood pooling in her mouth again, but she didn't care, pushing to her feet and running back to the bird. She saw the flash of Corsair and Kaiseln fighting together against a group of wraiths out of the corner of her eye, but they were quickly lost again, her entire focus on the vulture that was now drawing more corruption into its body, becoming bigger and bigger.

Its head almost reached the ceiling as it spread its wings wide and hissed loudly, but a soft gray light was beginning to emit from behind it, and Evelaine smiled, knowing what that meant. She dropped to her knees, sliding underneath its legs where the ichor had cleared as she thrust her blades to each side and into its sticky flesh right above its ankles. She didn't know if it was going to work, slicing its tendons like on a human, but it started listing and weaving on its feet, its weight unstable as she spun around and sank her sword into its back.

Falling forward, it landed with a thump that rattled the room, and she leapt onto its back, screaming as spittle of red flew from her mouth. She hacked at it, utterly crazed, and it rolled over with a heaving grunt, grasping her in its claws and lifting her away from it. Kicking, she tried to wiggle free, but its grip was too tight, crushing the breath from her.

Corsair and Kaiseln suddenly reappeared, though, and attacked it from either side as she tried to gulp in air, the talons cutting into her ribs like razors. Hissing again, it lashed out with its wings and managed to sweep Corsair off his feet, and he slid across the room from the force of it, but Kaiseln jumped nimbly and landed near its hip. They cut into it, trying to get it to drop Evelaine, but it doggedly hung on as it sucked more and more ichor into its body for protection.

Evelaine's sight was beginning to fade, air not reaching her lungs, but all of a sudden, her skin tingled as she became aware of pulsing energy at the rear of the room. She gasped, desperately trying to draw in a breath as she arched under the ecstatic feel of it.

Her blessing.

She could feel it budding within her like the first crocus after a long, cold winter and she moaned, drunk on the power of it as her hand instinctually opened. Dropping her now useless sword, she summoned a cascade of seeds that stuck to the sticky corruption across the vulture's belly and then ordered them to burst.

With bleary eyes, she watched as tendrils of green wrapped around the bird's body, rapidly hardening into vines of thick, rough bark and encircling over and over to pin its wings to itself. The creature screeched even louder, and its claws clenched tighter around her as her head began to spin. Then there was a shout beyond them, and she felt, more than saw, Corsair take hold of his blessing, too.

The room shuddered under the force of it, his roar deafening as he latched onto the metal surrounding them and commanded it to obey his will. Metallic creaks echoed, and Evelaine felt herself sway in the vulture's grip, her body going limp as her heartbeat pounded unevenly in her ears. She vaguely wondered if this was what Nees had felt, back in the plant temple as their body had been crushed under the ichor's impossible pressure.

Had their lungs spasmed like hers? Their fingertips tingling as blood flow had been cut off? Instantly, she felt closer to them. A shared bond beyond the tomb. She could almost hear their whisper, her incoherent thoughts struggling to make sense of the words, and her limbs twitched, warring with the persuasion to submit as her lips mumbled their name. The wilds of the burial grounds called to her, yet the growth was hers to control. She would be the one to gorge on the decomposing graves. Blindly reaching out with her blessing, she encouraged her vines to squeeze and felt the jerk of the bird's body as it fought for its freedom.

She couldn't see anything anymore, but she heard the impacts of Corsair's violence and the creature's agonized hissing, her body suddenly going into a free fall as she was released. Hitting the floor hard, she saw stars when her head slammed into it with a jarring snap as she tried to gulp in air. Her chest was heaving, her lungs aching, but she held onto her blessing for as long as she could, the sounds of fighting still raging on.

She heard gasps and groans, grunts and hisses, as her vision slowly returned and her body started to respond. Blinking up at the ceiling from where she had landed, she struggled to make sense of what she was seeing. Corners of metal panels had been bent, curling inward to reveal an intricate mess of complex gears, levers, and chains. She squinted against the pounding in her head, rolling so that she could see Corsair sneering with his hands outstretched. He was thrusting them through the air, sending clouds of shrapnel into and through the vulture's body as its form slowly melted away into nothing.

Letting her grip on her blessing relax, Evelaine pushed herself up with shaking arms as Corsair collapsed to his knees in the eerie silence. He stared blankly at the space where the vulture had been, his eyes wide and uncomprehending.

"Corsair?" she rasped, her throat raw.

He started at his name, his attention going to her.

"Are you okay? Where's Kaiseln?" She furrowed her brows, glancing around the space, but her heart stopped as she noticed her trainer slumped against the wall on the other side. They were lying at an awkward angle, their chest just barely rising as their mouth opened and closed with no sound coming out.

"Oh gods." Evelaine staggered to her feet, tripping as she rushed over. Kaiseln's hips were twisted the wrong way, indicating a clear break in their spine. "No, noooo . . ."

She reached for them but then drew back, suddenly uncertain. She didn't know how to make it better. She had to fix this. Their fingers fluttered in her direction, so she took them and bent down, trying to hear the faint whisper coming from their mouth.

"You . . . must . . ." She could barely make out the words. ". . . find . . . them."

"What do you mean? Find who?" she urged, her hoarse voice sounding unlike her own.

"The . . . guild . . ."

"What guild? What are you talking about?" She leaned closer, but nothing more came as a trail of air left Kaiseln and their jaw slackened. "Wait! What guild?!"

The eyes that met her desperate gaze were unfocused and cold, the life gone from them, and a sob caught in Evelaine's throat.

"No," she moaned, curling in on herself. "Please . . ."

She began crying in earnest, the full weight of everything that had happened to her causing her to collapse, and the tears flowed without end. Everything had gone wrong. It wasn't supposed to end this way. Was she truly destined to destroy everything she touched? Even those she loved? Snot mixed with blood and sweat and salt as she let herself go, wailing her anguish, but soon there was a hand on her shoulder, shaking her.

"Evelaine, look!" She heard Corsair's voice, but she refused to answer, curling in on herself further. He shook her harder. "Evie!"

She turned on him, her mouth opening to yell at him to leave her alone when she noticed what had caught his attention, or rather, who. A tall figure stood before them, and she instantly knew it was the Metal God, his brilliant silver gaze pinned on them. He simply stood waiting, wearing a suit of full plate armor. The molded gold was polished to a blinding shine, embedded with precious metals and gems, and she wiped at her running nose, unnerved.

There was a beat of silence as they stared each other down, Corsair's gaze bouncing between them.

"D-do you know who that is?" he whispered.

"The Metal God," she murmured. What was his name again? She had heard Tabriara say it when they'd been in her throne room. Urdan? Urken?

"I am Urkus, God of Metal, and I thank you and welcome you with my deepest immortal gratitude. It is because of you that my temple and sacred lands are now free and accessible to me once again," the figure intoned, his chin dipping ever so slightly in acknowledgement.

"Your temple," Evelaine muttered, her brows furrowing. "**Your** temple!"

She shoved Corsair off and pushed to a stand. "Your temple killed our friends!"

Corsair went to grab her hand. "Evie . . ."

"It's your fault they're dead!" she yelled, thorns weaving across her knuckles. "It's your fucking fault!!"

Urkus's lips thinned. "No, it is not."

"Yes, it is! You're the one that made this temple into a death trap! It wasn't even the corruption that killed them. It was you and this godsdamned metal MONSTROSITY!!" Her screamed accusation bounced off the walls, and he narrowed his gaze.

"Even an untrained metal blessed can navigate this temple with ease." He nodded in Corsair's direction, who winced. "It is no fault of mine that the contamination blocked his abilities."

"But you built this place! You let the corruption take over!!"

"No," he cut in harshly. "I did not."

"You gods are so fucking worthless!! Relying on us puny mortals to do all the dirty work for you! Why can't you just clean up your own damn messes?!" Was the screech that rang in her ears coming from her? It was so foreign, she couldn't tell.

"Evie—" Corsair tried again, his eyes wide.

"If you seek to lay blame for what has transpired, I can request an attendant bring a mirror, upon which you can find the true suspect," Urkus bit at her. "For whom was it that brought these friends of yours to this temple? Who was it that urged them onward despite the weaknesses that plagued them? Who was it that wrapped her own guilded trainer in unyielding vines until their bones rent?"

Evelaine gasped, her hand going to her throat. "No— No, it's not true!"

"The lies that fall from your lips spread like pappi on the wind. Not only do you deceive those around you, you delude yourself." He stalked toward her, stopping a few feet away as he loomed.

"You lie!!" she insisted, glaring up at him. Her chest heaved in denial. "You left us with no help! For centuries, our families have been abandoned, forced to fend for ourselves!"

"Abandoned? I show myself to you, intent on rewarding you for your deeds, committed to granting my boons, and this is how I am met? With vitriol and spite? Is that the answer you give your divine master?"

"FUCK YOU!!" Evelaine screamed, and Corsair backed up from them, focused on Urkus as the god's pearlescent skin began to shimmer.

"Ignorant, ungrateful girl," he pronounced with a sneer, then spun on Corsair. "Do you share her sentiment, boy? Do you refuse the power I offer? Do you reject your rightful crown?"

"C-crown?" Corsair looked stunned. "What crown?"

"You believe me to be indifferent to the struggles of your bloodline? You think I have not ached to set it all right?" Urkus slashed his hand through the air. "My brethren and I were prohibited from interfering. It was as it should be, she told us. We had no choice, but too far it has gone. Our blessed are being eliminated en masse and we can no longer stand by. We will raise our chosen, reinstate the elemental crowns, and fight back. Will you affirm it?"

"W-what?" Corsair asked, still confused.

"Will you further demonstrate your love and affection, power and ambition, and training and preparation in the defense of the temples of the gods and goddesses? Claim your crown, acquire an oathed, and confirm that all sacred lands are free from contamination?" The god's eyes were now glowing like molten silver, the metal walls of the room beginning to warp and melt.

"I-I don't know. I don't understand what you're talking about. I just wanted my blessing back. Evie asked me to—" Corsair looked at her helplessly, and she grabbed his arm.

"Don't listen to him. He just wants to control you, make you do whatever he wants," Evelaine pleaded, her mind spinning. She thought of the other blessed, the ones who were never there when it mattered. Those who had let all of her loved ones die without their help. "The crowns mean nothing. No one in Risten is going to give two shits about a crown. All they care about is money and power. We have our blessings back. We don't need anything from them. We can leave. Use your blessing and get us out of here."

"That is enough!" Urkus commanded. He abruptly lifted his hand and liquid metal rose over her feet, and then he swiped it to the side as the floor shoved her against the wall, where she stuck like an insect on flypaper. It began to absorb her, the silver panels flowing over her wrists and legs to hold her in place as she squirmed.

"You can't do this!" She panicked, fighting against the bindings as her thorns reached for him. "You have no right!"

"I am your GOD!!" he bellowed, her vines easily absorbed by the floor before they even got a chance. "You dare doubt my divine judgment? There is greatness within you, child, and still you refuse your path of destiny. The power of the gods, that which runs through your veins, IS the ultimate power. Any being who does not recognize that will fall to their own nescience. Open yourself to the truth!"

"Please," Corsair begged, dropping to his knees. "I'll do anything. Whatever you want. Just let her go."

The Metal God glanced down at his blessed, a sneer curling his lips, and opened his mouth to say something when a cacophonous boom shook the room. Jerking, he looked over his shoulder in surprise.

"URKUS! Free her at once!!" a voice demanded, another tall figure stepping out from behind the glowing gray crystal in the corner of the room. The Plant Goddess strode forward with purpose, her expression hard as Evelaine's breath caught. It was the first time she had seen her walk without using her conjured leaves for support and it unsettled her further.

"Tabriara," Urkus murmured, looking floored. "I have not seen you since—"

"I said, free her," she gritted between bared teeth, crimson leaves falling from her hair.

The Metal God glanced back at Evelaine, who had fallen still in her struggle, and waved his hand, a casual gesture that had her slumping from the sudden release. She scrambled to her feet and rushed to Corsair, gripping his shoulder and starting to pull him up, too.

"Leave him," Urkus ordered, his lips in a thin line once again.

"But—" Evelaine began to protest, but her goddess held up a hand, silencing her.

"Come with me, daughter," Tabriara said.

Evelaine hesitated, looking down at Corsair, but his wide gaze was glued to the Plant Goddess and he was trembling ever so slightly. She nudged him and he finally raised his eyes to her, but he just shook his head, silently telling her not to push their luck.

Not knowing what else to do, she approached Tabriara and awkwardly bowed as Urkus scoffed. Her goddess shot him a narrow-eyed look and his shoulders squared, the whole exchange too bizarre for Evelaine to even begin wrapping her head around it. Tabriara then turned and disappeared behind the crystal once more, Evelaine glancing over her shoulder at Corsair and his god one last time. They both watched them go, Urkus with an odd look on his face and Corsair with wide eyes, and it was all she could do to not turn back as she scurried after her goddess.

A DECISION

They entered a cavernous hall that was entirely carved out of metal, as one would expect from the Metal God, but Tabriara didn't go far, immediately turning to one of the walls and smoothing her hand across its gleaming surface. A green smear was left in its wake and Evelaine recognized it as algae, the plant material spreading quickly. It grew until it was the size of a doorway, a perfect arch with clean lines, and just as Evelaine blinked, it became an actual portal.

The familiar abundant hall of the Plant Goddess's palace could be seen beyond, and Tabriara walked through it without pausing, heading to the left with measured steps—this time with blooming leaves under her feet. Evelaine quickly followed, and when she glanced behind, the door was already gone. The usual moss-covered trees crowding the walls looked back at her impassively and she rolled her shoulders, nervous about whatever conversation was happening back *in the metal temple, but she turned to trail Tabriara, not wanting to get lost on her own in this winding passage.*

Eventually, they came upon the two trees that marked the entrance to the throne hall, and her goddess led her inside, inviting her to sit upon the mound of moss that she had occupied during her previous visit. As she lowered herself, it was only then she realized how sore her body was. She suddenly became aware of the blood smeared everywhere as well as the sorry state her clothes were in, burned away in great swaths, but somehow, she still gripped her oath dagger with white knuckles. Her fingers twitched open, letting it slip from her grasp as it fell to the moss, and everything came rushing back to her.

A sob caught in her throat, and then another. Before she knew it, she crumpled, her body shaking as she cried out her pain. Gods, she had lost so much. She had thought before that her chest was an empty chasm, but now? She was truly damned.

There was no coming back from the damage she had wrought. There would be no redemption for her. Not ever.

Had she truly been the cause of Kaiseln's demise? Had she blindly wrapped her trainer in vines along with the vulture? She hadn't been able to see anything, but that was a poor excuse. She should have known better. She should have been better.

The mounds of five new graves mocked her in silence as she wept into the dirt. None of their deaths should have happened.

It was all her fault.

She moaned, her tears watering the freshly turned earth, and long minutes passed as she exhausted herself, her cries echoing through the chamber. But Tabriara didn't say anything, letting her find a conclusion on her own as her pathetic whimpering eventually faded into depleted silence. She couldn't find the willpower to raise her head, though, until she felt a hand on her shoulder. Glancing up through sticky eyelashes, she found one of the palace's bark-skinned healers holding out a bottle of golden liquid for her to take with a sympathetic smile.

"Drink it," Tabriara urged from where she sat on her throne, nestled into the base of the colossal banyan tree.

"No." Evelaine groaned. "I don't deserve it."

"Drink." The tone brooked no argument, and Evelaine sullenly took the bottle but stalled, her hand dropping to her lap as she stared at it.

Gods, she was so tired.

The desire to fall asleep and never wake up again stole over her softly, like a warm blanket. It would be so much better that way. She would never hurt anyone ever again. She could lay her head down on the soft moss and let it cover her, nature wrapping her in its eternal embrace. Her bones could finally find peace, a happy ending after the nightmare that had been her life.

"Evelaine," Tabriara interrupted firmly, and her bloodshot gaze snapped to her goddess, the look on her divine face telling her she knew where her mind had wandered and didn't approve.

She sighed, her attention going back to the bottle as she slowly unstoppered it and drank it down in one go. Handing off the empty to the waiting healer, she lay back down on her mound and blankly stared out over the pond of lilies in front of her as the liquid healed her. She felt her skin stitch over and her burns mend, her lost tooth miraculously reappearing in its rightful place in her mouth with a satisfying pop. But the relief wasn't there, her chest still aching from the images that bombarded her.

"Did I——" she asked after a while. "Did I really kill Kaiseln?"

She heard Tabriara let out a long exhale from behind her before answering, "Yes, my dear one."

"Oh gods," she whispered, tears forming again.

"Let it not weigh on your soul too much, my love." Her voice was soft, understanding.

Her cheeks were wet, pressed against the moss. "How can I not? I have ruined everything."

"The deaths were unfortunate." There was a pause. "I believe you were right in directing your anger at Urkus."

"What?" Evelaine sat up, looking at her.

"That temple of his is dangerous. We all have our . . . preventative measures in place, but his especially so. He has always felt the need to protect what he considers his. Fiercely and without compromise." Evelaine almost saw her eyes roll, the twitch in her eyelids just barely there. "But there was nothing he could do. It had never occurred to any of us that we could be blocked from our own sacred domains."

"Will he hurt Corsair?" She asked the question that was worrying her the most.

"No." She looked off into the distance. "He loves his son as much as I you. He will push him to acknowledge the greatness that lies within him, as he tried with you, but it will not come to harm. He tests the limits, but his intentions are beneficent."

"Why us?" Evelaine rubbed at her wrists, remembering the cold slide of metal against them.

Tabriara's attention fell to her once more. "Did the Curacu elders never tell you of the balance between love and affection, power and ambition, and training and preparation?"

"They did . . . but I don't know if I—"

"The balance within you has been unsettled, that is true. Though, that does not mean it is not there."

Evelaine shook her head. "I don't know . . . ."

"You love deeply, do you not? You hold affection for those you trust close to your heart? You have immense power, blinding ambition, extensive training, and your journey has prepared you to make the decisions you must."

"But my choices always lead to the wrong thing. Only death and disappointment and betrayal."

"Perhaps some have, but only when you close your heart."

"But . . . it hurts." She thought of all the times she had let someone in, only to lose them. "They always leave me."

"The heart must be an open doorway, one through which those you love are welcome to pass freely. Chaining them inside will only lead to resentment and bitterness. A lesson not commonly understood, not even by some of us." The goddess's eyes trailed to the door of the throne room again, and Evelaine wondered if she was referring to Urkus.

"Is that what he meant when he said that the gods were raising their chosen?"

"Indeed." Tabriara's verdant gaze studied her. "You have proven yourself through every trial and tribulation. You persist despite all odds, and not all blessed have been able to do so. Yet you refuse your crown."

Tabriara had offered the Plant Crown to Evelaine last time she'd been here, after the hell that had been the clearing of the plant temple. After her goddess had restored her memories and she had had that total meltdown from the excruciating reintegration. Rakhmet and Hara had retired to their guest room for the night, and Tabriara had soothed Evelaine's fractured mind, urging her to drink teas and broths that the healers had provided.

Once Evelaine had regained her faculties, the goddess had told her the story of the crown. How it had originally been bestowed upon the first Plant Queen. How it had passed to the most capable heirs throughout the centuries, until the revolution had forced all elemental crowns to be hidden away. Evelaine had learned of the *crowning of the moon, sun, and water blessed, and Tabriara had offered her hers, but she had refused, telling her that she had no desire to rule from Curacu. Her plans for revenge had already begun to sprout by then and she had known that she couldn't stay in Talegartia for longer than necessary.*

"I am needed in Risten." Evelaine shook her head, the weight of her reparations heavy on her shoulders. "There are people I need to take care of."

"The crown will wait for when you are ready, my child," her goddess assured her. "What boon does your heart wish for instead?"

Evelaine stared at the lily pads, thinking, but there was only one answer that truly mattered. "My daughter . . . Estella, I don't want her to face the same fate."

"You speak of the sacred plant from which the blessing stems?" Tabriara tilted her head as Evelaine glanced at her, wondering if what she asked for was considered blasphemous.

"Y-yes, I don't know if—"

The goddess held up a hand. "I understand. You fear for your child, as is natural. You wish for her safety and comfort, for misfortune and pain to never befall her. Yet, a seed that is kept within its shell can never grow into the flower it is meant to become. It must break forth, thrusting its way through rock, clay, and compost, boldly declaring its right to flourish.

"The potential that lies within our sacred plant, the power that feeds the blessing can be harnessed in a multitude of ways. How it is directed and applied is the defining factor. To keep your daughter from this discovery will be a disservice to her. A mother may fertilize, cultivate, and nourish, but the discretion to bloom rests solely within the hands of the daughter."

To Reap What Is Sown

"How could I possibly guide her to the right path?" Evelaine felt the truth of the goddess's words but still felt inadequate. "All I do is leave destruction in my wake."

"Your hesitation is reasonable. I have mourned these many years that I have been unable to shepherd my blessed. Your mother was returned to me far too soon, and I was made known to you far too late."

Evelaine remembered the day that the Curacu elders had performed her initiation ritual with the goddess, something that should have been done when she had turned sixteen. It had been exhilarating, forming her connection with Tabriara and finally understanding the source of the power that ran through her veins. Otis had informed her that her blessing stemmed from the Plant Goddess, but meeting her during the ritual had made it tangible at last. An unseverable thread that assured her that she would never be truly alone. While the corruption had momentarily blocked her access, it had still lingered in the darkness. A latent seed waiting for its time.

"Estella possesses the potential to walk a different path," the goddess continued. "She may choose to initiate soon, if she so wishes."

"Before she reaches sixteen?" Evelaine gasped.

Tabriara dipped her chin, a subtle confirmation. Estella could go through her initiation ritual early and establish her connection with the Plant Goddess, who would guide and teach her so much more than Evelaine was capable of. There would be no need for her to ever travel to Talegartia to study under the Curacu elders. She could stay under Mason's protection until she was old enough to provide for herself. It was an ideal solution.

"How?" she asked before she let her hope blossom unfettered.

Reaching out a hand, the goddess waited as a vine dropped down from the branches above her and a leaf unfurled to present a small

215

shard of green crystal. It dropped into Tabriara's palm, and she held it between her fingers, inspecting it with a thoughtful expression.

"This comes from the crystal within my sacred temple, a piece of the whole. It will be sufficient enough to provide your daughter a channel of communication, to call upon me when she wishes. It will only work for those who have a direct connection to the bloodline, a failsafe that I have kept in case it becomes necessary. Yet, I have not had the opportunity to gift it until now."

"Will it hurt her? Initiating early?" She had to know.

"Intense and overwhelming, it may be, but she is your daughter, is she not? The tree may bend, but it shall not break."

Evelaine thought back to the vow she had made to herself: to make sure that Estella was empowered to be the master of her own fate. This was how she could ensure it.

"Th-that would be incredible." Evelaine breathed, relief lifting some of the weight from her. To know that her daughter would have direct access to the goddess? To receive guidance beyond what Evelaine's rotted experiences could muster? It was better than what any crown could provide.

"This is your wish?" Tabriara asked.

"Yes, My Divine Majesty." She bowed her head, filled with gratitude.

"Thus, it is so." The goddess held out the shard to Evelaine, and she took it with trembling fingers. There were still reparations that she needed to attend to, but at least she knew that her daughter would be able to walk a different path. That was what had haunted her above all else.

Staring at the piece of green crystal in her hand, she began making a mental list of the things she needed to do once she returned. First, she needed to make sure Corsair had survived his encounter with the Metal God. She felt guilty that she hadn't warned him about what to expect after they'd cleared the temple. She should have known that Urkus would show up and offer Corsair the crown. It was what had happened to all of the other blessed, after all.

"Why is reinstating the elemental crowns so crucial to raising your chosen?" she asked, lifting her head.

"Political power has its uses." Tabriara looked into the distance once again. "The crowns provide our chosen with influence and authority that the elemental blessings may not necessarily inspire. While the gods may recognize the potential for exemplary leadership in our chosen, the eyes of mortals are often blinded by ignorance, selfishness, and bitterness. They do not have the advantage of distance that the gods do, their perspectives limited and biased. As you are aware, many look upon the blessings with fear and mistrust, two qualities that do not an excellent leader make.

"The crown is simply an external signifier of a chosen's caliber that mortals may respect more so than the blessing itself. Each chosen is formed through the choices they make. Whether or not they bear a crown is irrelevant. It is a tool to wield wisely, yet not all blessed are inclined to use their powers for the greater good. The bloodline alone does not determine worthiness. It is why we place such importance upon the union of the six virtues.

"Our blessings are inherently attracted to those who have the potential for greatness, whether or not they are already part of a bloodline, and those mortals who demonstrate it through courage and action will, sooner or later, find themselves integrated into the bloodline that best aligns with their inner qualities. Like calls to like. The power we bestow coalesces in those that command it altruistically."

Evelaine thought of how much she had been judging the other blessed for so readily welcoming the privileged positions their crowns provided and how much she had been resisting her own acceptance of the Plant Crown. Was it because she somehow knew she wasn't ready to wield her power unselfishly? So much of her determination and planning since regaining her memories had been self-centered, focused on achieving vengeance against those who had hurt her personally.

But was that true? She had always fought for those she loved. She knew that for sure. And after all the injustice she had witnessed in the Tirdan Republic throughout her life, she had recently been forced to acknowledge the growing need inside of her to do something more. Something beyond the survival of her and hers within an economic and political environment that systemically oppressed the masses in favor of the privileged few.

Did that mean she was going to take up the crown Tabriara offered and use the influence it promised? She still severely doubted that it would do anything to persuade the affluent Ristenians to repent their crooked ways, but she could certainly use her blessing to throw some wrenches into their preciously held plans.

Especially with Corsair's help, if he was up for it.

She sighed, realizing that he might not even want to ever speak to her again after what had happened in the metal temple. There was a lot of apologizing she needed to do, and she was dreading breaking the news of Rikeland's death to Patia, but she had to face up to her involvement in all of it. She couldn't keep blaming everyone and everything but herself.

With the next day's tasks looming over her shoulder like the vultures they had slayed, all she could do was hope that her friends would accept her attempts at atonement.

DAY ELEVEN

Evelaine awoke to the smell of long-forgotten dust, blinking her eyes open to find herself in the darkened interior of the abandoned blacksmithy. The stone floor was cold against her back, and she couldn't help the shiver that pimpled her skin as she turned to find Corsair stretched out beside her. He was splayed on his stomach and snoring softly, deep asleep with his head nestled in the crook of his arm, as if he had simply landed there after a night of heavy drinking.

She almost didn't want to wake him, knowing that he was likely happier in the realm of dreams compared to the harsh reality that would hit him once he regained consciousness. So she lay there for several moments, studying the updated uniform he now wore. His formerly leather breastplate was now a shining silver, molded to his torso with exactness, and his long-sleeved tunic was a heavy, dark gray. She knew without even looking that there would be a symbol of his god engraved on his chest, just as she knew that there was a spiny seed pod on hers.

They had been claimed. Chosen.

Her weary sigh startled Corsair, who twitched at the sound, his eyes squinting at her in confusion. She let him come to his own conclusions, his expression changing as he remembered everything. There was surprise, then dismay. Anger, then coldness as he shut his emotions down. A hauntedness lingered as he slowly pushed himself up, his attention dropping to the new breastplate.

Frowning, he trailed his fingers along the ridges of the two crossed swords, but he quickly looked away, his hand slipping into his pocket and pulling out his tin of cigarettes. He lit one, taking a deep inhale with an arm propped on his raised knee as he stared into the distance, and she sat up, too, pulling over her pack to confirm that her pouch of coins was still there. It was, and lo and behold, her goddess had added the green shard as well as another handful of platinum for good measure.

She gently stroked the crystal and sent a silent thanks. It glimmered slightly, and she knew that the message had been received, a comforting thought amongst the dread that was crowding in on her, but she knew she had to ask.

Setting aside her pack, she turned to Corsair. "How are you?"

He huffed out a dry laugh but didn't answer, the smoke billowing around him.

She chewed on the inside of her cheek. "Did he hurt you?"

Scoffing, he rose to his feet and wrapped his cloak around him to hide the shining armor.

"Please, Corsair. I'm sorry for what happened. It didn't go the way I thought it would," she tried, standing as well and reaching for his arm. "I'll make amends."

He spun on her. "Amends? You think this can all be fixed with simple amends? We don't even have bodies to return, Evie!"

She winced. "I know. I-I'll give them what I can. I'll provide anything they need. We can take down Nydas and get all the—"

"Take down Nydas?! Is that still all you're focused on?!" He threw up his hands. "I can't believe you. You're still just thinking about yourself. After everything."

"No, I know it's not just about me. I've realized—we can do some real good in this city. I was thinking about it before we even went into the temple, after hearing about Patia's sister. We can take them all down."

"You think we stand a chance against them? They have power and influence that we can't even begin to touch."

"Well, I mean, so do we." The truth was beginning to dawn on her, but she hesitated. "Did . . . did you . . . The crown—"

"No," he said darkly. "I didn't accept the fucking crown."

"Oh." She was kind of surprised. "I-I didn't know if—"

"He offered. I said no. End of story." He bent to pick up his pack, slinging it over his shoulder. "Can I go? Or do you want to continue to drag me into your bloody death wish?"

"Corsair, please, I need your help with Nydas. I can't do it alone. We have our blessings back. We can—"

"Fuck you, Evie." He let out a hard sigh. "I just lost three of my closest friends down there. I . . . I need time."

"I know. I'm sorry." Her chest ached at the desolation on his face. "I'm so sorry."

"Yeah, well." He turned toward the front door then looked to the side, aiming his words at the wall. "So am I."

She couldn't find a decent response, watching as he flicked a hand and instantly unlatched the locks. He left her standing there in grim silence, the lingering smoke floating aimlessly. He would forgive her eventually, right? He just needed time, he'd said. She repeated that over and over to herself until she was almost convinced. Almost. And after a while, she managed to remember her plan, the desire to do the right thing just barely outweighing the apprehension that had torn a large hole in her stone wall.

Starting with the most painless piece, she headed toward Gimlet's house with detached determination, choosing to don the impassivity of her assassin days to get through the worst of it. It was easy enough to pick the locks and gain entry, the dealer's protections some that she had taught him over the years, but she refused to let her thoughts stray to the past as she quickly searched his quarters.

She found seven daggers, two crossbows, a quiver of bolts, three swords, eight darts, four throwing stars, five pouches of tobacco, a handful of unidentifiable substances, an entire cabinet of liquor, and two hundred gold and ten platinum coins. Grabbing everything but the alcohol (she would come back for that later), she also slipped his favorite cigarette case into her pocket for Corsair. She would sell as much as she could, but the case had been engraved with his initials, and she hoped that it would help toward the effort of getting her childhood friend to forgive her.

Again, she could only hope.

She sold all but the finest of the daggers at an open blacksmith on her way over to Rikeland's—well, she supposed it was Patia's bakery now. The thought depressed her as she stashed the ninety gold she had bartered for the weapons and headed southward, her heart growing heavier the closer she got.

It was in the pit of her stomach as she approached the counter window, watching as Orlah completed a couple of transactions before noticing her. The young woman's brows raised in surprise, her eyes darting to either side of Evelaine in search of her father, but worry began to creep into her expression when she didn't find who she was looking for. Evelaine tried to keep her lips curved in a thin smile but knew she was failing, Orlah's brows creasing even further as she rushed over to open the door.

"Evelaine, you've returned! Is everything alright? My father, is he . . . ?" Her words crowded together, the pitch rising as her anxiety turned to panic.

Patia glanced up from where she was working at a pile of dough on the counter. "Evelaine, back so soon?"

Evelaine swallowed hard, forcing the greeting out. "M-may I come in?"

"Of course, of course. Please sit. Is there anything I can get you? Tea? Coffee? I think we have some of those brown sugar scones. I don't know if Corsair will be coming along soon with Papa, but I can—" Orlah was babbling, her hands fluttering around her apron as she stepped back from the door to let Evelaine in.

"Please, don't worry yourself. Sit," Evelaine urged, ordering her feet to move to the table. Her hand felt as if it were a long distance from her body as she watched it reach out and grasp the back of a chair, pulling it out for herself. She glanced over to Patia as the woman rounded the worktable and waddled toward her, her hand pressed against her full belly. They exchanged a long look, and Patia's lips thinned, but her chin tipped up a fraction as Evelaine watched her steel herself for whatever news was coming.

Orlah was still hovering and Patia waved her over to help her settle into a chair across from Evelaine, keeping her daughter's hand clutched in hers as tense silence filled the space. Evelaine finally sat, folding her hands on the top of the table as she struggled to find the words. She opened her mouth, then closed it, and Orlah gasped, her hand pressing to her mouth as her eyes widened.

"*No*," she whispered, but Patia shushed her.

"Let's hear it," the woman said low.

Evelaine locked eyes with her. "I'm so sorry."

Orlah's next gasp turned into a sob, tears beginning to spill onto her cheeks, and Patia's teeth clenched, the muscles of her jaw flickering.

Evelaine turned to her pack, drawing out a heavy pouch. "I fully realize that this won't make up for your loss, but . . . this is five hundred gold."

She set it on the table between them, but Patia's gaze didn't leave hers as Orlah dissolved into heart-wrenching weeping next to her, folding in on herself.

"How . . . how did it happen?" Patia's voice was hoarse.

"It was the temple," Evelaine tried to explain. "We weren't prepared for the traps. It was worse than the previous one. Much worse."

"There's"—Patia attempted to clear her throat—"no body?"

Evelaine's stomach churned at the question. Why hadn't the bodies been returned? Nees's had been wrapped and waiting for her outside the plant temple, so where had Rikeland's, Gimlet's, and Andra's gone? She had been too upset to question it when Corsair had been yelling about it in the blacksmithy, but it was a glaring omission now that she was faced with Patia's stoic grief.

"It was lost, but I grabbed this before . . ." Evelaine drew Rikeland's notebook out of her pack, setting it next to the pouch on the table. Patia's attention finally dropped to it, her eyes shimmering as her shaking hand reached out for it. Her fingers closed over it, holding it there as if she were laying her hand on her dead husband's chest for one final goodbye.

"Oh, Papa, no . . ." Orlah sobbed into her hand.

Patia's eyelids fell closed and she took deep, measured breaths as Evelaine was assaulted by Orlah's wretched cries. She held onto her composure with gritted teeth, repeatedly swallowing back the knot in her throat as her skin itched to get out of there, but she waited until Patia's eyes opened once more, now rimmed red at the force of her grief.

"Please forgive me for being unable to express my gratitude for your . . . gifts," Patia rasped.

"Of course, I understand. I—"

"Forgive me, but you do not," Patia cut in. "You could not possibly understand."

Evelaine opened her mouth to protest, about to explain that she did know what it was like to lose a beloved partner, but closed it instead. Of course she could never know what it was like to have two children with someone and another on the way, only to be told that the new babe would never be able to know them. Never be wrapped in the warmth of their hug. Never feel the strength of their love.

"Right." She bowed her head in shame, the thick sap clogging her insides. "My deepest apologies."

"If you will excuse us, I believe we need to close up for the day." Patia's words were polite, but her tone slashed across Evelaine like a thousand thorns.

"O-of course." Evelaine pushed away from the table and stood, her movements wooden. She found herself at the door, her hand folding around the knob, but glanced over her shoulder one last time. Patia's hand still gripped Orlah's, the young woman inconsolable as she collapsed onto the table, but her other lay on top of the notebook as she stared at it with a distant gaze.

That was how Evelaine left them, her feet carrying her deeper into the city as she commanded her thoughts to home in on her final stop for the day. She knew she couldn't delay it, it would only haunt her until she faced the promise she had made, but her stomach still churned when the shining red facade of the Satine Rouge came into view.

Hardening herself with significant effort, she circled around to the back and made her way up the creaking metal staircase. Wexit and Rocan were on duty again and they let her in without question, the slash of her mouth warning them against it as she brushed past them. She didn't even remember the trip up the stairs, faced with the polished doors of the Mistress's office in no time. Her knock was perfunctory, her teeth still clenched as she readied herself for the negotiation she knew was coming.

Hearing the admission of entry from the other side, she entered and strode forward as the Mistress's eyes widened slightly from where she sat at her desk. Prim and poised as per usual, the woman dropped her attention to Evelaine's carved leather breastplate as she belatedly realized that she was still wearing it.

Whatever. Let her see the protection she had been granted by her goddess.

"I'm here to pay off Andra's debt," she stated with no preamble.

"Well, well, well." The Mistress recovered easily. "Isn't this a lovely surprise?"

Evelaine didn't even bother responding, crossing her arms and waiting.

"What? No greeting for your dear old mentor?" The question was purred, dripping with saccharine charm.

She barely held in her scoff, her lips curving at the suggestion. Mentor? She had lost her mentor back in the temple, dead by her own hands. Like hell this succubus in front of her was anything close to a mentor for her.

The Mistress's expression dropped a fraction and she sighed, her hand going to the desk drawer at her left.

Opening it, she rifled through a few papers. "Andra's debt, you say?"

"That's correct."

The woman placed a slip of paper on the desk in front of her, placing her glasses delicately on the bridge of her nose as she read over her notes. "Did our girl finally fly the coop, then?"

"You could say that." Evelaine shut her mind against the image of Andra falling to the floor inside the temple, her blood spilling out around her.

"And you are the one left to pay in her stead? How interesting indeed." The Mistress's keen gaze met Evelaine's over the top of her glasses, but she held her tongue, knowing that she was being baited. The older woman sighed again, placing the paper down. "It'll be a thousand gold."

Evelaine groaned internally. Nothing could be easy, could it? She didn't have that much, not even before she'd given Patia that five hundred. What the fuck kind of debt was this anyway? It must've been one hell of a favor the Mistress had done for Andra's sister to rack up that kind of payment.

Fuck it. "Six hundred."

The Mistress smiled. "Eight hundred."

She ground her teeth together. Reaching into her pack, she took out her backup plan and set the three vials and two pouches of substances she had found at Gimlet's on the edge of the Mistress's desk. "How much in exchange for these?"

The woman's brows raised, curiosity lighting her eyes. "You always were my favorite."

Leaning forward, she carefully plucked each one and examined it, giving a passing sniff or taste when needed. Her smile widened when she finished, sitting back and folding her hands once more. "One forty for the gifts, six sixty in gold."

Evelaine bit back her curse. "Five fifty."

"Six sixty, my dear."

Her hand clenched around the pommel of her dagger at her waist, barely resisting the urge to throw it. "I'll bring the remaining one ten in a few days."

The Mistress beamed at her. "You are quickly becoming my most cherished customer. It is such a pleasure to do business with you."

Evelaine tossed what she had on her desk with a sneer, not even justifying the comment with a response as she turned on her heel and strode for the door. She was officially down to six gold coins, a truly pathetic amount, but it only reaffirmed her plans for Nydas and the others. She swore she would bleed them dry before the week was out, in more ways than one.

Out the door and down the hall, she grasped onto her conviction with a thorned grip. She had to see it through. She had to keep going. There was no other choice. The puzzle pieces she had collected were beginning to show her a picture that she had never really accepted was a possibility for her. After spending a lifetime always under someone else's thumb, her dream had been simply to escape. To build a new life elsewhere, away from the oppressive forces that had exerted their will on her from the moment she was born.

She had dreamed of a selfish sort of freedom, one that didn't bear the weight of the others who found themselves trapped under the same systemic tyrants. But she was beginning to realize that maybe the reason why people had depended on her so much was because she somehow had the ability to not only withstand the forces, but actually defy them.

Her thoughts drifted back to her mother. Evelaine had been the one to nurture her, coax her brilliance to bloom again after being dulled each night spent in the service of the Rouge's clientele. A certain sort of quiet rebellion that had kept her mother from succumbing to the hardness that haunted the other courtesans. Then there was the Mistress, whose continued financial advancement Evelaine had ensured with great success. The proprietress's fortunes and influence had multiplied many times over once the plant blessed assassin had been placed into the field, firmly cementing her position as favorite.

The realization hit her as she was stopped in her tracks, halfway down the final staircase that would take her to the staff quarters. It was no wonder the woman had been so keen to bring Evelaine back into the fold and why she was delighted to negotiate with her further. Just in the last week alone, Evelaine had lined the Mistress's pockets with almost as much gold as the owner of the most prestigious brothel in the Tirdan Republic made in an entire year.

And Mason . . . he had snagged himself the ultimate prize when he had wedded her. A devoted wife and mother for his child who would protect her family with ferocity and cold-blooded competency that guaranteed they would never go hungry or be forced out onto the streets. Most of the working class in Risten could never aspire to make more than a hundred gold a year, maybe a little more if they were especially skilled. As the Mistress's favorite, Evelaine had brought in a little over two hundred. It had been nothing compared to the riches the affluent tossed around carelessly, but it had promised a potential for future upward mobility that very, very few could ever dare to reach for.

There was also Curacu and the villagers that she had given hope to. Tabriara's sacred land she had freed. She propped her hand against the wall, stunned by the sudden appearance of the understanding that was unfolding inside her. She had been chosen. She was the one her goddess had healed and empowered and soothed and aided. Even though the cost had been higher than she had ever imagined, one that continued to tear her soul to the quick, she was an agent of change. And after what had happened at the metal temple, she was now an agent of change with power and connections.

A crazed laugh left her. It had been a complete disaster, but it had worked. Her plan had worked. She and Corsair now had their blessings back and she was well on her way to paying her reparations. How exactly she would atone for the death of her trainer still haunted her, but she refused to let the lingering unease distract her. First, she just had to take down Nydas and a few stodgy old plutocrats who had no idea what was coming for them. He thought he had bested her in Port Werthine? She was the poisonous vine that kept growing back. She was the force of nature that would devour everything in her path.

Why hadn't she seen it before? She had been blinded by her hurt. Too consumed by the injustice of having those she loved ripped from her, but Tabriara had been right. To truly love meant to keep her heart open, so that loved ones could come and go. Why would she expect them to stay contained within when she knew deep down that her own wildness could never be controlled or chained? It wasn't right to keep the potential locked within a shell. The seed must sprout, grow, and wither all of its own volition, whether it was hers or someone else's.

She felt the buds of possibility burst through the stone wall as an idea blossomed with seductive vibrance, her feet moving quickly as she covered the last bit of distance to Corsair's door. Knocking once then twice, she didn't get a response, so she rapidly picked the lock and slipped inside. It was empty, but she noticed the shining armor shoved into a corner even though no signs of sweet smoke lingered in the air. Swinging her pack off, she dug through it to deposit all five pouches of tobacco, the fine dagger, and Gimlet's cigarette case on the desk. She then scribbled a note on a spare piece of parchment, pinning it to the surface with the blade.

Smiling to herself, she shrugged her pack back on and exited. The lock was reengaged with a flick of her tools and she was gone, striding down the hallway and out the back door as she nearly jogged all the way to her grandfather's apothecary. She didn't even bother going inside just yet, grabbing the hand cart that was stashed in the alley by the back door and hustling back to Gimlet's. The bottles of alcohol she had left were loaded and the sun was starting to set as she rolled her stash to the greenhouse, where she wedged it in a dark corner.

She entered with a pep in her step as Otis looked up from where he was stirring his stew for the evening, surprise and delight suffusing his expression. "You're back! How did it go?"

"Oh, Grandfather, you have no idea." She smiled, grabbing the loaf of bread he had waiting on the counter and taking a big bite out of it. "Do you have any more of that fire starter?"

He grew still as his brows creased, studying the look on her face. "I do, but . . ."

"Great! I need some." She glanced around, searching for the bottles as she chewed on her makeshift dinner. She would need the energy.

"Lainey, what happened?" He straightened, wiping his hands on a dishcloth.

"Don't worry about it. It's a long story." She waved him off, letting out a happy sound as she located the fire starter stored on one of his crowded supply shelves. Selecting as many bottles as she could carry, she began hefting them to the greenhouse door with the remnants of her loaf tucked under her arm as Otis grabbed her by the elbow.

"Why do you need the fire starter? Was the temple not cleared? Do you need to go back?"

"No, no. We took care of it." She shrugged him off, shouldering her way through the door, but he followed her, insistent.

"Then what do you need all this for?" His eyes bulged when he noticed the cart of alcohol as she set the fire starter down next to it. "Lainey, what in the world—"

"I told you. I have things I need to take care of." She began uncorking the bottles and pouring the liquids together.

"That is—good gods, Lainey!" He started grabbing at her hands. "You can't just mix those together!"

She swatted at him, but he squeezed his way between her and the cart, holding her wrists as tightly as he could. "Grandfather, please, I—"

"My dear girl, I will help you, I swear. Just tell me what you're trying to do and I will do my best to assist you, but you can't just combine these. The fumes alone could kill you," he pleaded, attempting to drag her away.

"Fine." She huffed, pulling her hands away as he pushed her back to the kitchen area. "Okay, okay, okay."

He managed to corral her out of the greenhouse and motioned for her to stay there before he went back and opened some windows to air it out. Shuffling back to her, he closed the door firmly and stood in front of it with his hands on his hips. "Tell me what's going on."

"I need firepower." She hesitated. "I don't want to tell you any more than that because the less you know, the better."

His frown deepened. "Is it for the temple?"

"No." She tossed her leftover bread onto the counter. "It's for something else."

"You were successful, then?" His brows only lifted a fraction. "You all made it out? Your blessings are restored?"

She winced. "Yes and no. I promise I'll tell you more when I get back, but I need to go take care of this first."

Sighing, he eyed her expression but relented. "Okay, fine. What kind of firepower are we talking here?"

"The biggest you got." She dipped her chin, her idea filling her with wicked glee.

He chewed the inside of his cheek, his gaze straying to his shelves as he thought. She could tell he wasn't happy, but he would help her—she knew it.

"Throwable. That's why I was using the bottles," she added.

His attention darted back to her, his wrinkled lips pursed. He sighed again and shook his head, scratching at his hairline. "Igniting on impact?"

"Exactly."

He took one last long look at her, then nodded and rolled his sleeves up. "Go grab the face masks. I'll grab the supplies."

She smiled, her eyes pricking as she fought back the relieved tears and hurried to follow his instructions. It took them a couple hours, but the Urdian Spire was chiming in the background as they filled up the hand cart with more than a dozen bottles with simple strips of fabric sticking out of the tops. She then traded her more identifiable breastplate for an inconspicuous one and hugged him one last time before wrapping her face in a dark scarf. With her cloak firmly tied closed and the cart covered with plain burlap sacks, she slipped into the empty streets and made her way to the Brookton District.

It was easy enough to keep to the shadows, most of the residences shuttered for the evening as it neared midnight, but she made sure none of the spare pedestrians roaming the streets saw her as she approached the grand estate that was her destination. Silent as a mouse, Evelaine tucked herself around a corner, breathing slowly and taking her time as she studied the thick, metal wall that ran along the perimeter that she was aiming to infiltrate.

Like most affluent families in the district, the Waltzins sequestered themselves inside a tiered manor, where those they'd hired to run the place lived in the lower quarters while the family luxuriated above, and she knew that just inside the wall was a carefully manicured garden that wrapped around the buildings. To make the impact she was looking for, she specifically located the corner where the top floors were closest to the wall, circling a few times until she found the perfect spot.

She could just see the faint glow of candlelight shining through the broad windows that overlooked the city, the spacious rooms showing no signs of inhabitants beyond the occasional pass of a servant or guard. There were a few armored figures who patrolled on the top of the walls, and she patiently waited as she learned their pattern, inching closer as she sensed her window of opportunity.

The moment one of them was isolated from the rest, she darted forward and urged a vine up the wall to lunge for their neck the second they glanced away. Wrapping it tightly around their mouths, she silenced them then yanked one by one, sending them falling over the side of the wall toward her, where she caught them in a soft bed of mosses. A handkerchief was quickly pulled from her pocket and slapped across their noses before they even got a chance to right themselves, a lesson she had learned from the man she was after.

Pulling them away, she stashed their unconscious, bound forms in an alley as she worked her way through the entire guard force. She barely stifled her giggles, the smile widening under her scarf as she moved to the second part of her idea. Rolling the cart over to the edge of the compound, she wrapped her bundle of bottles in a net of vines and set them aside, then hurried to hide her cart in an alleyway a couple streets back. When she returned, she scurried to the top of the wall and hoisted her bottles up after her, the burlap sacks preventing them from clacking together. Crouching, she examined the garden below as an errant servant passed by inside the house without even sparing a glance in her direction.

The corner she had chosen only held about ten or so feet of sculpted topiary, rows of delicate flowers, and a winding stone path dotted with a couple benches before the windows of the manor provided unobstructed glimpses of the rich furnishings beyond. It was truly moronic and elitist of them to think that their wide-open glass expanses were protected simply because they had a great, towering wall and some guards. Nydas might have been smart enough to build better protections into his warehouse headquarters, but who would dare assault the Waltzins at their home residence? They should listen more to the crime boss they were harboring, she wagered, but she knew she needed to test the windows first.

She said a soft hello to the nature below her, whispering its praises as it awakened to her call. It extended long vines toward the walls, slowly trailing up the facade until it reached the bottom corner of one of the panes. There, it pushed itself into the miniscule space where the glass met the frame and then expanded, a crack splintering the clear barrier. She complimented it, giving it her adoration as she urged it further, until the window was compromised enough.

Biting her lip to contain her laughter, she reached out and ordered more vines to follow suit, long tendrils of green snaking up the sides of the building and penetrating all manner of windows that were softly lit from within. When that step was finished, she compelled them to retreat into the dirt, giving thanks for a job well done, then reached for the first bottle at her feet. She pulled out her matchbox and held for another moment, watching for any movement inside, but there was none, the Spire finally clanging out midnight in the distance.

She gave one last smile to the stars above her then lit the strip of fabric, throwing the bottle with all her might toward the first broken pane. It burst through with a crash and ignited instantly, the explosion of fire covering the entire room as velvets and silks ignited. The start of a funeral pyre her friends would never get. Evelaine didn't even pause to watch as she grabbed the next one and lit it, lobbing it toward another expanse of cracked glass and watching it shatter.

Lights began to come alive in the lower levels, alerted voices reaching her in between her deliveries, but she moved faster and faster, not even waiting for a bottle to hit before she lit the next. Soon, the whole wing in front of her was inflamed, towering swaths of heat and destruction tearing through the manor as figures began spilling out doors at the opposite end of the compound. She ran the other way along the wall, carrying her last bottles with her as the fire stretched into the night sky. Voices were yelling, a cacophony of panic making the snickers finally spill from her lips as she gasped for air and tried not to double over in her mirth.

Sliding to a stop, she crouched out of sight and lit the remaining strips, flinging them in quick succession at anything they could reach. The crack, crack, crack of them hitting and the roar of detonation had her hiding behind the solid railing of the wall that kept guards from unfortunate missteps as she rolled with laughter. Her cheeks grew wet as she sobbed out her amusement, knowing she had to make a hasty exit sooner rather than later. It took her a second, but she managed to summon a vine to yank her over the side, another bed of mosses catching her on the street below.

No one was around, most of the commotion centering around the other side of the estate as she crumbled her creations to dust. Jumping up, she bolted into the nearest alley and let the shadows embrace her as she wound her way back to where she had hidden the cart. Her chest was heaving, but she slowly rolled it away as the shouts surrounding the Waltzin residence faded into the distance.

She passed a pedestrian here and there, weaving their own way through the dark streets, and desperately tried to keep her choking laughs to herself, keeping her hood low enough that she might just be mistaken for a drunken lunatic looking for somewhere to pass out. But eventually, she made it back to the greenhouse and tucked the cart back where she had found it originally before pushing her way inside and staggering into the rear of the shop on unsteady legs.

Otis was waiting up for her, his bony hands wrapped around a teacup, and shot to his feet when she entered, reaching for her as she fell forward. The cup fell to the floor, shattering as tea splashed across the tile, but his arms went around her as she slumped against him, shaking.

"Oh, Grandfather." She laughed, tears streaming down her cheeks. Her knees buckled, bringing her down.

"My dear Lainey, oh my dear," he murmured, lowering himself to her level as he nestled her head to his shoulder.

"The things I have done . . ." Her chuckles turned to sobs, her breath catching.

"It's alright. I've got you," he promised, her hood sliding off as he stroked her hair. "I've got you."

She clutched at him, trying to gulp in air as her cries shuddered through her. "I-it worked, b-but I still f-feel awful."

"What worked, my love?" he asked, starting to rock her gently.

"M-my plan," she wept. "B-but they d-died."

She felt her grandfather inhale sharply, his arms tightening around her. "Oh, Lainey. I'm so sorry."

"No." she swore. "**I'm** sorry. It's my f-fault. Co-Corsair won't forgive me and P-Patia was so mad. Orlah—Orlah—"

She couldn't even bring herself to finish the sentence, haunted by the echoes of Rikeland's daughter's cries. Shame and guilt thickened over her skin, a reminder of the deplorable sins that would mar her until the end of her days.

"I understand, but they will come around. I know they will," he assured her.

She shook her head firmly against his shoulder. "I will never forgive myself."

"That's okay. You don't have to."

That surprised her, her sniffles slowing as she sat up and scrubbed at her face. "W-what?"

Her grandfather smiled sadly at her, his hand cupping her cheek. "There are many things I haven't forgiven myself for, decisions I regret to this day. That's normal. Forgiveness is not a requirement for learning. Sometimes it is better to be reminded of our errors. Absolution isn't always the best teacher."

She stared at him with bleary eyes, trying to wrap her muddled mind around what he was saying. Maybe he was right, maybe he wasn't, but she nodded absently. He took the cue to get to his feet, his knees creaking as he reached down to help her up too, and she let him, exhaustion dragging her down as he led her to the cot she had been using. She flopped on it, and he wrapped the blankets around her, stroking her forehead as sleep rushed to greet her. She was absolutely depleted, but she did know one thing:

The Waltzins' estate was as blackened as her heart now.

DAY TWELVE

Evelaine's eyes were crusty and puffed to hell when she woke the next morning, mental images of the raging fire she had caused in her grief making her sit up in a rush. Had she really done that?

Otis glanced at her from where he was making breakfast as her head spun from the sudden movement, and she remembered that she hadn't really eaten much the day before. A possible contributing factor to the arson she had gleefully taken part in. As if reading her thoughts, her grandfather motioned her to the table, and she pushed back the blankets to shuffle over.

He set a full plate in front of her just as she plopped down, her fists rubbing away the lingering sleep, but they both jumped as banging came from the back door of the greenhouse. Otis leaned to the side, glancing through the glass door, and chuckled softly to himself as Evelaine craned her neck to see who it was. She couldn't see from her vantage point on the settee and huffed, pushing to a stand so that she could follow him as he disappeared into the rear structure.

She had just stepped inside when he opened the back door and Corsair entered, looking just as sleep-mussed as her. He wasn't even wearing a shirt underneath his cloak, his boots haphazardly shoved onto his feet with one pant leg up and one down.

"What in the—" she started as he threw his hands up at her.

"What the fuck did you do?!"

She opened her mouth, then closed it. The list of things she had done the day before was on the longer side.

"I didn't see your note until this morning." He huffed, stomping toward her. "What in the gods' names did you do?"

Ah, right. The note she had left him had been rather vague, she had to admit. The idea had been so exciting in the moment that she had simply scrawled, "The vultures' nest will burn tonight."

She lifted a shoulder, crossing her arms. "I may have . . . you know, sent them a message."

"Evie . . ." He narrowed his eyes.

"A strongly worded message," she amended.

Otis popped up in between them, blocking Corsair from leaning into Evelaine's space farther. "Come, come. Let's get some breakfast in you two."

He shooed them toward the kitchen door and corralled them toward the sitting area, where Evelaine dropped back into her seat and Corsair chose the armchair next to her. He leaned forward, pointing a finger into her face.

"Details. Now."

It was her turn to huff, sinking into the back of her seat and crossing her arms again as her grandfather deposited another full plate in front of Corsair. He dropped his attention to it, instantly distracted, and she could tell he probably hadn't had a decent meal in a long time either as he picked it up and started shoveling eggs, sausage, and potatoes into his mouth while still trying to scowl at her.

"What? Was your dinner of liquor and tobacco not filling enough?" she sniped at him, taking a guess at why he was so disheveled, but her stomach growled as if on cue and he smirked around his fork.

"Nice deflection," he grumbled, mouth full, as Otis sat with his own plate on the other side of the settee and let their argument volley back and forth.

She rolled her eyes, picking up her own plate and spearing a piece of sausage. Chewing, she eyed him. "Does this mean you're forgiving me?"

His expression flattened and he put down his plate, appetite dissipating. "Not until you tell me what the fuck happened. I saw you . . . left Gimlet's case and dagger. Did you ransack his place?"

She frowned. "I mean, I wouldn't say 'ransack' exactly . . . ."

He leaned back in his chair and propped an elbow on the arm, rubbing at his face. "Evie. Come on."

"Look." She gestured with her fork. "I had reparations to make. It's not like he will be using his stuff any time soon."

Corsair inhaled sharply, glancing away from her, and she grimaced.

"I'm sorry. I didn't mean it that way. I just . . . I know he was . . ." She sighed, struggling with the words. "I . . . had to use the resources that I had at my disposal. Both his gold and the money his weapons were worth went to Patia, plus some from my stash. I gave her five hundred in total."

Corsair's eyes darted to her as they widened. "Five hundred?"

"Yeah." She halfheartedly poked at a chunk of potato. "I . . . I had to do something for them. You should've seen Orlah."

He cursed under his breath, his head dropping to the back of the chair as he frowned at the ceiling.

"His . . . drugs went to the Mistress," she added, watching his reaction as his gaze slid to her. "As part of Andra's debt."

"Gods, Evie." He shook his head, focusing on the ceiling again.

"I paid off most of it. I need to get her another hundred and ten soon, then it'll be done. All I have left is six gold, so I figured . . ."

He lifted his head. "Time for Nydas."

"Time for Nydas." She nodded, dropping her eyes to her half-empty plate. "Gimlet's alcohol was particularly helpful for that piece."

She looked up in the grim silence that followed to find him staring at her expectantly but was unable to hold eye contact as she pushed around some eggs with her fork.

"I burned the compound down," she mumbled.

His fork clattered to his plate. "Excuse me?"

She lifted a shoulder. "At least a good portion of it."

When she glanced up at him, he was blinking at her, stunned, then a startled laugh left him as he rubbed his forehead. "Oh my gods."

"The plan was to smoke them out. They'll have to move into a hotel while the repairs are being done, which will be much easier to corner Nydas in. There was no way we'd be able to get into the estate without having their full guard force breathing down our necks, let alone whatever protections they have in place there. At a hotel, they won't be able to do anything beyond personal guard escorts. They'll likely only have one or two assigned to a room at any given time, probably on some sort of rotating schedule, and I doubt they'll put Nydas near the suites the family will occupy. If we can get into his room, we can isolate him."

Corsair sat quietly as she rambled through her explanation, but she eventually trailed off, waiting for his response. A long pause followed, his eyes glued to her as different emotions passed across his expression.

He finally shook his head, deciding on a question. "We?"

Her brows furrowed, anger rising. "Yes, 'we.' I need you to back me on this."

"Why?" he bit back. "You were perfectly capable of burning the fucking manor down by yourself. I'd only be holding you back, isn't that right?"

"What?" she asked, shocked. "Of course I need you. You're just as capable as—"

"As you?" He sneered. "Is that what you were going to say? Or am I just fodder for your vendetta just like Gimlet, Rikeland, and Andra were? Simply collateral damage?"

"No!" She gasped. "Corsair, I never thought of you all that way. I truly didn't know that it was going to be that dangerous. Even Tabriara said—"

"What did your precious goddess say, Evie? When she saved you from the big ol' mean Metal God? Did she tell you it was all justified? That all is fair in love and war?"

She snapped her mouth closed, studying the fury etched across his features. Once again, she wondered what Urkus had said to him. What had their conversation been like to produce such derision in him? He had been willing to do anything before Tabriara had appeared, yet he had refused the crown. She bet the god hadn't been pleased by that. Had they argued about it? Had he been punished somehow?

Reining in her temper, she took a deep breath. "This isn't just about me anymore. This is about balancing the scales. I need to pay off the Mistress so that Andra's debt can be cleared, otherwise her sister will likely suffer the consequences. Plus, I wanted to provide some money for Mason and Estella. I abandoned them for too many years. I need to do what is right."

She thought about what Tabriara had said about the blessed using their powers for the greater good. "We can do something worthwhile here, Corsair. We can get information out of Nydas and figure out how to hit the Waltzins, and maybe others, where it hurts. They have to be protecting him for some reason. Maybe he knows something. Something big."

He let out a long, beleaguered sigh and dropped his head back on the chair, so she pushed her opportunity.

"Yes, I could do this by myself, but I'm better with you. Together, we can be smarter. More effective. I've made too many mistakes on my own . . . cost too many lives." Her voice hitched on the word. "You're far more intelligent than you give yourself credit for. I've seen the way your mind works, but you hide it behind that carefree attitude of yours. You numb it with smoking and drinking and fucking—"

His head snapped up and he glared at her, but she kept talking.

"I've known you my entire life, dude, and I know you care just as much as I do about the state of this fucking city. It's a mess." She bored her gaze into him, urging him to understand. "If we have learned anything in the last few days, it's that Risten is yours. It's the sacred metal lands and you're the blessed that has been chosen to do something about it."

"You fucking sound just like him." He scoffed, looking away.

She couldn't believe she was saying it, but the puzzle pieces were undeniable. What her goddess had told her had been lingering in the back of her mind. "You may not bear the crown, but this is your city. Are you going to let those assholes crush everyone they deem lesser than under their heels? Are you going to let people like Patia and her sister and Andra's sister suffer just because they weren't lucky enough to be born into wealth? Don't think I don't know about your little donation habit. You **care**."

He ground his teeth together, the muscles flickering in his jaw as a tense moment passed. He glanced back at her with a scowl. "And you're expecting me to do this for free? From the good of my heart?"

"You can have whatever money we find. All I ask is that some is set aside for Mason and Estella. The rest you can distribute as you wish. I trust you."

"And what if I just decide to run away with it all?" he challenged her.

"You won't," she said softly, and he dropped his eyes, knowing she spoke the truth.

Long minutes passed as he braced his elbows on his knees and stared at his feet, one pant leg still awkwardly caught in the top of his boot. He threaded a hand through his hair, realizing midway through that it was still tangled to shit, and huffed, yanking his fingers out of the snarl and tossing it over his shoulder as he leaned back and dropped his head on the chair. He scrubbed his face, hard.

"How are we going to get into his room?" he finally asked, his voice muffled from behind his hands.

Her heart bloomed with relief, a sly smile curving her lips. "So I was thinking . . ."

She laid out her plan for him as he slowly sat up and focused on her, and she could see the wheels turning behind his sharp gray eyes despite the red rims that indicated his overindulgences from the night before. She briefly wondered where he had dragged himself off to in order to soothe his own grief while she had relied on arson to process her unwieldy emotions. Whatever. All that mattered was that he was here now, pressing his lips together as she finished explaining her idea.

"I don't know if she'll be up for it," he eventually said.

"We can set aside some of the money for her. Your mother will be the perfect ruse. Nydas's men already know what I look like."

He gave her a wry smile, shaking his head. "She does need a little excitement in her life, I guess."

She sat up straighter, only barely containing her urge to clap happily, but was instantly sobered at the reminder of her friends' faces flashing before her. Corsair tucked back into his meal as he thought, finishing off the plate and then also the seconds that Otis immediately fetched for him as Evelaine slowly chewed hers, hoping beyond hope that she was making the right call. She had been completely honest when she had said that she had made too many mistakes, but maybe aiming her efforts toward a goal that benefitted the greater good instead of just her was the pivot she needed.

The realization that had hit her in the stairwell the night before was resting uncomfortably within her, not yet fully integrated. Maybe being the one others relied on was a strength, not a burden. Maybe she was uniquely equipped to do something meaningful with all of the experiences that had shaped her into who she had become. Maybe nature actually was a continual process of destruction then construction, over and over as all material things fell to the test of time.

Was it her time to build instead of destroy?

Before she could do that, though, she had one last task to attend to:

Nydas Sutherland must die.

They finished their breakfast and hustled over to the Rouge, finding Seraphine and outlining their plan to her. She was hesitant at first, but the light of adventure soon glowed in her expression as they assured her of her safety and the money that would follow. She was the one who had instilled the unquestionable precociousness in Corsair as a child, after all. A quality that made him as resilient as the element that flowed through his veins.

She was excitedly choosing her outfit when Evelaine left them to make her own preparations with Otis, a few choice chemicals and tonics necessary for their plan to go smoothly. By the time the Spire was striking eight that evening, Evelaine was back at the Rouge with her supplies in hand and shrugging on the baker's outfit Corsair had procured for her.

Corsair and Seraphine took the lead as they left, her in a dazzling gown of silver silk and he in his guard uniform, while Evelaine trailed from a distance, keeping to the shadows with her trusty cart. They had confirmed early in the day that the Waltzins and their immediate entourage were staying at the Golden Crest, an expensive hotel that sat on the edge between the Gildan and Brookton Districts. A perfect midway point for those who wished to partake in the titillating experiences of the entertainment venues while also seeking the entitled quiet of the wealthier neighborhoods.

Once they arrived, Evelaine split off toward the back of the establishment and Corsair and his mother entered through the gilded front doors, greeted by gentile doormen and welcomed inside as recognizable visitors from the Rouge. It wasn't uncommon for courtesans to spend their evenings inside the Crest, servicing the clientele who didn't care to be seen entering the brothel, so Evelaine had known that it would be easy for them to gain entry, a beautiful paramour and her guard casually inquiring where they might find her companion for the night.

Evelaine, on the other hand, snuck her way into the staff hallway in the rear, blending in with the rushing attendants as they hurried from one task to another on a busy weekend shift. She even slipped into the kitchen and grabbed a basket of bread, giving her an excuse as she found her way to the upper levels where the guest rooms were. No one noticed a thing, her presence nearly invisible as just another paid hand delivering a request from one of the patrons above. She almost laughed at how simple it was turning out to be but didn't dare curse their luck when they had only just begun.

Her steps slowed as she located the plush hallways, lined with rich green brocaded wallpaper and busts of important-looking figures set on credenzas that had been polished until they reflected the candelabras, glowing on the walls. She patrolled the first floor but found nothing, moving to the stairs again to ascend higher. Listening carefully as she walked, she wandered until she caught the distant sound of light humming, a sign from Seraphine as they dallied in the corridor where they had been directed to find Nydas's room by the front-desk staff.

She scurried over and peeked around the corner, finding her two allies very slowly pacing the hallway as if they were simply admiring the artwork as they passed. Whistling low, she alerted them to her presence as they glanced in her direction then nodded.

"Room two fifteen," Corsair mouthed to her as they approached the correct door.

Seraphine lifted her chin and straightened her shoulders, then knocked delicately. "Delivery for Mr. Nydas Sutherland."

Evelaine ducked back around the corner, intently focused on the gruff voice that followed as the door creaked open. "What is this?"

It was him. She recognized the rumble instantly, her skin prickling from the rush of memories. Her thigh ached where the javelin had pierced her and her breath caught from the phantom sensation, but she caught herself, focusing in on the end of whatever Seraphine was answering.

". . . for the evening? It would be my pleasure," she purred, her charms well-honed.

"And who's this?" The sneer was clear even though she couldn't see him.

"Just my guard, don't mind him." She giggled lightly, and Evelaine could imagine her in her mind's eye, brushing a hand against his bicep and fluttering her eyelashes just as Evelaine had seen her do a thousand times in the Rouge's great hall.

There was a huff, but it wasn't as forceful as it could've been, and Evelaine knew they had him. The door creaked again, opening farther. A pause followed and then she heard the click of the lock sliding into place. Peeking around the corner, she found the coast to be clear and hurried over.

"*Come on, come on,*" she whispered, her hand on the doorknob. There was a long minute as she heard another giggle from Seraphine on the other side, then the lock slowly clicked again. Corsair had timed it just as another peal of feminine laughter rang out.

She wrenched it open, sliding inside and closing it quickly as she held out the bread basket with a smile. "You requested bread, sir?"

Seraphine had gotten Nydas to sit on the edge of the bed while she had positioned herself leaning against the dresser across from it, her hands seductively trailing down the sides of her torso in some sort of precursor to a strip tease. The second the words left Evelaine's mouth, she sprung forward when Nydas's gaze was slow to leave the figure in front of him, reluctantly sliding to the rush of movement at his right. His eyes widened as recognition hit, his lips parting to yell just as Evelaine reached him, shoving a doused cloth over his mouth and nose.

He gasped, trying to twist out of the way, but Corsair was right there, pinning his arms as he pushed him down on the bed. They both fell on top of him, using their weight to subdue him as his struggles ebbed under the effect of the sedative Otis had mixed up for her. There wasn't even a guard in the room with him, and she couldn't help but laugh as his eyes fell closed. The idiot has been lulled into a false sense of protection, believing that he was safe after she had been lost five years ago far across the sea.

Fucking moron.

She sat up, straddling his chest as she looked down at his relaxed face with the pock-marked skin she remembered so clearly, and cackled again, slapping him hard across the cheek as his head simply lolled to the side. Backhanding

255

him, she smacked him to the other side as Corsair gripped her arm to stop her from another.

"Evie," he warned, "we don't have time for this."

"Right, right." She chuckled, smiling broadly and climbing off him. When she glanced at Corsair's mother, she was watching Evelaine with a strange expression on her face but straightened her shoulders and moved toward the door.

Evelaine pulled the small potion bottle they had prepared out of her pocket and leaned over to pour it down Nydas's throat, then left Corsair to watch him as she started searching the room. These kinds of hotels always provided safes for their patrons, and she began in the closet where—yup, there it was. She shook her head at the predictability. These arrogant pricks, thinking they were so above everyone else. Untouchable in their lavish rooms. What attendant would dare think they could get away with stealing from them?

"Corsair." She jerked her head in the direction of the safe and the metal blessed glanced over his shoulder, waving a hand as the locking mechanism clicked. Biting her lip in anticipation, she opened it but frowned in confusion. It was empty.

She looked around the room, finding Nydas's suitcase, and stood to rifle through it. Just some clothes, boots, a few daggers. Normal stuff. Her frown deepened as she ran to the dresser and started throwing open the drawers, but they were empty too. He hadn't even bothered to unpack anything, the lout.

Turning to Nydas, she dug through his pockets and found a handful of coins, mostly gold, a few silver, and one platinum. She thrust them at Corsair then began tearing the room apart, searching under the mattress, in the pillowcases, behind furniture.

Nothing. There was nothing here.

There was no way the Waltzins would leave their fortune in their burned-out home. They would've at least carried enough with them to spend comfortably while they were away. Sure, most of their money had to be in banks, but they had to pay Nydas, right? He had to receive some sort of allowance or salary as part of their staff, unless . . .

She studied the prone figure on the bed, his fingers beginning to twitch as the sedative wore off. He groaned, his eyes blinking open groggily as his tongue stumbled over grumpy sounds. She couldn't afford to fret over the details just yet. It was time for the next step.

After she nodded at Corsair, they both slipped an arm under one of his shoulders and hefted him to a stand. He wobbled on his feet, slurring at them as Seraphine hurried to open the door and they hustled out into the corridor and toward the staff staircase. It was awkward, maneuvering his drugged weight, but they managed as best they could while Corsair's mother used her charms on anyone they encountered along the way.

Her client had had too much to drink, she said. He didn't want to be seen like this by leaving the hotel from the front, she insisted. She wanted to keep an eye on him overnight to make sure he didn't come to any harm, but had to return to the Rouge or else her employer would come looking for her. She had to take him with her, of course. It was only right.

Evelaine kept her head low, shadowing her face under the bulk of Nydas's shoulder, the other attendants' eyes passing over her baker's uniform and accepting it at face value. Once they made it outside, they slipped into a nearby alley and recovered Evelaine's hand cart, slumping Nydas into it as he mumbled incoherently at them. She summoned a seed to grow into vines that wrapped around his head, covering his mouth to keep him quiet, and then threw a blanket over him for the journey.

Corsair and Seraphine split off after she nodded as Evelaine donned her cloak and pushed the cart through the shadows toward the southwestern corner of the Industrial District. It took a while, traversing the entire length of the city with her load, and by the time she got there, Corsair was waiting for her at the back entrance to the abandoned blacksmithy, having dropped off his mother back at the Rouge safe and sound. Neither of them wanted her to witness what would come next.

Another wave of his hand and the chains locking the basement doors were easily freed, but Corsair didn't smirk in his triumph, his lips in a grim line as they opened them and began the process of moving Nydas. The doors were locked once more, and Corsair lit the torch he had retrieved upon returning to the brothel, using one hand to hold it out while the other helped Evelaine support the headman down the long staircase.

It was eerie, being back in the space that had been the death of their friends, but neither of them dared mention it. It was as if they had reached a silent accord not to make this situation any more difficult than it had to be. As much as each of them would like to say that it was something they'd never done before, torturing someone for information was a messy task that they had agreed a long time ago to never discuss at length. It just was what it was.

She felt the change come over Corsair as they neared the platform where they had placed a chair and implements earlier in the day. It was almost as if his skin hardened into armor, his affinity for his element taking over his countenance as his expression became a blank panel. She recognized it, his personal protection for what they were about to do, and she understood the need. For her, she felt vines begin to wrap around her knuckles, wrists, and forearms, sprouting thorns as they went.

They reached the platform and pushed Nydas into the chair, Corsair calling metal to circle his wrists and ankles. Evelaine shucked her cloak, letting her vines crawl farther up her arms, onto her collarbones and into her hair, while Corsair sat on the lower steps and began methodically sharpening their blades. There, she stood and waited for Nydas to come to, only the sound of their even breaths and the swipe of Corsair's whetstone filling the space.

It took about twenty minutes before Nydas's head stopped lolling to the side, his neck muscles tensing as he regained his awareness and tested his restraints. Once he realized he was truly stuck, he lifted his gaze to study them suspiciously. His eyes narrowed on Evelaine's face, his lip curling in disgust, and Corsair slowly stood, raising a hand that had a wall of metal shutting off the staircase to give them complete privacy. Nydas's attention darted behind her, his brows twitching up in surprise, him not expecting the move as he shifted uncomfortably in his seat.

Evelaine unsheathed the oath dagger, letting it dangle in her hand as she began to circle the chair nonchalantly. "Hello, Nydas. So nice of you to join us."

He growled, refusing to answer.

She tsked softly. "Now, now. Aren't you pleased to see your old friend? What has it been, five years now?"

He spit at her feet as she came to his front once again. "Friend? Hah. I left you for dead."

"And where exactly was that? Hmm?" She tapped the end of her blade against her lip. "I can't seem to remember the details."

"You weren't supposed to remember anything, bitch." He sneered in contempt.

"And yet, here we are." She lifted a shoulder. "How strange, indeed."

He just stared at her in challenge, his glare landing on Corsair, who was not so subtly examining the man's measurements with clinical detachment as she strolled out of his perspective again.

"What was your plan for me, I wonder? It seems as though it didn't quite work out, now did it?" she asked casually.

"Apparently," Nydas muttered.

"The Waltzins weren't too happy about that, were they?" she guessed, coming back into his periphery and tilting her head curiously.

His attention slid to her, the briefest flash of alarm showing before he smothered it.

"They knew that the Mistress would send her favorite assassin to take care of you when you began stealing those shipments. That's why you did it, wasn't it?" His eyes evaded her, and she pressed further. "They told you exactly what protections to set up."

She lunged forward, pressing her blade to the side of his head underneath his ear as he jerked back at the sudden movement. "How did they know?"

His lip curled, but he stayed silent so the dagger began to slice into the soft flesh of his lobe, and he inhaled sharply.

"How did they know?!" she demanded, not letting up as she started to hit cartilage.

He gasped against the pain, gritting his teeth but still not giving in.

In one swift move, the ear was severed and a holler left him as he tried to wrench away from her. The fleshy bit fell to the floor with a soft slap, and she stepped back as he panted with bared teeth.

She raised a brow at his obstinance, then turned to Corsair and nodded. He approached Nydas and held out his empty hand, the metal that held Nydas's left wrist lengthening and pushing it up toward the metal blessed. It kept him restrained but forced the headman's hand out to where Corsair could easily reach it as Nydas squirmed.

"What the fuck?" he bit out. "You freak."

Corsair chuckled low. "Want to find out how true that is, friend?"

He gripped one of Nydas's fingers in between his own, wedging his dagger into the crease at his knuckle. Without warning, he flicked and the finger was dislodged as Nydas screamed again.

"You fuck!! You will pay for that!!"

Corsair's lips twitched into an unnatural smile as he readied his blade against a second finger. "Is that so?"

Another twist of his wrist and another finger joined the other bits on the floor as Nydas howled, his chest heaving in fury.

"YOU BASTARD!!"

Corsair's smile widened. "See how easy it is to tell the truth?"

Evelaine took her cue to lean forward, sliding her dagger across his jaw to tilt his head up so that he looked her in the eye. "How. Did. They. Know?"

Red dripped down the side of his face, his gaze enraged as it swept across her mild expression. "You fucking freaks are nothing but mutants. Monstrosities! You deserve what's coming for you!"

"And what's coming for us?" she asked, slicing a thin line across his cheekbone as he tried to jerk away. Corsair lifted his hand and another piece of metal wrapped around Nydas's neck to hold him in place.

Nydas laughed, the sound a bit choked from his restraint. "You don't even know. You have no idea, do you? Fucking stupid bitch."

Evelaine saw a quick movement out of the corner of her eye and the headman yelled as another finger joined the pile on the floor.

"Whoops," Corsair said mildly.

"Please, do enlighten us." Evelaine drew her blade across his other cheek, another line of blood following in its wake.

"It doesn't matter if you kill me. They're coming for you." Nydas panted. "They'll shut that fucking smart mouth of yours and tear you into pieces. I only wish I could be there to hear you scream!"

Corsair changed tactics, coaxing his metal to circle the man's knees and pulling them apart as the headman struggled. He settled his blade against the sensitive appendages located there and Nydas's eyes bulged, his breath quickening.

"And you!" he accused. "You're the metal freak that they told me about. The fag whore who follows this one around like a lost pup. You should just fuck the bitch and get it over with before they—"

He didn't get a chance to finish as Corsair's hand twisted, and Nydas screwed his face in an infuriated howl, red beginning to pour from his crotch.

But Corsair simply held him there, his own lip curling. "Might I remind you, friend, it's the whore who has a blade wedged in your ball sack. Mind your manners."

"Just do it." He gasped. "Just kill me. I'll tell you nothing!"

Evelaine gripped the side of Nydas's face, slipping the fine tip of her dagger underneath his eyelid as he tried his best to flinch away. It only made her cuts more jagged as he began screaming in earnest, blood splashing across his face. His clamor echoed loudly around them, bouncing off the metal walls, but soon there was a final pop and his eyeball fell to the floor.

"Try again," she ordered as he groaned.

He tried to clench his teeth, but Corsair dug his blade deeper and he began to screech.

"Fr-Frandae was only—" he choked out. "Only the beginning. They'll come for you!"

Evelaine blinked, stepping back a pace as she stared down at him. Frandae. Her mind dug up a distant memory that had been buried, something Rakhmet had told her back when she'd been Esia. The Nalliendrans were adamant in their quest to eliminate all blessed ones, he had said, and they had begun with conquering Frandae.

She quickly glanced at Corsair, who was eyeing her with a question hidden deep within his carefully blank expression, and nodded.

He was fast, not even hesitating for a split second as his dagger slipped across the major artery in Nydas's inner thigh before arcing up and slicing the man's neck open. Blood gushed out of him, slicking the floor in a rapidly increasing puddle as Nydas's jaw dropped in his final gasps.

Corsair urged holes to form in the metal panels beneath them to drain the liquid, preventing it from staining their boots as the criminal twitched and then fell still. They watched him for a few more moments, but he was gone, leaving behind tense silence.

Day Thirteen

In the early hours of the next morning, Evelaine found herself in the staff's bathing chambers at the Rouge, washing away every speck of bloody evidence, as she had on countless occasions before. She could hear Corsair in the shower stall next to her, the splash of water against the tiles the only sound as they each performed their absolutions. He had buried the body, still strapped to the chair, underneath the metal platform in the temple. A strange sort of offering to leave behind, and she didn't know how he felt about it. They hadn't said a word to each other yet.

She honestly didn't know how to feel about it herself, either. There was certainly some relief. Knowing that Nydas was taken care of was the culmination of the very first plan she had made since regaining her memories, but other plans had somehow sprouted between then and now. She should be happy. She should feel complete. Satisfied.

But she didn't.

Instead, she felt uprooted. The foundation that she had built all her motivation upon had been shaken. Disturbed like swaths of freshly tilled farmland, broken and torn roots reaching helplessly toward the sky from mounds of soil. Where she had assumed that her journey was entirely separate from the rest of the blessed, it was, in fact, the opposite. She was as firmly woven into their motives as they were. Apparently, everything led back to Nalliendra after all.

She shook her head, toweling herself off and putting on a new set of clothes that she had grabbed from the storage closet before emerging into the larger bathing chamber, where Corsair was combing through his wet hair. He stood in front of the bank of sinks, his gray eyes meeting hers in the mirror in front of him. He was shirtless per usual, and she could clearly see the tattoo on his back moving as his muscles bunched and shifted. She supposed it must be active again, the two crossed swords glinting ever so slightly in the low light.

He finished as she approached him, jerking his chin to the exit to indicate that they'd talk once they reached his room for privacy. She nodded, following him down the hallway and closing the door behind her as he lit the candles on his desk. Reaching for his tobacco and papers, he sat at the head of the bed and began rolling as he waited for her to begin.

Letting her pack fall on the floor, she took up her spot at the other end. "Have you heard about the Nalliendran war?"

"Bits and pieces," he replied, sealing the cigarette with his tongue.

"I don't know if it's common knowledge, but one of their main goals is to eliminate the blessed ones. They began with Frandae."

His brows rose as the match flared. "I hadn't heard that part."

"It's something that Rakhmet, the fire blessed, told me. It sounded like they were slowly making their way west, into South Endrian. Maybe farther. He said that the Endrian Coalition of Rulers was building a defense against them."

He studied her through the smoke. "So the Waltzins are colluding with the Nalliendrans? To get rid of the blessed?"

"Sounds like it." She glanced out his dark window. "Which means they're coming east as well."

"How are they managing that? I didn't think they had that big of a military force."

Her skin itched, the feeling like they were missing something. "I don't know."

He tapped his cigarette into the ashtray on his desk, thinking. "And they wanted to kidnap you? That was their plan?"

"I guess so. He said that I wasn't supposed to remember anything, which is why they used that sedative that gave me amnesia. My grandfather said that it was super rare, something they probably wouldn't've been able to buy in the Tirdan Republic." She paused. "I wondered if that meant that Nydas had international ties, which would make sense if he got it from the Waltzins, who might have gotten it from the Nalliendrans. But why take me to Talegartia?"

"You don't know what they had planned for you there?"

"No, I . . . I don't remember much." She frowned, digging through her hazy memories. "I woke up in some sort of bedroom. I think it was an inn or something. I had this overwhelming need to escape, so I climbed out the window using the bedsheets and ran. I was still in my clothes that I had been wearing when I had first found Nydas, but they stunk to high hell, as if they hadn't changed them the entire trip across the Cortan Sea."

There had been fresh bandages on her injuries, though. They had wanted her to survive, but to what end? Why hadn't they simply killed her on the spot?

"And that's when you found the plant village?"

"It took several days, but I just knew there was something important waiting for me." Her frown deepened. "I don't know how to explain it."

He stared at the burning tip of his cigarette. "I think I understand."

"What do you mean?"

"The blacksmithy . . ." He searched for the words. "I didn't feel it the first time we went. I think it's because my blessing was still blocked. But tonight? Or yesterday, I guess? I didn't even have to try to remember where it was when I was coming to meet you. I just knew. And stepping inside? It felt . . . It felt like it was mine."

She grimaced, remembering what they had done in there. Spilled Nydas's blood. Heard his screams. "Did we—do you regret what we—"

"No." He was quick to shake his head. "No, it needed to be done."

"Are you sure? I'm sorry to have dragged you into all of this, but I needed—"

"No, I understand." He met her eye. "This is bigger than you and me, Evie. Way bigger. If they're coming after all blessed, then . . ."

She reeled back, realizing what he was saying. They would come after Estella. Sooner or later, they'd set their sights on her daughter.

"Do you think they already know?" she asked in a rush. "Do you think the Waltzins—"

"I don't know." He shook his head sadly, reaching for his tobacco again. "You know more than I do. I still don't understand how they knew about us."

Her attention drifted to the window. How had they known? Had the Waltzins notified the Nalliendrans of the presence of two blessed in Risten? Or had the Nalliendrans sought out the Waltzins to be their intermediaries? There were far too many missing pieces.

"We need to find out more. We have to investigate them. See what they know."

He glanced up at her, lighting his next cigarette. "I know."

"Plus, we need to get you the money. I still need to pay off the Mistress for Andra."

"And now my mother is involved, Evie." He stared at her, lips in a thin line.

She drew in a quick breath. Of course. They had known that Seraphine would likely be questioned about the disappearance of Nydas and they had been prepared for that, but with how deep this went with the Waltzins and Nalliendra? It was dawning on her that they wouldn't stop there. Nydas had been valuable enough for the Waltzins to keep alive and protected. He had known highly confidential information about their collusion with foreign powers, something Risten's political elite might not take to kindly considering Nalliendra's current attempts at widespread domination.

While Nydas might not have recognized him at first, it was no secret that Corsair was the courtesan's son. With how rare it was for children to be raised under the Rouge's roof, the gossip had been spread for years. They would soon guess that the metal blessed was behind the loss of the criminal somehow, and apparently the Waltzins had already known that Corsair and Evelaine had been close in previous years. Would they make the logical leap to figure out that Evelaine was seemingly back from the dead? Would they go after her and Corsair first? Or strike at Estella to draw them out?

She dropped her face into her hands, cursing. The situation was supposed to be resolved with Nydas's death, that had been the whole point, but now it was even more complicated. Mason would have no way to protect Estella from a family such as the Waltzins, even once she gave the green shard to her daughter. There was only so much her goddess could do from far away to prepare Estella for what would happen if she were to be targeted. But would Evelaine's presence help or hinder? Maybe they didn't even know about Estella, and by going back to the woodshop, she would be leading enemies right to her daughter's door.

The Mistress could protect Seraphine far better, with the dozens of guards and protections she employed in and around the Rouge, but her influence wasn't limitless. She had nowhere near the power of the Waltzins, and it still meant that Seraphine likely couldn't risk taking on clients for the foreseeable future. Which meant that they needed to replace her income in addition to the other plans they had for pilfering the Waltzins' money.

"I'm so sorry," she mumbled. "This is a mess."

Looking up when she didn't get an answer, she found Corsair staring at the tip of his cigarette again, lost in thought. His usually handsome face was haggard, the impact of everything that had happened to them in the past few days causing deep lines to appear. His gaiety was nowhere to be found, leaving behind the haunted expression that he allowed very few to glimpse. She watched his bare ribs expand as he took a deep breath, blinking at her as he recognized the expectant silence filling the room.

"Right." He agreed to a question she hadn't asked, rubbing at his neck with his free hand. "I've got almost two hundred gold saved up. I can give you the one ten to pay off Andra's debt."

"You don't have to—"

"No, we need to get it out of the way. We need the Mistress on our team," he insisted.

She reluctantly nodded, accepting his logic. His mother needed the Mistress's protection. That was beyond clear. "Of course."

He leaned over, rummaging underneath his bed before brandishing a full pouch and tossing it to her. She took out the correct number of coins then handed it back, ordering her mind to set aside her worries and focus on a plan.

"Our best bet would be to search the estate while the restoration project is underway. We could possibly dress up as construction workers if we wanted to try during the day, or slip in at night to hopefully avoid detection altogether," she offered.

He dipped his chin to agree but pinned her with his gaze. "You need to talk to Mason. He deserves to know."

She dropped her attention to the floor. "I know."

He shifted to the edge of the bed, reaching for the tobacco as he jerked his head toward the door. "Go. We can talk about the next steps later. We both need the sleep."

Her mind spun as she thought about everything that had happened, but she stopped herself. Temple. Blessing. Reparations. Devastation. Vow. That had been the plan, and she supposed she had accomplished it, though not exactly as she had intended. Or at least, it hadn't reached the conclusion she had expected. There was still so much she had to do. More impossible decisions to make.

"Right." Sighing, she stood and gathered her pack. She glanced at him one last time, his back hunched and features shadowed by the candlelight as he rolled his third cigarette, but he mustered a halfhearted wink for her, letting her know that he would be fine. So she closed the door softly behind her and made her way to the Mistress's office, knowing that the proprietor would still be up as the Rouge below her bustled with activity.

It was a quick exchange, the woman smiling with satisfaction as Evelaine deposited the remaining balance on her desk. Andra hadn't been important enough to warrant a nondisclosure agreement, which Evelaine was immensely grateful for considering the circumstances. Yet it galled her to know that Andra's name would live on as just another entry on the Mistress's long ledger of income and expenses. Another red line turned black, all in the name of the woman's continued financial success.

She was in a sour mood by the time she returned to the apothecary, but Otis hugged her in relief, finally retiring to his own room after staying up for her. As she slumped into the cot, she focused on her breathing and reined in her trailing thoughts until she felt her eyelids fall closed. It would do her no good to consider the thousands of what-ifs that plagued her. The only way forward was to focus on the next step, no matter how much it made her stomach turn.

Sleeping late into the day, she tried to delay the inevitable as much as possible as she listened to the sounds of Otis shuffling around and opening the apothecary for business. But after she forced herself to choke down an early dinner of perpetual stew, she dragged her feet to the woodshop that had haunted her dreams.

She made sure to take the back alleys, keeping a careful eye out for any followers but spying none as the display window with its carefully polished toys, chairs, and shelves came into view, and her pace became even slower. Every time she returned here was a risk—she knew it. Swallowing back the dread that was winding its way up her throat, she told herself she had to go through with it. It was the right thing to do.

Her hand landed on the doorknob, her eyes finding Mason through the small window as he straightened the legs of a table in the rear of the shop. His back was to her as he squatted, his thick fingers fiddling with the joint where the carved pieces met the bottom of the tabletop, and she took a moment to steady herself. The blond mop of hair was exactly as she remembered it, speckled with sawdust and as unruly as it had been when he had woken that morning, she was sure of it. Mason was not one to take much care with his appearance, and she bet that the comb on the expertly crafted dresser in the bedroom hadn't been touched in days.

She couldn't let herself fall into memories, though. They would prevent her from doing what she knew was necessary, so she commanded herself to harden, the protective bark around her heart thickening in preparation. Once her determination was as solid as the stones beneath her feet, she pushed the door open as the shop bell tinkled above her. His head raised, turning to the side as he huffed out a customary greeting, then he brushed his hands on his apron as he stood.

His lips were parted as if he were about to say more when his gaze landed on her, shock freezing him in place. The sound that left him was part surprise, part hurt, as if he had been punched in the stomach and lost his breath. His wide blue eyes darted over her face then trailed down to her shoulders and limbs, him seemingly assuring himself that she was whole and unharmed.

"It's good to see you," she began, breaking the silence.

"Evelaine," he murmured. His hand reached for her as he shuffled forward, but he stopped, catching himself. "My gods, where have you been?"

She smiled sadly. "It's a long story. I'm so sorry I haven't been able to return until now."

"It's—" he started to say. She could tell he wanted to tell her it was okay, but they both knew it wasn't.

"It's good to see you, too," he finished instead as he continued to inch toward her, like she was a timid animal about to bolt. "Where . . . Or, I guess, what . . . ?"

She shifted on her feet, and he noticed the movement, his progression stalling. "Can we . . . talk? Alone?"

"Of course," he was quick to respond. His attention went to the door behind her. "I'll close up, but Estella's . . ."

He trailed off again, and she could see the flash of guilt in his expression. Here it was. The impassable canyon between them. Biting the inside of her cheek, she waited for him to say it.

"She's at the florist's." He tried to hide his grimace unsuccessfully, and she felt sick to her stomach. She had no right to feel this way, she told herself.

"That's probably for the best," she finally said haltingly.

His brows creased. "Don't you want to see her? She would want to—"

"No." She winced when his head jerked back. "I mean, yes. Eventually. But we need to talk first."

Wariness crept over his face, mixed with a touch of disappointment, and her heart dropped, but he moved to the door as she stepped out of the way, careful to keep a bit of distance between them. The hurt was obvious as he side-eyed her. He had never been good at hiding his emotions, they were always engraved across his features with no attempt at artifice or deceit, and it was another punch to the stomach to know how deeply she had betrayed his guileless trust. She lowered her gaze as the locks clicked into place, and he propped the closed sign in the display window. Turning, he gestured for her to head to the workshop, a separate room beyond the shop floor where his tools and workbenches were.

She tried to keep her steps casual, but nervous energy was budding in her veins as she approached one of his stools and perched awkwardly. Her gaze was still downcast, her finger trailing through the thick layer of sawdust on the table as he settled on a stool across from her.

"What's going on, Evelaine?" he asked, his voice low and laced with apprehension.

She took a deep breath. Gods, she had to say it. He more than deserved to know the truth. "One of my jobs for the Mistress went wrong, horribly wrong. They kidnapped me and took me to Talegartia." His brows shot into his forehead, but she pushed on. "The sedative they used stole my memories and I was stuck there until a few weeks ago. I came back to Risten as soon as I could. I-I've been staying with my grandfather."

"Otis?" He frowned. "For how long? Why didn't you—"

"I couldn't. Not just yet." She urged him to understand. "There were things I needed to take care of first."

"What sort of things?" She watched as he struggled with the questions that surged inside him.

"The man who kidnapped me . . . I had to . . ." She left it unsaid as his frown deepened.

He glanced to the side, knowing that there were things she had hidden from him about her duties for the Mistress, then determinedly met her gaze. "But it's taken care of? You're back now? For good?"

She fought the trembles in her hand as she forced herself to say it. "Not exactly."

It was too dangerous to keep coming back to the woodshop. Sooner or later, the Waltzins would track her down. They would find Estella, if they didn't already know about her. She couldn't do it. She wouldn't. Even though the thought made her want to rip out her hair and scream to the stars, she had to be the strong one. She had to protect her daughter at all costs.

"What does that mean?" he rumbled, anger rising. "Estella has missed you. She needs you. I need you."

Latching onto frustration that answered his, she gritted her teeth. "She may need me, but you obviously don't."

"What are you talking about?" He glared at her, but it was forced. The answer to his own question was in his expression.

She refused to tiptoe around it. "Frederica."

The effect was like a bucket of ice water to his face as he flinched back. "H-how did—"

"I saw her. In the shop the other night. I saw the way you looked at her." She tried to breathe, burying the hurt. It couldn't matter. It shouldn't.

He dropped his gaze, ashamed. "I'm sorry. I didn't know—I thought that maybe—I didn't intend for it to—"

"I know." She sighed. They didn't have time for this. "I understand. I'm not . . . I don't . . ."

She couldn't bring herself to say that she wasn't mad, that she didn't blame him. Because she was. She did. But that wasn't what was important.

"Mason, you need to know something. About me. About Estella." She had to tell him. She had to reveal the poisonous roots she had spent years desperately trying to hide from him. She had to impart the importance of protecting their daughter from what was coming for her.

He darted his eyes to hers, immediately concerned. "What about her?"

Her ribs expanded to draw in a deep inhale. "Have you ever heard of the blessed ones that wield elemental powers?"

His brows furrowed. "Elemental powers?"

"Have you ever noticed how Estella is drawn to plants? How random seeds show up in her sheets?"

His expression went back to shocked. "How—"

"The plants in the greenhouse. They respond to her, right? Bloom under her care?" She watched as he sat back, the wheels turning in his wide gaze. "She wields the plant blessing . . . just as I do."

His mouth opened, then closed as he studied her closely. It opened and closed again, the words not coming.

"My mother had it, I have it, and now Estella has it." She leaned forward, rushing through the explanation. "It runs in my bloodline. There's nothing I can do to stop it. I hoped that it would skip her, but it was inevitable. I can help her though. Tabriara can help her."

He shook his head in disbelief. "The Plant Goddess? What are you saying?"

"You can't deny that she is connected to plants, Mason. Grandfather told me that her blessing is beginning to manifest. She must complete her initiation ritual soon." Her voice was pleading. "There are people coming after her, they wish her harm, but Tabriara can guide her."

"What people?" His face was instantly drawn, his blue eyes bright with anger. "Who's after her?"

"This is so much bigger than you can understand. There are forces at play here that even I don't know about. The Waltzins are the biggest threat right now, the closest ones at least. The man who kidnapped me was in on it and I took care of him, but I don't know how much other people know. I don't know if they know about Estella, but I can't take that risk." She reached for his hand, gripping it tightly. The feel of his callouses brought back hundreds of memories and her head spun, but she forced herself to focus. "We have to protect her."

"The Waltzins—" he began, but the sound of a lock turning and the shop bell tinkling interrupted them as both of their heads twisted to the doorway that connected the two rooms. Her heart began hammering as she jerked to a stand, dropping his hand and stepping away from the table.

"Papa?" She heard a girl's voice call, and Mason's attention slid back to her, looking truly alarmed.

"Yes, dear." He cleared his throat, not looking away from Evelaine. "We're in here."

"'We'?" The response came and Evelaine's legs trembled as she slowly faced the doorway. Light footsteps neared until expectant teal eyes peeked around the frame, glancing around as they landed on Mason and then shifted to the side and widened.

Estella's mouth popped open, freezing in place just as her father's had upon seeing Evelaine. A rush of emotions passed across her face. First surprise, then excitement, followed by nervousness and a slight tremble to her bottom lip.

"M-mama?" The question was quiet, tentative, and it shattered Evelaine's blackened heart into a million pieces.

Her vision began to blur as a sob caught in her throat, and she reached out a hand. "Baby."

Her daughter rushed forward, throwing her arms around her as Evelaine crushed her to her body. Their limbs shook as they pressed closer, Evelaine tucking Estella's head into her shoulder and barely holding them upright as they swayed.

"Mama!" The girl cried into her neck. "Mama, I thought you were—you were—"

"Shh, it's okay." Evelaine wept, stroking her hair, her cheeks, anywhere she could reach. "It's okay, baby. I've got you. I'm right here."

"Oh, Mama . . ."

They murmured to each other, their voices thick with emotion as they held on tightly, not wanting to let go. A rush of praises and reassurances fell from Evelaine and all of her careful reservations fell away as Estella sobbed her grief and happiness in equal measure. There was nothing between them, their souls rising to meet one another in their reunion. Her baby, her flesh. The missing piece she had tortured herself for forgetting. How could she have possibly left behind such an integral part of herself?

The need to protect her was prickling her skin, calling forth her blessing before she could suppress it as seeds ached to be released. It was time for Estella's vow. She jerked back, holding onto Estella's shoulders with white knuckles. "Baby, I need to tell you something."

Her daughter blinked up at her, tears streaming down her wet cheeks. "Wh-what is it?"

Evelaine kneeled in front of her, clasping her hands between hers. "I know about your connection to plants. I know about the seeds and pollen."

Estella gasped, eyes going wide. "B-but—"

"It's your blessing, baby. I have it, too, so did my mother. It runs in our bloodline." She opened one of her palms and let a seed grow, the vine slowly wrapping around her hand as Estella's jaw dropped open. "We're blessed by the Plant Goddess. By Tabriara. And she wants to meet you."

"Meet me?" Her voice was so small, barely audible.

"Yes, you, baby. You're the next generation. Our hope. Our dreams. She asked me to give this to you." She reached into her pocket and drew out the green shard, placing it in Estella's hand and wrapping her fingers around it with her own. "Do you feel it?"

Her daughter gasped again as the crystal throbbed with light, the reflection of it shining in her teal gaze.

"If you speak to her, she will hear you," Evelaine urged, desperately needing her to understand. "She will help you develop your blessing."

"*I-I thought something was wrong with me,*" she whispered, staring down at the shard as it pulsed again.

"No, not at all, baby. You're perfect," Evelaine insisted. "Do you understand? There's nothing wrong with you.

281

You have a power that others can never touch. A power that could change the world as we know it."

Her daughter met her gaze with a worried look. "Will you help me?"

A sob caught in Evelaine's throat as she worked to swallow it down. She slowly stood, putting space between them that made the pieces of her heart shudder. Gods help her. The words fought her tongue, not wanting to be released, but she would protect her daughter even if it killed her. "I can help you through the initiation ritual, but— But I can't stay."

"Wh-what do you mean?"

"It's too dangerous, baby. There are very mean people out there who are looking for me, who might be looking for you, too. Because we are blessed by the goddess, they wish us harm, and I couldn't bear it if I accidentally drew them to you." She glanced over at Mason, who was standing to the side, his expression utterly distraught. "You need to stay with your papa. He will keep you safe."

"You're leaving us?" Estella cried, her eyes going wide. "Again?"

Her shoulders began to shiver, traveling down her torso like an animal shaking with fear, and Evelaine moved before she made the conscious decision, wrapping her in her arms. "Shh, it's okay, baby. It's okay, my love. You are so strong. You'll be strong for me, right?"

"We'll be alone, Mama!" The girl gasped, her voice choked as she clung to her. "I n-n-need you!"

"You won't be alone, I promise," Evelaine desperately tried to reassure her. "Your papa and Tabriara will look after you and you'll grow into the tall, unbreakable tree you were always meant to become. And I'll return. Some day. After all of this is over. After I make sure none of the mean people will find you, I'll come back for you. Okay?"

Her daughter wept into her shoulder, crying out for her mother as Evelaine soothed her hand up and down Estella's back. She whispered promises of returning, of the goddess's support, of a bright future where they could truly be free, and it became crystal clear that Evelaine couldn't deny the truth. No matter how she had felt about Mason and Nees, how deep her care and devotion had been for each of them, her heart was right here, in her arms. The love that bloomed within her for her daughter was something that could never be pruned, grafted, or cloned. It was the only love that mattered at the end of it all. It was the only love that would keep her moving forward.

In that moment, she knew that the promises falling from her were not empty ones. They were not lies. She couldn't bring herself to fool her own flesh and blood, and she would pay any price to make sure her daughter was nourished and empowered. Strengthened into a force to be reckoned with. A leader that could truly embody the six virtues in a way that Evelaine knew, deep down, she herself never would be able to. One day, if Estella wished it, she would bear the Plant Crown and be the benevolent, wise, and powerful ruler that would demand the respect she deserved.

She would bend to no one.

After what felt like hours, the girl quieted, exhausted as she blinked up at Evelaine with red eyes. She sniffed, rubbing her nose with the back of her hand. "You'll come back?"

"I promise," Evelaine swore, the oath vining its way around her ribs.

Estella studied her mother's face for a moment, nodding when she found evidence of the pledge, then glanced down at the shard she still held clutched in her hand. She turned it over, looking at its many facets as it pulsed gently. Her breath caught at the beauty of it, her fingers trailing along the sharp points with a sense of awe.

"Can you feel it?" Evelaine asked softly, sensing Mason approaching slowly in her periphery. Her eyes met his as he neared, his hand landing on Estella's shoulder in solidarity, his expression set even if concern still lingered.

"*Yes*," her daughter whispered, mesmerized by the crystal.

Evelaine returned her focus to her. "We need to complete your initiation ritual, okay? It'll make you stronger, so that you can protect yourself."

Estella's gaze lifted, a flash of worry crossing her face. "Will it hurt?"

"Maybe." She couldn't sugarcoat it. "It will require a test of your determination and faith."

Her own ritual had been a feat of patience, a warped slice of time that had felt like centuries in the span of mere minutes. It had been a testament to the longevity of nature as she had watched buildings, cities, and civilizations crumble and decay while the vines and flowers had continued to bloom, spread, and feed. It had meant to show her that the grasses did not care for the transient, fleeting lives of animals, for they would all eventually return to where they had come.

That was the amaranthine cycle.

"Th-the Plant Goddess . . . is she nice?" Estella asked, twisting her fingers nervously around the shard.

"Yes, she has taken very good care of me, and I know she will adore you. She loves all of her blessed," Evelaine was quick to answer. "She told me herself that she wishes to know you."

"Really?" Her daughter's eyes brightened.

"Of course, she will guide and protect you. Teach you how to be strong."

Estella nodded again, slowly this time as she squared her shoulders. "Okay, I will try."

"I'll be right there with you." Evelaine's attention darted to Mason, who looked as resolute as she felt. "And your papa will be, too."

He dipped his chin in confirmation, and Evelaine straightened, gripping her daughter's free hand. "Let's go to the greenhouse. That'll be the best place for it."

She insisted on taking point, her eyes swinging in every direction as she searched for anyone that could be watching them. There was an errant pedestrian or two, but none that stared at them for too long. Evelaine tried to convince herself that they were harmless, yet she knew she couldn't trust that their movements were not being tracked. It was a matter of when they found her daughter, not if, and she'd be damned if she didn't get the chance to take them down before they struck.

If that happened, she truly would become the poison. Nothing and no one would be able to stop her.

Time was of the essence as she hurried them into the back door, calling to Otis as they entered and locked themselves in. Her grandfather's shuffling steps soon arrived, and she briefly explained what was happening as he greeted Estella and Mason with a broad smile. Evelaine instructed him to close up shop while she gathered the supplies, following the whispered suggestions that came from the shard in Estella's hands. While her daughter couldn't yet hear it, Evelaine was well aware of Tabriara's soft voice even though she wasn't even holding the crystal herself. It was as if the goddess herself were bent over her shoulder, her directives the barest of exhales against the shell of her ear, and Evelaine felt the urgency in her bones as she collected the necessary herbs.

Eventually, she positioned Estella in front of the lemon tree Evelaine had been drawn to in her blind panic eight days prior. She felt the Plant Goddess's presence most strongly there, now that her blessing had been restored, and could tell that Estella felt the same as she instinctively thrust her fingers into the soil at its base without prompting. As an expression of bliss crept across Estella's face, Evelaine wondered what it had been like for her daughter to have had her burgeoning blessing dampened by the corruption at Corsair's temple in recent months. It would've awakened for her the second the first corrupted vulture fell, and she desperately wanted to ask how it had felt for her.

There were too many questions that pressed against her throat, so many conversations untouched that would have to wait. Her presence just by itself was a danger to her loved ones, let alone bringing Estella and Mason to the apothecary. She knew that after this ritual was done, she would have to cut herself off from them completely for their safety until the threat of the Waltzins and Nalliendra was taken care of. It was the only way to ensure that Estella remained hidden from their malicious plans.

Tears sprouted in the corners of her eyes, but she forced them back, focusing on the mixture of herbs she was pounding with a mortar and pestle. A heady fragrance bloomed as it slowly turned into a paste, woody and flowery and spicy, then she scraped it into a stone bowl she had found in Otis's cabinets. Turning, she found that he had arranged candles as she had asked in a large circle around her daughter and the lemon tree. Evelaine took her place in front of her and motioned for Mason and Otis to sit on the other side of Estella to make a triangle.

She met her love's gaze, the girl's jaw set with bravery that Evelaine immediately recognized as kin to her own, and her heart swelled with pride. The emotion that passed between them was so intense that she began to feel the blackened flesh flake off like a birch shedding its bark, each beat reviving the shriveled organ. A vision of greatness flashed before her and her breath caught as Estella's teal irises started to emit an ethereal glow that signalled the first chord of connection. The single note that initiated the call to bond.

Placing the now rapidly pulsing shard in the center of the herb mixture, she reached for her matches and struck a light with shaking fingers. The second it touched the incense, a burst of green flames came to life and Evelaine felt the chant sprout from her lips unbidden, a script that was written in the core of who she was.

"Nurturing Mother of Flowers, Goddess of Plants, Keeper of Seeds, we beseech thee.

"Divine Majesty, we are your humble daughters of plants and we are eternally grateful for the blessed love, strength, and guidance that you have granted us.

"We are Evelaine and Estella Peonille of Tabriara, at your honored service."

The candles flickered as her voice rose and Estella's eyes rolled back, her hands digging deeper into the soil.

"Nurturing Mother of Flowers, Goddess of Plants, Keeper of Seeds, we beseech thee.

"Bless your chosen, Estella Peonille, and gift her your guidance."

Smoke the color of moss twined with gold filled the space and branched toward the glass ceiling like towering boughs, but it wasn't choking them. Evelaine breathed in deeply and felt her tension ease, a sense of ecstatic rightness causing her eyelids to flicker. Her back arched, her skin humming.

"Nurturing Mother of Flowers, Goddess of Plants, Keeper of Seeds, we beseech thee.

"Your blessed daughter is awaiting you and wishes to submit herself wholeheartedly to your divine embrace."

She heard her daughter gasp, now completely obscured, but she trusted, without a shred of doubt, that she was safe. Protected. Supported.

Evelaine knew, deep within her soul, a new seed had thrust forth, breaking its shell to boldly declare its right to flourish.

Seventeen Hours Earlier

Corsair felt his expression fall the second the door clicked closed behind Evie and he slumped to the floor like a sack of potatoes, his forearms propped on his bent knees as he dropped his head onto them. Gods, he was so tired. He barely managed to flick his finger toward the lock, blocking out the rest of the world as he let himself descend into the existential exhaustion that weighed down his limbs like iron manacles. Like the thick strips of metal that he had used to hold Nydas in place and . . .

Nope, he wouldn't go there. He couldn't. He blocked it out, shutting the vaulted door and spinning the spoke handle. It was no use reliving the past twenty-four hours. Fuck, the last three days were better off completely wiped from his recollection. The desire to go knock on the Waltzins' hotel door and beg for the sedative that had stolen Evie's memories, or maybe even a solid blow to the head was overwhelming.

Good thing he literally could not bring himself to move from his position on the floor, because his bad ideas were not seeming so bad at the moment.

He did manage to lift his head and take a drag of his dying cigarette, however. At least there was that.

Hauling his arm up with a grunt, he swiped the pouch of tobacco and papers off his desk and began rolling another. Once it was lit, he took another deep inhale as he fumbled around underneath his bed until his hand landed on the cool glass of a bottle. He tugged it toward himself, thumbing the cork out and lifting it to his lips. Down went three big gulps, and he didn't even bother to wince at the burn as the liquor made its way down his throat. It landed in his empty stomach with a foreboding slosh, and he vaguely wondered when the last time he had eaten was.

Was it at the apothecary? Yes, that was it. He remembered shoveling two plates of breakfast into his face as Evie had tried to wave off her not-so-subtle arson party she had had without him. Rolling his eyes, he stuck his cigarette between his lips and let his head fall back on the edge of the bed. It wasn't like he had had any intention of burning the Waltzins' estate down, but she should've at least included him so he could've been there to watch her back.

He couldn't blame her, though. He'd been pissed to hell when they'd argued in the blacksmithy, yelling at her for still wanting to go after the criminal. He'd been hurt and confused, still nursing the gaping holes in his heart, and while she had funneled her grief into reckless action, he'd pushed her away when he should've pulled her close. It was just like her to mourn by burning someone's house down while he drank, smoked, and fucked his way through the emotions that pierced every breath he took like a hundred daggers.

What a fucking loser.

Ripping the cigarette from his mouth, he glared at it and moved to crush it into the ashtray by his head, but stalled at the last second. He couldn't even stop it as his limbs moved, giving him another puff and another swig from the bottle. Even his cock twitched to life, sensing where his thoughts were stumbling, and he cursed himself. He was a godsdamn mess, yet he still craved the release.

It had been all too easy to find someone to fuck furiously the night before. Multiple someones, in fact. His spinning thoughts and aching chest had momentarily left him in peace for a blissful couple of hours in that loud music hall, the rolling beat of the drums pounding through him as he'd slammed himself into some nameless guy's ass in a dark corner before finding another one in the bathroom.

Had there been a third after that? Fuck if he knew.

It didn't matter.

Maybe he should go tell the Mistress he was available for whatever was left of the night. What was it? Two? Three in the morning? There were bound to be some drunk stragglers that he could coax into bed and earn some coin to start replacing what he had given Evie, but he knew before he even finished the thought that he wasn't in the right mindset. The clientele would want the charming version of Corsair, who whistled his way through life with a pep in his step and a gleam in his eye.

That Corsair was nowhere to be found.

The man that now sat slumped on his bedroom floor was broken. A shattered mirror that only reflected the nightmarish scenes of his friends bleeding out before him and the ghostly remnants of a terrifying figure who had towered above him, demanding he step up, claim his crown, and prove himself worthy. The glaring shine of the god's armor had blinded and dazzled him, and he had blinked up at him in bewilderment from where he had landed on his knees.

He still didn't understand what had been asked of him. How could he? The god's—his god's?—expectations were so far beyond anything Corsair had ever imagined for himself. Claim the Metal Crown and become the ruler of the Tirdan Republic? What the fuck did that even mean? He was the bastard son of a courtesan who had no future beyond following in his mother's footsteps and fucking strangers all in the name of the slim hope of maybe, somehow, possibly earning enough to retire someday. A fool's dream that many a whore had deluded themselves with.

That was exactly what he was, after all. A misguided prostitute who also just happened to be able to control metal and swing a sword like his life depended on it. He had no idea what the hell the god was thinking to insist that he was the one to be a paragon of excellence or whatever the fuck he had said. Lifting the bottle, he drank deeply and sighed as the heat finally began to melt the sharp edges of the blades in his ribs.

He blinked blearily at the cigarette stub in his fingers, wondering when it had gone out. Whatever. Another was soon made and lit, the movements so rote that he barely noticed as he shifted to stretch out on the floor. He rolled his ankles, twisted his hips, and arched his back, hearing the joints pop and crack as his body relaxed. The room was thick with tobacco smoke, but it suited him just fine, creating a layer of camouflage that helped him hide from the harsh reality that was waiting for him outside the door.

While he dragged on the new cigarette, his traitorous mind brought him back to the day that he had first met Gimlet. He had been a thin scrap of a man, but it had been the look of devious cunning in his beady brown eyes that had had Corsair itching to get underneath his skin. Somehow, he had instantly known that Gimlet would end up being one of his most creative lovers, a man who had known exactly how to get Corsair all hot and bothered with verbal and physical sparring in lieu of foreplay. It had taken Corsair all of six months to circle him, slipping under his defenses and luring him into touches that had been more than friendly until the dealer had finally let the blessed in.

It had been one of the nights where Gimlet had snuck a bit of something or other from the Mistress's stores and had just been reckless enough that he had let Corsair corner him in the weapon storage room as they had both disarmed after their guard shifts. One of Corsair's arms had been propped against the wall over Gimlet's shoulder, the dealer's back to him, as his other hand had curled around the man's side and slipped the dagger out from the sheath at his hip. He had loved how he could tower over him, the bulk of his torso creating a solid mass that Gimlet had not so subtly backed into as Corsair had lazily trailed the tip of the blade up his stomach and chest.

"You better watch yourself," Gimlet had warned, his voice low.

"Or what?" Corsair had breathed into his ear, a slow smile spreading as the man had shivered from the hot air on his neck.

"I won't be responsible for my actions if any blood is drawn."

Corsair had moved his free hand from the wall and had brought it down to Gimlet's other hip, gripping him in place as he had brought the flat side of the dagger to the man's chin and had used it to turn his head so that their eyes had met. "Why? Is it one of your kinks?"

Desire had radiated from those brown eyes, but he had refused to give in so easily. "Like you could handle my kinks."

Corsair's hand had shifted from Gimlet's hip, sliding across the front of him until he had found the man's erection straining against his pants. He had palmed it, squeezing, and his grin had turned sly as the dealer's pupils had darkened and lips had parted in a silent gasp. "Oh, but I so enjoy feeling what I can do to you."

"Fucker," Gimlet had gritted out, his teeth clenched.

"Yes." Corsair's smile had widened. "That is the plan."

The dagger had then nicked at Gimlet's jaw and Corsair had brought the bloody tip to his mouth, letting his tongue curl out as he had slowly licked it clean. It had been the last straw as the dealer had spun in his arms, attacking him with a brutal kiss, and before long, Corsair had had him pinned against the wall, penetrating him with primal thrusts as their rasping moans had echoed in the small space.

It had been a beautiful thing while it had lasted, their vicious unions occasionally allowing room for whispered tenderness in the privacy of their bedrooms, and their combined pleasure had climbed to inventive heights until it had all corroded away after Gimlet had been fired from the Rouge. Corsair had sought him out for a night or two here and there, but it hadn't been the same, the lingering tension of secretive flirtations while on the job no longer keeping the forge of interest stoked.

The mental image of blood beading along the blade had Corsair rolling over and tucking his knees into a fetal position, his dead cigarette falling to the floor beside him as he choked against the stab of pain in his chest. He watched as it rolled to a stop and rocked for a moment before stilling, the movement far too similar to how Gimlet's dislodged fingers had shivered in the abrupt absence of their owner in the temple. He could still hear the man's screams, see the panicked look in his eyes in the last few seconds before the panel had closed.

How could he have known that he would witness the moment the fear of imminent death had stolen across Gimlet's stark features? Lines of doom scrawled on the planes of his face that had spelled a fate that neither of them could stop. If he had only had access to his blessing, it could've all been prevented. Gimlet's dawning terror. Andra's fatal misstep. Rikeland's unfortunate fall.

But who was he kidding? He had had full access to his capabilities as Kaiseln had been crushed to death. He had just been so focused on shredding the vulture to pieces that he had missed the screams that had been coming from the other side of its grotesquely corpulent mass. It was his fault they were all gone and there was nothing he could do about it.

He shot upward, patting around for the bottle of liquor and sucking the rest of it down. The thoughts needed to stop. The doom that had wrapped itself around him like a hundred pounds of plate armor had to go, but his dizzy gaze caught on the corner of a shining breastplate that had been shoved into the corner behind his bookshelf and he scowled at it. Throwing the empty bottle aside, he scrambled toward it on his hands and knees, the room lurching around him, and tugged it out.

"What the fuck do you want from me?!" he yelled, shaking it as it reflected back his enraged face. He could see evidence of wetness on his cheeks and it infuriated him even further. "WHAT MORE COULD YOU WANT?"

There was a banging on the wall to the left, his neighbor protesting his raised voice, and he jerked as if he had been slapped. Right, of course. He was at the Rouge. In his room. Surrounded by other staff members looking to tuck in for the day after a long night of servicing others.

What had happened at the temple felt like a fever dream, and he was still waiting to wake up. His ass found the floor and his knees bent to the sides awkwardly as he stared down at the molded metal in his hands. It had been shaped to fit him exactly, the feel of it unlike anything he had ever worn before. Light. Agile. Almost like a second skin.

He could easily destroy it. Use his blessing and melt it into a bulbous glob, but he couldn't bring himself to do it for some reason. There had to be a reason, though. What was it? Where was it? It felt important, but he couldn't put his finger on it.

Was there something he was forgetting?

His sluggish brain provided no answers. What could he possibly do? The intense need to fix things was making his blessing roll under his skin, begging for release, and he felt his tattoo itch. He shifted, trying to suppress it as his shoulders bunched, but he felt the blades begin to emerge despite himself. The feeling was incredible. Incomparable. Every time, it was as if his power were releasing in an orgasmic burst, and he dropped the breastplate, unable to resist its call.

He stretched, reaching for the pommels on each shoulder, and gasped as he pulled forth his swords for the first time since his blessing had been restored. The throb of pleasure traveled through his entire body. Gods, it felt so good. He had been denying himself, making himself wait because he didn't think he deserved it after everything that had happened.

They lowered in front of him, his fingers wrapped around the engraved handles as if caressing a long-lost lover, and he marveled at the feel of them. They were long, curved, lightweight, and perfectly balanced. The ideal weapons, in his opinion.

The image of them had come to him in a dream and he had immediately known that they were his somehow. It had taken him years to save up the money, but the day had finally come when he had provided his rough sketch to a talented tattoo artist. His vision come to life.

Later, in the privacy of his room, he had curled his fingers over his raw shoulders. Even though the skin had still wept after the hours and hours the artist had spent carving the design into him and his head had still spun from the endorphins pulsing through his veins, he had torn the blades from himself for their very first appearance. His back had split open under his urging, an elemental birthing that had felt so right. A release that he could never replicate.

The swords were a part of him. A part of his blessing. A part of his past, present, and future. And it was entirely too fucking ironic that the same image had been engraved in the Metal God's breastplate. Now Corsair's, too.

It almost cheapened it, realizing that the vision hadn't been truly his. That it had all been because of the divine connection that he knew next to nothing about. Just another absent father figure that had determined what his life would end up being, without Corsair's involvement or consent.

He needed to take control. Fix things. Take back what had been taken from him. But that was impossible, wasn't it? It's not like he could bring his friends back to life. They were dead. Gone. There was nothing he could do about it.

His fingers tightened around the pommels, his teeth gritted against the molten rage inside of him. He had told Evie that people died every day and that they might as well make it count for something, but he hadn't known what he would be asked to sacrifice. The selfish ass that he was, he had only been thinking about himself. His life had never meant anything in the grand scheme of things.

What truly mattered was his mother. Patia, Orlah, and Sorlene. Andra's sister. Rikeland's unborn babe. The injured sister-in-law and nephews that had been tossed aside by the insatiable cruelty of industry and profit. They were what mattered. Not his useless existence, a prized stallion locked in a cage only to be trotted out when his body was needed to race or breed.

He was supposed to be the scaffolding, the reliable structure that supported their happiness and protected them from harm. And yet, he had failed.

Andra had just a few weeks ago confessed to him why she had entered into a contract with the Mistress. They had been drinking and decompressing after a particularly long guard shift where they had been forced to intervene when a client had gotten too rough with one of the courtesans. It had brought up old memories for Andra, whose sister had been a courtesan for the Mistress up until a little under seven years ago, and Corsair had learned that she had been one of those who had been kidnapped by the Aldaran pirates.

Her sister had been brutally beaten and raped when she had tried to escape their clutches and had required extensive reconstructive surgeries in order to regain the use of much of her right side afterward, a cost that Andra had begged the Mistress to pay in return for her promise of employment as a guard at the Rouge. The Mistress, however, had lost one of her best courtesans in the process and had insisted on Andra also paying back the missing profits that her sister would have earned if she hadn't been disabled for life.

Andra had demanded that Corsair not tell a soul about it, knowing that it would embarrass her sister to learn that her former coworkers knew about the low level of poverty that she and Andra were forced to endure with

Andra's scant earnings that didn't go directly into paying off the debt. He had tried to get her to take some of his savings, but she had refused on principle. Even so, he had started leaving a gold coin or two in her pockets whenever he could sneak it. Now, he would never know if she had noticed.

The blades trembled in his hands, his muscles shivering under the driving need to do something, and the metal flickered with the reflection of the candles on his desk. His whole life had been lived in the service of others, but his recent actions had only put his loved ones in danger.

He could do better.

He would do better.

The answer rang within him with the suddenness of a clanging bell. He would become the protective armor that shielded, the wall that defended, and the sword that cut. Where he thought he had been training simply to be the Mistress's tool, he would now set his sights on something bigger.

Reaching up with shaking hands, he absorbed the two weapons into his back and felt their power meld with the vibration in his veins. He vowed to himself that he would no longer be someone else's instrument, but the apparatus that would carve a stronghold for the weary and downtrodden into this rotten city.

His city.

FIN.

ACKNOWLEDGMENTS

Well, here I am once again, leaving the writing of the acknowledgements to the very last minute. This time, I can't help but ask: Is writing simply an act of love at the end of the day? At least for me, it feels like a continual practice in recognizing and honoring the communal support that it takes to write, publish, and sell a book (let alone multiple). Truly, it takes a village, and I am increasingly in awe of the encouragement I receive from sources near and far.

First, I must always and forever thank my team: My beloved editor, Norma Gambini, for both her professionalism and her enthusiasm. My exacting formatter, Samantha Pico, for her unerring attention to detail. And my insightful cover artist, Carlos Ortega-Haas, for his uncanny ability to pull my characters out of my head and onto paper.

Second, there are my amazing beta and reviewer teams: H.P.T., Aiden Murray, Camri Kohler, Kenneth Creech, Bridgette Portman, and many more. They are the ones that help me feel a bit less delusional on this journey of mine as I navigate that thin line between confidence and competence.

And, finally, I want to thank the countless others who have crossed my path at all of the amazing events I am so lucky to be able to take part in. From the San Francisco

Writers Conference, to the Write Women Book Fest, to WorldCon and beyond, I have had the wondrous privilege to nerd out with writers and readers of all kinds. Your passion fuels my own every single time.

Together, we can move mountains.

Glossary:
Gods & Goddesses

Dishiru | God of Wind
Temple somewhere unknown.
Blessed Bloodline: unknown

Furaro | God of Fire
Temple near Zahar, a desert city in South Endrian.
Known as the Fire God, his power controls all forms of
flame, and he lives in a palace surrounded by a source of
magma. His tapestry features a phoenix and a flaming
tree.
*Blessed Pyrantus Bloodline: King Rakhmet Pyrantus and
his father, Pharosos*

Gamarna | Goddess of Earth
Temple somewhere unknown.
Blessed Bloodline: unknown

Hazu | God of Life
Temple near Aepol, the northern pole in North Endrian.
Known as the Sun God, his power is the gift of life
and healing, and he is married to Hecatah. His tapestry

features a sun, a tree of life with interconnected roots, and two lions with the wings of an eagle.

Blessed Sintal Bloodline: King Roe Sintal

Hecatah | Goddess of Death

Temple near Supol, the southern pole in Brindt. Known as the Moon Goddess, her power involves overseeing the death process and the passage of ghosts and spirits. She is married to Hazu. Her tapestry features a moon in a winter landscape with a cypress tree and two owls in flight.

Blessed Makaanis Bloodline: Queen Kelah Makaanis

Sirenia | Goddess of Water

Temple on Tusi Island, the northernmost of the Bourisian Islands to the east of South Endrian. Her power controls all forms and bodies of water, and she rules over all marine creatures from her palace at the bottom of the ocean. Her tapestry features an expanse of coral, crowned by a crab in a sea of green and blue.

Blessed Rutrulan Bloodline: Queen Nasima Rutrulan and her grandparent, Ohn

Tabriara | Goddess of Plants

Temple near the village of Curacu, east of Lythenea in Talegartia on the western coast of South Endrian. Her power controls all forms of plant life, but her special plant is the castor bean. She rules from her palace decorated with a cacophony of plants, and her tapestry features a red-purple leaf and spiked seed cluster.

Blessed Peonille Bloodline: Evelaine and Estella Peonille

Urkus | God of Metal

Temple in Risten, the capital of the Tirdan Republic. His power controls all forms of metal and he rules from his metal palace. His tapestry features two crossed silver swords in front of a gold shield.

Blessed Bloodline: Corsair Manadion

GLOSSARY:
MORTAL COURTS

The Makaanises

In the past, they protected and honored the Moon Goddess's sacred land and temple near Supol, the southern pole in Brindt. There is a single blessed one per generation and they can see, speak to, and command spirits.

> *Moon Queen: Kelah Makaanis*
>> *Partner: Roe Sintal*
>> *Oathed Guard: Zandira Gwendi*
>> *Mother: Molla Makaanis (deceased)*
>> *Father: Beret Makaanis (deceased)*
>> *Brother: Lienn Makaanis (deceased)*

The Manadions

In the past, they protected and honored the Metal God's sacred land and temple in Risten, the capital of the Tirdan Republic. There are multiple blessed ones per generation and they are connected to and can wield all forms of metal.

> *Metal Blessed: Corsair Manadion*
>> *Mother: Serpahine Gustave*

The Pyrantuses
They protect and honor the Fire God's sacred land and temple near Zahar, a desert city in South Endrian. There are multiple blessed ones per generation and they are connected to and can wield all forms of fire.

> *Fire King: Rakhmet Pyrantus*
>> *Father: Pharosos Pyrantus*
>> *Grandfather: Diemani Pyrantus (deceased)*
>> *Mother: Oyah Pyrantus*
>> *Oathed Guard and Partner: Hara Gamal*
>>> *Advisors: Viceroy Emat Nehitet, Vicerah Nerfera Semitep, Viceroy Nikat Tuthakht, Vicerah Duae Setaemtir, Viceroy Kay Ramsey, Viziera Niankha Hotep, Vizier Desher Sekhem, Viziera Meruka Kagemni*
>>> *Ambassadors: Arad Shivash (from Gheseruti), Tellis Risais (from Talegartia)*
>>> *Other Members: Nebehet Tuthakht, Inenekah Hotep, Khenti Kagemni*

The Rutrulans
They protect and honor the Water Goddess's sacred land and temple on Tusi Island, the northernmost of the Bourisian Islands to the east of South Endrian. There are multiple blessed ones per generation and they are connected to and can wield all forms of water.

> *Water Queen: Nasima Rutrulan*
>> *Partner: Cassandra Mertusa*
>> *Oathed Guard and Partner: Cassandra Mertusa*
>> *Mother: Charo Rutrulan (deceased)*

Father: Jameson Wulf, Captain of the Golden Inquirer

Grandparent: Ohn Rutrulan

Spouse: Rochelle Willan

Other Members: Dumadi Tongse, Annisa Tongse, Arika Tongse, Kai Tongse

The Peonilles

In the past, they protected and honored the Plant Goddess's sacred land and temple near the village of Curacu, east of Lythenea in Talegartia on the western coast of South Endrian. There are multiple blessed ones per generation and they are connected to and can wield all forms of plant life as well as produce poisonous seeds and pollen spores.

Plant Blessed: Evelaine and Estella Peonille

Mother: Elemona Peonille (deceased)

Oathed Guard: Nees Rasa (deceased)

Guilded Trainer: Kaiseln Arturi (deceased)

The Sintals

In the past, they protected and honored the Sun God's sacred land and temple near Aepol, the northern pole in North Endrian. There is a single blessed one per generation and they can wield healing abilities.

Sun King: Roe Sintal

Partner: Kelah Makaanis

Daughter: Venara Sintal

Mother: Osmia Sintal (deceased)

Other Members: Brishna Reconi

DISCOVER MORE IN THE NEXT BOOK OF THE THREADS OF DESTINY SERIES!
Coming Halloween 2026

Photo by Holli Margell

Claire E. Jones | Existential glitter bomb. Dog mom. Bookworm. Romantic. Nerd. Creative AF. Dancer. Only child. Goof. Introvert. Blonde. Artaholic. Entrepreneur. Clairvoyant. Homebody. Prochoice. Philanthropist. Stoner. Intellectual. Visionary. German. Lithuanian. Welsh. Pansexual. Millennial. Intuitive. Progressive. Prounion. Humanitarian. Pegan. Pagan. Witch. Anti-capitalist. Seattleite. Former Midwesterner. Pisces Sun. Pisces Moon. Leo Rising. Mercury in Aquarius. Five planets in Capricorn.

CONNECT ONLINE
www.claireejones.com
@clairjoyance